SHOWDOWN AT
ROOKVILLE MALL

NO MAN OUGHT EVER witness a rail-thin Viking warrior wearing glasses as thick as his broadsword.

"You will hand over the prisoner!" Geordi repeated, enhancing the irritability of his voice with a nasal twang.

Haz stood in the midst of his troop, Taggart beside him. Not to be outdone, Haz held a megaphone in one hand, which he raised to his lips. In the other hand, he held what appeared to be an Uzi.

"You will *go fuck yourself*!" Haz yelled into the megaphone.

An astonished gasp followed this as Geordi's convention-attendees shuffled anxiously, eyes widened.

Geordi hit his response button a moment too soon. There was a sigh, followed by: "You have chosen your fate, Son of Earth!"

Haz hefted his Uzi, frowned briefly as if considering what to say, then dropped the megaphone and decided to let his weapon do the talking for him.

LETTERS TO AN EDITOR

LETTERS

TO AN

EDITOR

DAMIAN STEPHENS

FOURTH MANSIONS PRESS

LETTERS TO AN EDITOR

FOURTH MANSIONS PRESS, LLC
Charlottesville, Virginia

fourthmansions.com

ISBN: 978-0-578-50518-3

Cover art and interior illustration of Bash by Pantelis Politakos
Cover design by Fourth Mansions Press, LLC

"Everything in the universe is merely letters to an editor."

— Bash

to
all creatures orphaned
(sheltered or homeless)
I dedicate this
modest offering of hope

CONTENTS

PART ONE

QUOD EST INFERIUS

FOR EXAMPLE," THE STRANGE creature said, grabbing another cookie from the pile set before him, "here is a rather useful spell that I enjoy: it makes use of the fact that time only exists as a constructed aspect of space."

The creature—he called himself "Bash," or that was what Martin could make of the polysyllabic utterance—proceeded to hold the cookie in one small, four-fingered hand level with his eyes in the air before him. It reminded Martin of a larger version of the gentle paws of a hamster or similar rodent. Bash's peculiar reptilian eyes narrowed as he focused on the cookie; he began to mumble some-thing, a set of words that caused the air around the cookie to warble and warp.

Bash removed his hand. The cookie remained in its place, levitating a few feet above the cinder block Bash used as his dining room table. The creature grinned, showing a row of teeth designed for grinding and tearing vegetable matter.

"Now here's the cool part," Bash said. He began mumbling again, and Martin marveled at the sight of the cookie beginning to rotate through numerous axes, like an old-school model of the atom, until its center began glowing—first white, then ever-brighter, until its radiance appeared as an after-image of the Sun when one gazed at it too long.

In moments, the cookie had become, for all intents and purposes, a miniature *planet*. Martin could make out swathes of forest and snow, large land masses separated by even larger oceans, not to mention meteorological phenomena indicated by the presence of swirling clouds.

Martin let out an inadvertent gasp. Bash laughed.

"Is that how...?" Martin attempted to formulate a question about cosmogony, but Bash waved it away.

"Oh, I guess, sometimes," he said, plucking the small Earth out of the space between them. "And then, I suppose—" Bash popped the planet into his mouth and crunched loudly.

Somewhat aghast, Martin found himself laughing in response.

THE FIRST COURSE OF Martin's day inevitably tasted like bacon too dry and eggs too wet.

He found himself once again at a desk of faux mahogany, the grains of which bristled with a chorus of seething, silent mouths. He wanted to throw it through the window behind him. Extracting a dull, red pastel crayon from the front desk drawer, his gaze fell like sterile gleet on the barren field before him.

> The significance of isolating these variables in the context of Euclidean space is not only useful but can also help us in understanding why these simple functionals are so useful. A magnification utilizing a metric that exceeds what would commonly be used in this procedure makes use of a particularly useful notion outside of which its use becomes negligible, i.e., it cannot be used for

> anything except rendering infinite magnifications
> of curves useful in these types of calculations.

Martin made a few tentative marks with the crayon, trying to ignore a creeping headache.

> The significance of isolating these variables in the context of Euclidean space is not only useful but can also help us in understanding why these simple functionals are so ~~useful~~. A magnification utilizing a metric that exceeds what would commonly ~~be used~~ in this procedure makes use of a particularly ~~useful~~ notion outside of which its use becomes negligible, i.e., it cannot ~~be used~~ for anything except rendering infinite magnifications of curves ~~useful~~ in these types of calculations.

He allowed his eyes to rise up and his hand to droop down. A scent like chamomile and tastefully burnt coffee ghosted into his nostrils from a memory linked to the ketchup stain irremediably plastered to the ceiling of his office. What an intergalactic fucking *mess* that had been to clean up—lunch *everywhere...*

Their constellations—so much different than ours! But our bodies—so much the same! Parisa—no, it hadn't been *her*, had it?—hell-bent mentally and physically to obtain the "juice" (she pronounced it "zhoos," in the manner of electronic devices), prodding and pressing and pulping him like an orange... He was a carrier pigeon with a message of life-or-death, the scroll tied to his ankle with knotted piano wire.

When it came undone, at last, she shone translucently, silvery data, caramel skin aching with labored breaths.

That version of the dream had not occurred since before the accident. Now those dreams were so much...

darker. Sorrowful.

Who had that been? *Parisa*. Parisa. Right. Had to have been.

He had eaten the remaining French fries in exhausted silence.

Here and now once again, the stain was gone.

Martin blinked, twice, three times. He rubbed his eyes. Gone.

He took several deep breaths.

Martin returned, reluctantly, to the page of drivel before him in real time. Differential geometry. His dissertation had focused on differential geometry; not even his advisor had understood it fully. Martin knew, because if he had, he would never have accepted it, would have argued against it, would have consigned it to sewer or shredder without a moment's hesitation.

That was before he left that world and came (after a brief detour in Fall County Jail) to this one. He remembered Pamela had licked her lips when she first saw him, had lingered with her eyes on his trouser-front for a moment (several moments) too long, had inveigled him in her cosmic agenda the day she hired him.

"We've always got work for a PhD in math," she had said. "I'm practically stuffed with it."

This was in the Last Years of Parisa Parviz, on the First Day of the Sputtering Hesterian Fire, in the Month of the Ending Star.

"THIRTY-FIVE ERRORS ON THE *first page alone*!"

Samantha Salieri rushed into Pamela Stoyanova's office at Ever, Nevers, & Co. on Monday morning, trying to plead her case.

"Lovely!" Pamela responded, paying more attention to her computer screen than to Samantha. Martin could hear the ex-Playboy playmate in her voice every time she spoke. "Make sure there aren't any *more* than that. I'd suggest going through each page at least three times, especially with an error rate that high."

Samantha made a sound that lay somewhere between a cow's moo and a rumble of thunder. Martin Ready's unique vantage point—the second small office down from Pam's corner one—made him the next go-to spot, since Vic Toronto had left the firm.

Well, not exactly "left"—he had been found raving like a lunatic in the middle of Fifth Street three weeks ago, covered in purple house paint and insisting that people help him find the "little sonofabitch who stole my car!" Terrible ravings about not letting "them" drag him into the "lightless room" followed, merely to his detriment.

"Marty!" Samantha stepped into his office and lowered her voice, but not by much. "Marty. Please. You've got to talk to her. We've got to drop this motherfucker."

Samantha stood there in her standard "I-don't-give-a-shit" outfit: sturdy grey skirt, white T-shirt, and black cowboy boots. She held a single typed manuscript page out in front of her like a piece of rotting Swiss cheese. Arcane runic inscriptions in scarlet covered it. Standard editorial graffiti. Martin noticed several large question marks and at least one instance of "NO!" splattered across the page.

"What do you want me to do?" Martin asked, his voice diminishing *sotto voce* in a reverse crescendo. NLP training. Dissolve conflict when you're able. Leave when you can't.

"Can we kill him?" Samantha asked, pushing closed

the door and sitting down in the single tattered wood-frame "client's" chair in front of Martin's desk.

"Hypothetically?" Martin answered, smiling. "Sure. I guess we could get Vic to do it. Break him out."

Samantha responded with an unconscious grin, which she literally wiped from her face with a sweep of one hand. "I'm *serious*, Marty," she said, pointing at him. "When was the last time we made any money off this fucking monkey? A decade ago? Where does he get off sending us this dog vomit?" She crumpled the paper into a ball and threw it in a little dark-grey trash receptacle with one swift behind-the-head motion. Impressive.

Martin chuckled, sliding open his bottom desk drawer. "I know what you need," he said, hefting a bottle of Laphroaig 10 Year onto the desk.

"Oh, no," Samantha said. "Not right now. I can't."

Martin, ignoring her, followed this action with setting two small glass Scotch tumblers on the desk. He noted that Samantha had not stood up to go. He uncorked the Laphroaig.

"Ah!" he said dramatically. "Smell that! Like goddamned *smoke* from a camp fire! Please let me help you with your problem, Samantha." He filled each glass with a dram of the whisky and slid one over to her.

"Fine," she said, grabbing the glass. "Whatever." She downed it in one gulp, grimaced briefly, then brightened. Martin lifted his glass and tipped it to her. "May we all die happy deaths. May we all find love in every breath." He took a sip. Good. *Perfect.*

He should bring a bottle of this back to Bash sometime.

"How do you stay so fucking calm?" Samantha asked, placing her empty glass back on the desk. Martin raised his eyebrows at it, and she slid it closer. He obliged with a refill.

"I'm only calm at work," he said. "Once I get home, it's like a fucking epileptic fit. Did you know that I don't even own plates? I smashed all of them."

Samantha giggled and took a modest sip of the refill. A single lock of black hair from the mass pinned up on her head fell uncausatively over one of her piercing blue eyes.

"True story," Martin continued to lie, raising his glass into the air. "I've never worn the same outfit twice. I burn each one in the fireplace as soon as the sun goes down. Every fucking night. For *warmth*, you know?"

"That's a lot of clothes, Marty," Samantha said, laughing. "You're worse than a girl."

"Oh, I *am*, Sammy!" Martin insisted. "Far worse than any girl or boy you could conceive of. So bad that I deign at this moment to visit your ill-mannered motherfucker of a client," Martin drained the glass dramatically. "But I will need something first."

"What's that?" Samantha asked.

Martin pointed up at the space above his office door, behind her. Samantha turned to look and immediately burst out laughing. It was a plaque with an actual handgun affixed to the center of it, beneath which were embossed the words: "WHEN IN DOUBT."

"Where the *fuck* did you get *that*?" Samantha asked, still laughing.

"I made it in shop class," Martin said. "Hey, look, I will, though. I'll go talk to Mr. Graham. Tonight if I can. Or tomorrow. In the meantime," he whisked the two empty glasses and the Scotch bottle away, "work on those Pepperwood manuscripts. Those are easy."

"Are you sure?" she said. Ah, the guilt. First step in the repayment process. "I don't want you to—"

"Solve this problem?" Martin finished for her quickly. "Thank *God* for that! All right! I was just kidding about all that stuff, anyway."

Samantha stood up, frowning at him.

Martin smiled. "Just kidding! Jesus," he said. "Go chill out. Eat something. Leave Mr. Graham to me."

MARTIN DECIDED TO CHECK out from work just a tad early and head over to Rosewood College for a little bit of digging before his meeting with Thomas Graham. Pam's secretary Whitney had somehow magicked it into happening that evening, a Friday night.

"Is there anything else I can get for you at the moment?" the girl—Gracie, by her name tag—asked him after rolling up a library cart loaded with archival boxes.

"No," Martin said. "I'm good."

Gracie—not much younger than him, in fact, and a grad student—smiled at him and withdrew to the office at the front of the library holdings division.

The Thomas Graham Collection had originally been a priceless jewel of Rosewood College, in the ornate Reading Room of which he now sat. Martin was almost certain, however, that he had seen Gracie the Grad Student stifle a laugh when he had filled out the request form earlier.

"Wow," she had said unenthusiastically, glancing at the form. "We don't get many calls for *that* stuff these days."

Martin managed a little grin. "Call me old-fashioned," he had said.

Thomas Graham had become a worldwide success just a bit too early to avoid the big head that usually attaches to such things, perhaps. But was that the *real* reason he had failed, and continued to do so? There were enough "crash-and-burn"-type stories in this business, Martin supposed. But it just seemed a bit too *easy*, for some reason. Martin hoped to dig up some clue before his meeting this evening. Who knew? Maybe even *help* the old guy out?

Martin had realized on the drive over that he knew *just enough* about Thomas Graham to function as one of his occasional representatives at Ever, Nevers, & Co.— in the sense that, well, a grad student, for example, in modern English literature might know *just enough* about Shakespeare to pass exams or teach a survey course.

The Krixwar Saga. That was his breakout hit. Three novels published in three successive years: *Krixwar*, *The Going of Jacinta*, and *The Devil Escapes*. They had made Thomas Graham and Ever, Nevers, & Co. famous and rich. Frank Fleurety—who had been chief editor back when *Krixwar* came out, in 1972—had done a notorious job of blanketing the world in advertisement and promotion.

Despite their popularity—perhaps because of it— Martin Ready had never read the beloved *Krixwar* trilogy.

Their fame and popularity had been compared to various other beloved works of fantasy literature; however, such a comparison was—at least according to Frank Fleurety—"unfair...Graham's work speaks to us from *within* that other world. There is...not an ounce of self-consciousness in his depiction of the City of Kept Promises; indeed, in its careful delineation, and the account of its rise and fall, Graham functions more in the role of transmundane prophet than mere mortal pen-wielder."

This last from a press release stuffed into a folder in

the first of the archival boxes, now splayed out on the large wooden table before him. He dug further.

Letters, original manuscripts, Christmas cards. Photographs. Thomas Graham age 23, promotional photograph. A black-and-white image of the building where the offices of Ever, Nevers, & Co. was (and remains) housed, 1973. Official notice from the Department of the Army: Mr. Thomas Graham of 718 Colonial Hill Road, unfit for service due to complications of asthma, scoliosis, etc., etc. Privately schooled in the UK. No college education. Worked in the New York offices of a chemist—Dr. Ellington Mayhew, D.Phil., FRS, etc., etc.—in some unspecified capacity.

Mayhew... Didn't he start that candy company?

Here was a picture of Thomas Graham and Frank Fleurety standing behind a table at a press release with all three volumes of *The Krixwar Saga* on display before them. A hospital release form dating from around the time the first book came out—oh, but this was for Frank Fleurety. "Released to the care of Mr. Thomas Graham..." *Why in the world...?*

Several more international bestsellers. One book three years after *The Devil Escapes*; its title seems appropriate: *Hesitancy*. Martin remembered seeing his mother reading that one, in fact. *What's that book about? Oh, it's super-weird...what did you do in school today?*

Martin paused and leaned back in his chair. *What was he looking for?*

He should talk to Bash about this.

More promotional photos, more letters—lots of back-and-forth with the editorial staff. It seemed like they started having problems with him in the 1980s—oh, a letter from Pam Stoyanova, dated 6 March 1988: *Dear*

Mr. Graham, Many thanks for the explanations. I'll try and pass these along to the copyeditors. Do you think we could get together to discuss the material, though? Perhaps at Frank's this weekend? Yrs. sincerely.

Martin began shaking his head inadvertently. Wow. Gracie's sentiment seemed perfectly apt.

Martin riffled and scanned, occasionally perusing and re-reading, moderately perplexed but mostly bored, for the better part of two hours before he found a reference that seemed—*maybe*—to point in a direction of interest.

Dear Frank, the letter read. It was dated 23 May 1992. *Thanks for the vote of confidence. I am doing reasonably well, given the circumstances. Your review showed true insight where others saw nothing at all. I think perhaps I may try to vacate for a little while—you know what I mean. GQ stuff just outstanding. Fill you in when I get back. Best, TG.*

"*GQ?*" Martin quoted aloud inadvertently. He glanced around the empty reading room in response to his own voice.

Vacate...?

It was perhaps significant that there were no further letters or materials from Thomas Graham for the following three years, until the last of his three-and-counting mega-failures had been published, in good faith, by Ever, Nevers, & Co.

The archive material ended in late 1996. So here Martin found himself, just two years later, wondering where in the hell Thomas Graham had "vacationed" starting in 1992.

And, even more curious, why he had bothered to return, only to become one of the most publicly dismal failures the world had ever seen.

THOMAS GRAHAM LIVED IN the stateliest possible estate
Martin ever laid eyes on. A full moon rose behind it,
casting into relief shadows of pointed turrets and the
crazed angles of physics-defying architecture.

"This makes perfect sense," Martin said to himself as
he sat in his Toyota, feeling like a stick of gum in a Hot
Wheels car. The readout on the digital clock displayed
"9:00." He hesitated before pushing the button that would
presumably open the intricately scrolled gatework before
him.

The button buzzed. "Mr. Ready?" A voice stately
enough to be part of the stately house crackled through
the little tin box.

"That's me," Martin said ineffectually.

The gate hummed into life, opening inward, and a
row of small, occulted lamps lit up suddenly beyond,
indicating an expensive-looking driveway of patterned
concrete.

"Okay," Martin said, feeling awkward at the lack of
verbal response. "I'm heading in now, I guess."

He crawled forward in his toy car, heading directly
for a discussion he fully intended to fail in the purposes
of. Samantha would be fine; Martin had already decided
to take over the project himself, and attempt to make the
catastrophically bad "latest novel" of former bestselling
author Thomas Graham at least moderately readable.

He thought about Bash. This would make a good story
to tell him. Bash loved a good story.

And if all else failed, he supposed, he could just take
Bash up on his offer to try a full, material transfer into
Yuttelborough "the old-fashioned way"—circuit boards
and wires and whatever that crazy kid was cooking up.
Might be fun, at least—quit this super-weird world of

death and taxes for good, one way or another.

"MORE WINE, MR. READY?"

Jesus. A fucking butler. Martin hadn't ever dealt with a butler before. Well, not in this way at least. He had tried waiting tables while he was in college, but that only lasted three days. Hardly professional.

"Sure," Martin said, holding up his glass. Without missing a beat, the butler removed the glass from his hand and presented him with a brand-new one, filled halfway with a rich, ruby-colored liquid.

A modestly dressed older woman knocked before entering the library, where Martin sat enveloped in a delicious dark leather couch before a fire, crackling in the immense hearth. She passed the several heavy wood tables and staircase spiraling up to levels two and three of the library, crammed with thousands of books, each of which was almost certainly more valuable than Martin's car, or even Martin himself, on her way to silently bow and hand a small white envelope to the butler.

The butler bowed in return stiffly, and unfolded the envelope. He read silently for a moment.

"Mr. Ready," he spoke as the woman disappeared the way she had come. "Mr. Graham regrets that he will be somewhat later than expected this evening, and invites you to enjoy the library and any evening repast you might desire. Is there something I can fetch for you?"

Martin's eyes lit up. The wine had loosened any worry that remained, and this extraordinary pronouncement implied that maybe, just maybe, if he could just *will* Tom Graham to *not be able to make it at all...*

"Ah, no," Martin answered. "The wine's good." He

stood up. "Where's the restroom?"

The butler turned and led Martin to the dark hallway through which they had entered. "To the left, sixth door. Would you like me to accompany you?"

Martin did a doubletake. "Accomp—? Oh, *no*! No thanks. I'm sure I can find it." He hoped that was what he meant, at least.

The restroom turned out to be basically another elaborately constructed room that happened to have a toilet and a sink in it. There was a selection of current magazines in a little rack off to the right of the toilet, monogrammed hand-towels that looked like things you shouldn't ever touch for any reason, a selection of soaps labelled painstakingly in calligraphic French...

Martin noted the window near the ceiling, through which bright moonlight shone. It was cracked open; a minuscule current of air filtered into the room from the wilderness that the Graham residence backed up to. Feeling terribly poor, Martin relieved himself quickly, flushed, and chose one of the soaps at random with which to wash his hands. Unwrapping it, he noted that it smelled like a weird combination of patchouli and lavender.

"So what's the old man got that I don't have?"

Martin gasped and turned to the window. Bash sat on its edge, grinning at him.

"Christ, dude!" Martin whispered harshly. "Don't *do* that, okay? Scare the hell out of me!"

Bash gave him a look of exasperation. "Whatever," he said. "Anyway, I checked the house, but you weren't there. So I thought: 'Where would Martin be if I knew where he was right now?' And I got it! Surprising how that works."

"Yeah, I guess," Martin said. He lathered and rinsed

his hands. "I don't know what I'm trying to accomplish here. How do you say, 'Hey, man, you were great once, but now you suck'?"

"You just say it," Bash replied. "And accept the consequences."

"What if you don't want the consequences?"

"*Everything* has consequences," Bash said wisely from his perch. "Doing or *not* doing. Which is just 'doing something else,' really."

A crash sounded from outside. Bash spun around.

"I have to go!" he said. "Don't tell him I was here!"

"Tell *who*?" Martin asked, but Bash had already leapt through the window, his little bipedal half-lizard/half-cat form shimmering into silvery mist in the glow of moonlight.

Martin stood there with wet hands. A knock sounded at the door.

"Is everything *quite* all right in there, Mr. Ready?" inquired the butler.

Martin sighed. "As good as it can be," he answered. "Be right out."

"CAN YOU *IMAGINE* SUCH a thing?" Thomas Graham shouted, lifting the silver lid off a gigantic pot roast. The scent alone seemed to supply Martin with enough nourishment for weeks, months, years.

"I stood there in the midst of the desert," Thomas continued, "and I witnessed heaven open, a cataclysmic deluge. I thought I might drown in it. And I feel that, perhaps, I *did* die, you know—at least a little bit."

Martin nodded. "I know what you mean," he said, feeling lame and absolutely uncertain of the meaning of *anything* Thomas Graham had been saying for the past fifteen minutes. "I've—had experiences like that myself."

Thomas frowned. "Indeed," he said as the nameless butler miraculously caused several flawless slices of pot roast to appear on Thomas's plate.

"I mean," Martin said, trying to dig himself out, "not anywhere near as overwhelming."

Thomas's grin returned slightly. He lifted a fork and prodded at the pot roast.

"In fact," Martin continued, "I might say that what you've told me qualifies as perhaps one of the most *astonishing* experiences I've ever heard."

Thomas lifted his fork into the air. "Indeed!" he shouted, smiling broadly now at Martin. "That's what you must understand! *Every word I write is a revelation*—a *gift*, Mr. Ready! Once imbibed, absorbed, digested, there is little else one must do except *wait*!"

Martin looked down and was, in fact, astonished to find his plate filled to the brim with the evening's main course. Pot roast and buttered biscuits and some sort of cold pasta that melted in his mouth with a cheesy aftertaste.

He washed down his first bite with more of the exquisite wine Thomas seemed to have on tap. Although he had been pacing himself since his first glass, it seemed to be catching up with him rapidly. He returned to the pot roast and attempted to act moderately civil while devouring it in hopes of second and third helpings.

Martin didn't recall seeing Thomas take a bite of food or chewing at all, though when he glanced over, it seemed that Thomas's plate had already been consumed by half.

"I would caution you, Mr. Ready," he said, "to be wary of any *alterations* made in the writings." He glanced up at him, set down his fork, and lifted his wine glass. "There are those without the necessary..."

Martin watched as Thomas appeared to fall into a trance, gazing into the midst of the red wine in his glass. A stroke, perhaps? Thomas seemed paralyzed, frozen. Where the hell was the butler?

Martin was about to clear his throat or attempt some other modest interruption when Thomas returned to life, continuing to speak as if nothing had happened. "Sensitivity required for these sorts of things."

Martin nodded, relieved that Thomas had not actually died in front of him.

"So tell me," Thomas continued. "How do you like the wine?"

The remainder of the evening passed in a cascade of mundane tellings and re-tellings. By the time he got back to his car, Martin felt unsure of whether or not he could actually drive home.

The night air, though, served to convince him of his capacity...although it could also have been the fact that he seemed to come to in his car, sitting just outside the gates to the Graham residence, with the digital readout on his clock displaying in perfect innocence "9:00."

He shook his head. "Damned battery," he said, rubbing his eyes. He looked back at the clock. "11.32" it now read.

He backed out of the driveway, onto the dark twisting private lane that led ultimately to I-64 and to his house at the other end—the more discreet end—of Rookville.

Something hidden in the darkness surrounding the residence watched him go.

"WHAT WAS *THAT* ALL about?" Martin asked Bash when he got back home.

Bash was seated in front of the radiator with a large mug of hot cocoa, reading a paperback. *Too Many Horrors!* it read on the cover, above an image of an adolescent with his hair standing on end.

"Oh, *gods*, what a mess!" he said, not looking up from the book. Rowley, Martin's Norwegian forest cat, purred happily beside Bash in her raggedy cat bed, and opened her eyes in brief cattish attentiveness. "That guy needs to get a handle on what he's doing."

Martin set his jacket over the back of the kitchen nook chair. "Maybe you should tell me why you've never mentioned him before?"

Bash shrugged and set the paperback down in an inverted V-shape on the rug. "Sure," he said. "What do you want to know?"

"What do I want to *know*?" Martin repeated rhetorically. He opened the refrigerator. One-half of a turkey sandwich with avocado, mayonnaise, shredded cheese, and tomato. The bread looked a little soggy, but still edible. One mostly empty two-liter of Cherry Coke. The remains of an Olive Garden salad from delivery at work earlier that week, which he hefted with the intention of throwing out.

Aha! Cold pizza behind the salad!

Bash leaned back against the base of the couch and began to idly scratch Rowley's furry neck, which the latter accommodated by stretching luxuriantly. "All *right*," Bash said. "Just playin' with you. I occasionally have to make it at least *seem* like we're in a novel, you know."

"What?" Martin said, taking a bite of pepperoni pizza.

He closed his eyes, savoring it.

"Never mind," Bash said. "Thomas Graham. Let me see. How best to put this?" He took a sip of the cocoa. "Got any Kahlúa?"

Martin nodded and fished out a bottle from the cabinet above the refrigerator. "Did you eat yet?" Martin asked. "I think I might order something. Maybe more pizza?"

"Do it!" Bash said. He took the Kahlúa bottle from Martin and drizzled a shot—then another—into the cocoa. He took a sip, grimaced briefly, and then nodded. "A thief," he continued. "The sonofabitch stole one of our prized codices during that little internecine conflict we all know and love."

Martin nodded knowingly. "You're welcome," he said.

"And many thank yous, as always," Bash said. "At any rate, the *Krixwar* books—"

Martin suddenly realized what Bash had said. "Wait, *Thomas Graham*—"

"A thief, yes. A visitor to the fabled land of Yuttelborough, indeed," Bash confirmed.

"Thomas *stole* the fucking *Krixwar* books?" Martin said, reeling.

Bash was nodding his head. "You're lovely human family sincerely enjoyed gloating over the exploits of our lineage," he said. "All the dirty secrets fit only for the High Priest of Yuttelborough."

Martin sat in the fraying wicker chair opposite Bash and gazed at him, astonished. "Thomas Graham stole the *Krixwar* books," he said again. "I can't believe it. Why didn't you tell me this before?"

"Oh, pardon my ignorance, Martin," Bash said affectedly. "It looks like we're just now getting to it. Everything has a time."

Martin scowled at him. "I guess it wouldn't have made much of a difference," he said.

"Not until now, at least. Anyway, he's not exactly on the list of people held in high esteem by our population," Bash said. "His whole career's a joke, a lie. Plagiarism, in the deepest and most unappealing sense." He sipped from his mug of Kahlúa cocoa. "Any chance we can get that pizza order in?" he asked.

Martin started, having fallen into a trance in consideration of the news while staring at a Bosch print on the wall above the couch. *Cutting the Stone*. "Oh, right," he said. "Hang on."

He went to the kitchen phone and hit Speed Dial #2: Pizza Hut. The window just above the sink showed his reflection against the night beyond: pale, dark blond hair, glasses. Other than the little scar that jutted out from the part in his hair—an old, nearly forgotten wound—he looked like a librarian. Perhaps a corpse stand-in for a movie, if he slackened his jaw and stood still enough. Certainly not a second-ranking editor—gods, no.

Martin returned to the living room of the duplex with a mostly full pint of Jameson's, an open bottle of Bordeaux that had been hiding behind the Kahlúa, and two glasses.

"Fantastic!" Bash said, setting aside the cocoa. "Mixing alcohol! Talk about favorite pastimes. What's the special occasion?"

"Tomorrow's Saturday," Martin said. He filled both glasses with a generous helping of the Jameson's. "And this story is fucking *amazing*. Hell, I might even get cupcakes later, if you keep it interesting enough."

Bash practically leapt out of his seat. "Your attention will be *rapt*, sir! This I swear, on my honor as former Apprentice Sorcerer to the Greater Grash-Bash

Yuzzutah!"

Martin smiled at him and tipped his glass before taking a sip. Whatever it was that Bash had said, the title sounded important. Anyway, he knew Bash wouldn't dare lie to him if cupcakes were at stake.

"IT WORKS OUT THIS way," Bash took another of the colored markers Martin had provided for him and continued illustrating his explanation, "magic is not a *thing*, it's a *result*. You don't 'do magic' any more than you 'do' what you see." He drew a red X through the blue line leading from the word "MAGIC" in the middle of the whiteboard to an image of an eye. "This is all essential to understanding what Thomas Graham did and why he is considered the Ungruh-Mainyoosh."

Martin had switched from alcohol to coffee around one in the morning—roughly the time he decided to take a brisk walk, sober up a little, and purchase a dozen cupcakes at the Needman's on the corner. The remains of their extraordinary repast lay spread out on the coffee table, beside which Martin had propped an old whiteboard for Bash to assist in his lecture. Bash stood hardly taller than the whiteboard itself, which occasionally made him look like a clever illusion that someone had pasted on it.

"In any event," Bash swiped another cupcake from the box and took another huge, frost-laden bite, "getting to other worlds really doesn't differ overmuch from your notions of space travel. How 'foreign' a thing is seems to depend mostly on how far you've traveled to reach it."

Martin nodded. "Like going to your usual grocery store in another city thousands of miles away," he said.

"Sure," Bash responded, tossing the remainder of the cupcake into his mouth and chewing thoughtfully. "Anything that you do *now* affects what you experience *later*." He lifted his half-empty glass of Bordeaux, grinned, and drained it. Martin couldn't fathom at what speed Bash's metabolism must function in order to process that much poison without any real signs of intoxication, especially given his size. He could unquestionably drink Martin under the table, any time, any place.

Bash continued. "So if you do something super-weird *now*, that will make what you do *later* seem strange, even if it's not," he said. "But who makes the call about what's 'strange' or not? There is a sense in which a foreign language spoken by one's own species, for example, could be considered merely an extreme dialecticization of one's native tongue."

Martin sipped his coffee. "So you're saying that what we call 'magical' really boils down to very extreme alterations in our perceptions of things?"

Bash nodded enthusiastically. "Yes!" he said, waving his hands in the air. "Indeed it does! But be careful here. The true understanding of this goes further. Your psychologists have done a splendid job of annihilating the true causes and means of magical phenomena, which were much easier to effect before their discipline became popular. *The magical perception* is *the actual fact*. I think one of your early philosophers said something similar."

"Okay," Martin said. "But that doesn't exactly explain how Thomas made it to Yuttelborough. I mean, it *does*, in a sense—"

"Oh, well, *that* part," Bash poured the last of the Bordeaux in his wine glass and leaned against the back of the couch. Rowley had scuttled away when the pizza had arrived, and returned at this point, sniffing the air and formulating a plan to steal some small portion of it. Bash tossed a piece of pepperoni on the floor, for which Rowley made a beeline. "*That* part still baffles me, somewhat. I know how it *might* be possible—but how he *actually* did it, especially from *this* side... Well. I'm not sure."

"I see now," Martin said. "So, you basically explained to me what you've got. But we need a few more clues to piece together his actual *modus operandi*."

Bash sipped his wine. "Once again, my friend, *you* come into the picture, cast expertly in the mold of a hero to my people!" He winked, indicating the sarcasm, but raised his glass to show that the praise was tendered honestly.

"Well, what should I do?" Martin asked. "Go back to Thomas's? Give him a little dusting-up? Threaten to not read his books?"

Bash laughed. "Perhaps," he said. "But I think there's another person of interest in this matter."

"Who?" Martin asked.

"That thing lurking about Thomas Graham's estate earlier like he owned the place," Bash answered. "I tried to catch up with him, but he slipped past me somehow."

"Any idea at all what that might have been?" Martin asked further.

"I would merely be guessing," Bash said. "I don't want to be hasty in judgment. Could be another refugee like me." Bash shrugged his shoulders. "Could be the bastard that sold us all out."

DESPITE THE REVELATIONS AND promises of adventure— invited or not—Martin's eyes began to close without permission. Bash insisted that he get himself to bed, and even volunteered to do the cleanup (which, given the ease of doing so by generating sorcerous pockets of localized negentropy, wasn't all that generous).

After a quick shower to wash the weirdness of the day off of him, Martin collapsed into bed, followed quickly by Rowley, nestled deeply in the sheets in the crux of his arm. Delta waves engulfed him superabundantly, followed by fragmented dreams.

Bash descended to the alcove he and Martin had set up in the basement as his not-so-temporary home.

What strangenesses beset him in this peculiar turn, this twist in what he had always suspected would be the plot of his life! Yuttelborough—gone, for all intents and purposes. A few (he hoped!) straggling children of its parentage escaped into *this* world, Earth and humans and all that. The safety of New Yuttelborough still to be decided.

Thank the *yuzzutahs* for Martin Ready, and for those like him. Bash suspected he would be cowering in some dump—possibly literally—making each day a sequence of escapes and stealing food by teleporting inside closed restaurants and grocery stores.

But Bash was an eternal optimist. Although his training was unfinished, he knew *something* of how the multiverse functioned, something of the mechanics behind its appearance. Which made Thomas Graham's access to and absconding with the *Gah Quinkwe* that much more peculiar. What did the human know that Bash seemed wont to discover? What was Bash himself perhaps taking for granted that might solve this whole mystery and dissolve the villainy that even now resulted from Yuttelborough's missing pieces?

A world missing a piece—a *single* piece—could not exist. The concept of "missing" something seemed, indeed, utterly abstract. Unless...

Bash himself sank into a restful sleep, unsettling thoughts of the *Krixwar* and its obviously extra-human provenance notwithstanding.

THE NEXT DAY, MARTIN awoke to the scent and sound of bacon frying. He entered the kitchen to the sight of Bash assembling an extraordinary breakfast on the kitchen table: scrambled eggs smothered in cheddar cheese, thick bagels slathered in butter, and a mountain of the promised bacon on a gigantic serving plate.

"Help yourself!" Bash said. "I got hungry again."

Martin smiled and poured himself fresh coffee. Rowley had already settled down to a small plate of eggs and bacon, lovingly set out in her dining area.

"Where the hell did you get all this food?" Martin asked. "I—"

"Late night trip to the grocery store," Bash said, and winked. "Got a little carried away—maybe."

"Not in the slightest," Martin said, and dug into a bagel that dripped butter. "Although I will probably regret this meal in half an hour."

"I can take care of that!" Bash said. "Don't worry. Mix you up Yuttelborough's equivalent to Pepto-Bismol!"

Martin chuckled. "I accept the challenge, then," he said.

"By the way," Bash said, "I think I may have something of a plan."

"Okay?" Martin said, shoveling another forkful of scrambled eggs into his mouth. Bash's culinary artistry was in full swing this morning.

"During my theta-wave activity I allowed several apparently incongruous data-sets to encounter one another," he said. "In short, I dreamed some weird stuff. But, as with any of these manifestations, any encounter tries—quite desperately—to generate a degree of logical coherency. If the data-sets are sincerely incapable of any degree of feasible combination—well, I think a basic human summary would be: 'If they don't jive, then make shit up.'"

Martin laughed aloud. The bacon was *incredible*...

"At any rate, that's precisely what I did," Bash continued. "I put some things together, and I realized that there *ought* to be a sort of manual for dealing with crises of this sort! I mean, this can't be the first time that the capacity for an innocent world to thrive has been thwarted by villainous machinations—intentional or otherwise. There really *ought* to be a rule-book, a guide-book, something you could use to—"

The phone rang.

This being a Sunday morning—and Martin's friend group being mostly limited to one fugitive from another world and some old college friends with whom he spoke perhaps once a year—Martin's anxiety level skyrocketed instantaneously.

Third ring. Fourth.

"Um," Bash said. "Are you...?"

Martin dropped his bagel, stood up, and proceeded to the phone. He hesitated on ring number seven, then picked it up.

"He—hello?" he said.

"Martin?" A tinny metallic version of a female voice sounded from the other end of the line. "It's Samantha."

"Hey," Martin responded. Bash's eyes were wide with inquiry. Martin shrugged and raised an empty hand. "What's up?"

"I'm sorry to have to tell you this," she said. "But Thomas Graham died last night."

Stunned was not the right word. Astonished didn't work either. Lightning-struck, perhaps?

"Martin?" Samantha said.

"Oh! Um," he said. Bash was goggling, apparently having overheard the news. "That's, uh. Wow. Holy shit."

"Yeah," she said. "I feel pretty shitty right now about how I was talking yesterday. Who could have known? Did he seem sick last night, or anything?"

Martin sat down heavily in the chair at the kitchen office nook. "No," he said. "He seemed—fine. I guess. Jesus. What the hell? Do you know how he died?"

"Heart attack," she said. "It was on the morning news. I figured you wouldn't hear about it until Monday unless I called you, since you never watch that stuff."

"No, no, you're right," he said. "That's—tragic. Weird. Tragically weird. Wow."

"Yeah, well," Samantha said. "Just thought you should know. Hey, I'll see you at work, all right?"

"Right," Martin said. "Thanks for letting me know."

Bash was speechless when Martin returned to the table.

"Okay," Martin said. "One world-destroying villain down. What do you want to do tonight?"

"THIS IS WHAT YOU need."

The guy in the dark, *dark* clothing and sunglasses had been skulking about at the back of St. Albertus's

Church since before the service started. Martin noticed him immediately upon entering, and felt his gaze on him throughout Frank Fleurety's flawlessly cadenced and moving eulogy. When the congregation (large enough, given Thomas Graham's once-international acclaim) proceeded to Berryhill—"the cemetery for rich people," as most of those around Martin referred to it—the guy had cornered him.

He handed him a brown paper bag, folded over. It contained a book. Bash's words from several days ago sprang into his mind unbidden. *There really ought to be a rule-book, a guidebook...*

People filtered past the two as Martin gazed from the man to the package and back to the man. "Okay?" he said.

The book was an old hardcover, its dustjacket hardly more then shreds, but Martin could make out the title. *Occult Architectures of Memory.*

"Read it carefully," he said, and presently disappeared into the throng.

Martin stood for a few moments, as if awaiting further instructions. He gazed back down at the book in his hands. The author's name had been badly obscured on the dust-jacket. He opened the book. A bookplate: *Ex Libris Ward Chapman.* The title page:

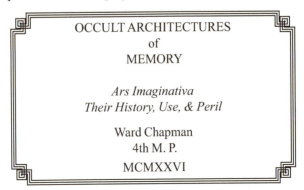

OCCULT ARCHITECTURES
of
MEMORY

Ars Imaginativa
Their History, Use, & Peril

Ward Chapman
4th M. P.
MCMXXVI

Author's personal copy. But what in the name of—

Someone jostled Martin. He closed the book and looked up.

"Hey, weirdo." It was Samantha Salieri, looking petite and pretty as always. "You going to the"—she hushed her voice and leaned closer to Martin's ear, grinning—"*after-party?*"

Martin grinned. Pretty girls always smelled like peppermint and vanilla. "Depends on how many"—Martin lowered his voice substantially—"*bodies we're burying.*"

Samantha giggled. A few stragglers were still in the vicinity, ignoring them. "Frank's hosting the wake," she said.

"And they're having it at Thomas Graham's mansion?" Martin said.

Samantha nodded. "I guess Frank's inheriting the place?" she said.

Martin reeled. "That's so fucking typical."

"Right?" Samantha headed out into the gray daylight with Martin in tow. "Looks like Frank's investment paid off."

Martin scanned the crowd as it flooded into the parking lot like tide waters over a beach of many-hued shells. Where had the guy who had given him the book gone?

"You want to ride with me?" Samantha asked. "I'll take you back here to get your car later." It was obvious that she felt somewhat awkward in the circumstances.

"Sure," Martin said. They proceeded to the parking lot. "Hey, did you see the guy with the sunglasses—"

"The guy that gave you that book?" Samantha said. "Sure. Opportunist. This *is* Ever, Nevers, & Co., after all.

You gonna trash it?"

"The book?"

"Yeah."

"Why would I do that?" Martin asked.

"Because it's going to be *crap* is why," Samantha answered. "It's *always* crap."

Martin shook his head as they got into Samantha's pristine blue VW bug. "No," he said. "It's not a manuscript. Just an old book."

"Ah," Samantha said. "Reprint opportunity. Fell out of copyright."

Martin gazed down at the paper bag holding the book in his lap.

"Maybe," he said. "Could be."

THE BURIAL PROPER PROCEEDED without incident. Martin kept straining to find sunglasses-guy in the crowd, to no avail.

There seemed to be twice as many people at the wake as had attended the funeral.

"Jesus," Samantha said, angling the little bug into a spot amongst the crowd of other vehicles. "Big party. You think Frank brought out the good stuff?"

Martin laughed. "You think Frank owns any *bad* stuff?"

He left the book on the passenger seat of the car. There was a short walk down the tree-lined avenue to the mansion's gate, which stood open, admitting the many curious funeral attendees.

"I'm surprised they're doing it this way," Martin said. "I mean, sure, it's been over a decade since his last hit book, but he's still famous. Isn't Frank afraid that people will try to steal keepsakes and shit?"

Samantha pointed subtly at two individuals standing beside the arched, oaken doorway of the mansion. "Looks like some money went into security detail," she observed.

"Yeah," Martin said. "Weird trick. They look like statues, but you can't get a thing past them."

Martin happened a glance to one side of the long drive. Bash peeked out from behind a tree trunk, hidden in the semi-darkness. He made a quick little move with his head indicating that Martin should meet him at his hiding place.

Martin made a little show of looking behind himself and squinting his eyes. "Hey, I'll catch up with you in a second," he said to Samantha.

"What? Who is it?" Samantha asked.

"Hang on," Martin deflected. "One second."

"Um—" Samantha said as Martin separated from her and darted back past a couple of small groups of people toward the entrance. Samantha looked back at him momentarily, shrugged, and then continued on into the mansion.

Martin reached the entrance gate to the drive, double-checked that Samantha had entered the mansion, and waited his chance to slip off the drive and into a little darkened cove of trees.

"Nice moves," Bash said from a spot farther on in the darkness. "Who's the chick?"

"Co-worker," Martin said. "The girl who called the other day. What's up?"

"The usual trouble," Bash answered. "I was able to pinpoint the location of the murderer using a variant of the associative oscillator spell."

Martin's eyes widened. "*Murderer*?" he repeated.

"Yes, murderer," Bash said. "Thomas Graham was old and wealthy—incidentally the easiest type of person to kill and get away with it. Nobody investigates *too* much when they're all getting a cut of almost a billion dollars."

"Who's the murderer?" Martin asked directly.

He noticed Bash shake his head in the dim light. "I don't know. All I know is that he, she, or it is *here* at the wake. Right now."

Martin felt slightly frantic all of a sudden. "What else do you know?"

"The person in question *was* at the funeral," Bash said.

"Okay, well," Martin said, deflated. "That narrows it down to about a hundred people from several demographics."

"Yeah, I know," Bash said. "Sorry I couldn't get more specific. I knew you were coming here, and I think that whoever it was realized that someone—i.e., me—was trying to track them using that spell. They put some sort of cloaking device over the area. I can still determine the location within a block or so, but I can't quite pinpoint the precise *spot* where the individual's standing." Bash paused. "Yet."

"Should I keep my eye out for anything specific?" Martin asked.

"Short of a 'Hey, I'm the murderer!' T-shirt, I don't know what to look for," Bash answered. "Anything suspicious, I guess? I just thought I should warn you— keep you informed, you know."

"I definitely appreciate it," Martin said. "And I can tell you right now that the only 'suspicious' person I've seen is some guy dressed completely in black who was at the funeral. He gave me a book and said that I should 'read it carefully.'"

Bash looked concerned. "What book?" he asked.

"It's called *Occult Architectures of Memory*," Martin said. "Have you ever heard of it?"

Bash shrugged. "Nope," he said. "Do you want me to take a look at it?"

"Come to think of it, yes, I do," Martin said. "It's in Samantha's VW bug down the street. On the seat in front. Can you get it?"

"Unlocking's a piece of cake," Bash said. "I barely need any magic to do that. I'll grab it and do some 'vesti-gatin'!" Bash hurried off into the underbrush, taking the long route back to the street.

Martin watched carefully for his chance to get back on the drive without being noticed, and stepped out.

"Martin."

It was his boss's voice. Pamela Stoyanova.

Martin turned around and faced her. She stood there, smoking a long, black cigarette out of a long, black ciga-rette holder in her long, black dress. Everything about her was dark except for the heavy blonde curls falling in cascades down her back and around her shoulders.

"I'm glad you could make it," she said.

"Yeah, right," he said. "Super-weird situation, huh?"

"No doubt," Pamela said. "Thomas had his troubles, but he was a dear, dear friend of mine and Frank's. You had just taken over his latest project."

She simply stated it as a fact. "Yeah," Martin said. "I was here on Friday night to discuss it with him over dinner. He didn't seem like he was in ill health at all."

"Yes, well," Pamela said, snuffing out the cigarette beneath the toe of one black high-heeled shoe. "Whom-ever suggested that death has a conscience never met the man."

Martin wasn't sure whether she was talking about Thomas Graham or "death." She strode past Martin down the drive. Without turning around, she said, "See you inside."

BASH WAS THREE-QUARTERS OF the way through *Occult Architectures of Memory* by the time Martin got back home.

Oddly, Samantha seemed to have completely forgotten about the book when they had both returned to her car after mingling for half an hour at the wake. Martin assumed that she had made her estimation of the book— boring, waste of time—and left it at that. Not notable.

"*Who* gave this book to you?" Bash said immediately as Martin entered and divested himself of wallet, keys, and jacket. "Mr. 'Ward Chapman' has basically *nailed* the mechanics of portal technology here!"

"Of the *portal*?" Martin repeated. "I thought it was a book about memory. Mnemotechnics, memory tricks, or whatever."

"It *is* and it *isn't*," Bash said. "Listen to this passage."

> Once context is established—i.e., the premises upon which the field of play orients itself—then it is the familiar rules of *logic* that orchestrate the results. The Practitioner simply *allows* those rules to make all necessary connections amongst various facets of the contextual premises. Left to its own devices, this context gradually takes the place of an existing *Weltanschauung*.

"But here's the kicker," Bash continued. "'The *speed* with which such a context replaces that which is extant depends almost entirely upon the Practitioner's degree of conviction.'"

Martin sat down heavily in the wicker chair across from Bash, his usual spot. Rowley had gotten up moments before to finish the last of her supper in the kitchen.

"Fascinating," Martin said, leaning back. "I'm assuming that you're going to tell me what this actually means?"

"It means that Thomas Graham's trek to Yuttelborough had precedent," Bash said. "But I've never heard of this 'Ward Chapman' character. Did he write anything else? Is he still living? I suppose it's possible, technically."

"Wait, wait," Martin said. "I'm not sure I fully understand the situation as it is. 'Once context is established,' for example—what the hell does that mean?"

Bash placed the book on the floor beside him and settled into lecture mode. "Think of it this way," he said. "What you experience really boils down to a set of causes and effects that accord, for the most part, with what you *accept* as possible. These things that happen *actually can* happen in a given set of circumstances. If you set up a particular *space*, however, within which the usual rules don't apply—or within which you *add* or *subtract* various rules or aspects of rules—you can get people to go along with it for as long as they're willing to play the game."

Martin nodded. "Okay," he said.

"So suppose you can somehow keep a game going long enough, or expand the domain within which game-rules hold far enough, to the point where those within the boundaries of the game *forget* that it's a game they're playing. You just keep the game with those rules going until people start to act *as if* those were always the rules, all along."

"Then you have created a new reality," Martin said, "a pocket in the reality you had before where things work in a certain very specific way."

"Right," Bash said. "And you need to set up safeguards at this point against people ever straying outside the physical-mental boundaries you established. Enter a *ruler*—someone who *measures out* the actual parameters of the playing field."

Martin suddenly realized what Bash was describing. "Everything," he said simply. "What we call 'everything' is actually just the limits of measurement."

Bash nodded ecstatically. "Precisely!" he said. "And you simply make it *so* believable *within* the established parameters—even if it's not exactly *comfortable*—that those who have forgotten they are simply playing one type of possible game within those parameters basically do your policing *for* you. They *excommunicate* those who say, 'Hey, guys! Look out there! There's actually something *beyond* the spot where the king said there's supposed to be stuff!'"

Martin began to understand something of the implications of what Bash said. "Who was it that gave me the book?" he asked.

Bash's smile faltered slightly. He paused momentarily, then brightened.

"There's someone *writing* this at this very moment," he said. "And, at the same moment, someone *reading* this."

"What?"

"What formulates our assumptions?" Bash asked—rhetorically, Martin hoped. "Why do we think that we're *not* being written or read?"

"Okay," Martin said. "You didn't exactly lose me, there. But aren't you engaging in a sort of logical error?"

"Which one?" Bash asked.

"The one where you presume something that *doesn't* need to be presumed?" Martin said.

"You mean to say that I'm not applying the principle of scientific parsimony," Bash responded. "Occam's razor."

"Something like that," Martin said.

"Hm," Bash responded. He stood up and began to pace. "Suppose I decided to *stop* pacing right this very moment," he said, and continued to pace. "Would my continuing to pace be an indication that I possessed *no* free will?"

Martin thought for a moment. "I don't see how this relates to Ward Chapman," he said, finally. "Or Thomas Graham. Or whoever *murdered* Thomas Graham."

Bash laughed. "The ultimate wall, the one with all the answers," he said, "lies *right at the edge* of what you can experience. The page upon which these words are written—and I say this to the author, as well as to the reader—defines the existence of that 'wall' between us. Some of my words get re-written, practically as I say them. And Martin here gazes at me as if I've finally lost my mind. But I think the most extraordinary thing about this whole story is that it exists *at all*."

Martin stood up from the wicker chair and smiled. "Why did I stand up and smile?" he said.

"Because the author's trying to prove a point," Bash said. "And the simplest way for him to do it is to give you *direct proof* that you're in a story."

"Okay," Martin relaxed and let his smile drop. He smiled, then frowned, then relaxed again. "I don't really find that this proves anything."

"That's because the man writing about us at this very

moment (I saw that re-write, by the way!) is, in fact, being *written by us* as well," Bash said. "The person reading these words right now? That person is being *read* by us as well!"

"Existence?" Martin said, hardly knowing why.

"'To stand outside of,'" Bash quoted. "I think we've exhausted the poor man. And I fear that he will probably decide to re-write this *whole* section unless I tell him not to. *Please remember us!*"

Martin decided to pace as well. "It's the next day in that other world, isn't it?" *Who was making him say this?*

Bash shrugged. "Probably," he said. "I don't know *everything*. But I *am* beginning to get a sense of the extent of inventiveness. Every solution, every problem, every *context*, is invented. But it only lasts as long as you 'take it for granted'—that is, as long as you *actually believe* in it. Not just a spouted belief; not just something you use as a rationalization. An actual *understanding*. Like when you can explain *why* a certain theory of physics makes sense in context—not just calculate using it."

Martin suddenly felt elated—like the weight of an entire world had been lifted from him. He was, somehow, mysteriously, *getting it*—no exceptional maneuvers really seemed all that necessary in order to "make" the world what he wanted it to be...though one slight observation gave him pause.

"But to simply 'perceive' another *universe*—doesn't that presume the existence of that universe?" Martin asked.

"Yes, of course," Bash said. "But I see what you're getting at. The answer to your hidden question is to *note the areas in your thinking where you assume existence as primary*. If, instead, you note your own ability to *perceive* as primary—"

"Your new assumption, your new understanding, functions as the means by which you experience *everything*," Martin finished.

Bash laughed.

"How do we test it?" Martin asked. "I mean, if this holds *true*, then how do we test such a thing?"

"There's the problem in a nutshell," Bash said. "And I'm not trying to 'cop out' on you, either. The notion of 'testing' something derives from the fundamental assumption that keeps you stuck in one world rather than another. You don't *test*; you simply *do*. You don't *exist*; instead, you *insist*—on the world that you 'now' experience, the one you want, with no thought or recognition of that 'other' one except perhaps as one of many possible fictions."

"It makes sense," Martin said. "It actually does. What we 'wake up to' is, in a sense, the result of actually random processes that get linked together logically into a story. The more *investigation* we do into *that* particular story, the more 'real' it becomes—*because we treat it as such*. But to *truly* shift into another world—one where your wildest hopes and dreams exist as *truths*—requires both no effort and maximum effort at the same time."

Bash clapped his hands. "You're *getting* it, Marty!" he exclaimed joyously. "Let's just hope that all this exposition is worth it to those reading it!"

Martin laughed, feeling oddly reminiscent of something. "I guess I'm going to just take your word for it," he said. "Consider it! Hell—just *let* the new world be!"

Bash and Martin were both standing, practically floating on air, when a knock sounded from the door.

Bash's eyes widened. He scooped up *Occult Archi-*

tectures of Memory and made a dash for the basement. Martin waited a few beats, and then proceeded to the front door and gazed through the eyehole. Rowley sat on the windowsill in the kitchen, looking a little anxious and inquisitive.

What he saw was peculiar enough: a cowled, cloaked, and bearded figure standing there, dimly illumined by the yellow porch light. What he heard made him open the door.

"Martin Ready?" the figure whispered in earnest at the door. "It is of vital importance that I speak with you. You and the Yuttelboroughian."

"I HAVE REASON TO believe," the old man had said, seated now on the couch in Martin's living room, utterly unfazed by the presence of Bash beside him, "that you and Bash here have come into rather *concrete* understanding of the Wisdom protected by my Order."

"An Order whose function is to ensure that the information we *just now* figured out is hedged about with all sorts of oaths and obligations." Martin summarized what the old man had yammered about when Martin had let him in. After the shock of hearing a stranger speak about Yuttelborough—and a brief conference with Bash—he had decided that there was really no point in trying to keep a mere door shut on the fellow.

Besides, he looked a lot like an old wizard, like Gandalf or something—and Martin just *had* to know. It turned out his name was Loah-Dath, and he "never minded a coffee, no matter what the hour."

"That is correct, in part," he said. Martin glanced at Bash, who leaned back against the couch cushions, resting his elbow on the arm of the couch and his head on the palm of one small hand. Martin couldn't tell whether Bash seemed unsettled or just baffled.

"There are occasional, highly unusual confluences of events," Loah-Dath continued, resting his coffee mug meditatively in his lap and holding it with both hands, "that trigger our arrival. The first was the traffic accident you suffered several years ago, resulting in your seemingly inadvertent rescue of Bash from the destruction of Yuttelborough."

Martin unconsciously raised a hand to the sole remaining evidence of that night's reality: a three-inch scar, only the tip of which protruded from beneath his hairline.

"The second was the continued presence of Bash," Loah-Dath said. "We did not intervene at that time because—well, it seemed that you got along well with one another. Bash's orphaning could not be helped. At least, not until the construction of New Yuttelborough is completed. And the third," he took a sip of his coffee and savored it for a moment. "The third was the death of Thomas Graham, *if occasioned by the presence of Ward Chapman.*"

"The book?" Martin asked.

"The book, indeed, is of supreme importance," Loah-Dath confirmed. "We thought that all copies of that book had been confiscated shortly after its appearance. There was a rumored errant copy which, thankfully, has now been located. As you spoke understanding of its contents, I was sent to ensure that the information is...contained."

"Wait a second!" Bash chimed in, sounding annoyed. "You can't just take that book *back*! And not just because I haven't finished *reading* it yet!"

"Be calm, friend," Loah-Dath smiled. The man seemed imperturbable. "I will not confiscate the book, provided I obtain your word that its contents will not be discussed with any individuals who presently lie outside this room."

"Okay," Martin said, noticing that Bash had started to formulate an argument. "We'll figure that out. You said that the book is of 'supreme importance.' You *didn't* say that it constituted the 'presence of Ward Chapman.'"

"Correct," Loah-Dath said. "It was Ward Chapman who *gave* you the book. Probably the only person in existence who *could* do such a thing."

"The guy at the funeral?" Martin said. "But he didn't look more than maybe forty or fifty years old—"

"Looks are quite obviously deceiving," Loah-Dath said. "Ward Chapman defected from our Order nearly three hundred years ago, after our stint as the Invisible College of the Rose Cross. He was known under a different name, then."

"Is it this person—Ward Chapman—who killed Thomas Graham?" Bash asked.

"It is highly doubtful," Loah-Dath answered. "As the death of Thomas Graham appears to have—as you would put it—thrown a substantial wrench into the gears of his plan."

"Which is?" Martin asked.

"The total dissemination of our Order's secret wisdom," Loah-Dath said plainly.

Martin remembered his own forgotten mug of coffee and retrieved it from the table before them. "The *Krixwar* saga..."

"Indeed," Loah-Dath said. "Graham's success was unprecedented. We were quite taken by surprise when it was reported to us that Ward Chapman had succeeded in bringing off a major part of his scheme in the most ingenious manner—namely, he simply made it all look like fiction."

Bash had a look of consternation on his face. "Doesn't seem all that ingenious to *me*," he said. "It's been done before. Many times."

"Yes," Loah-Dath said, "but in each of those cases we were able to subtract some vital piece of the puzzle before the world got wind of it. In this case, Chapman was able to distract us with a rather extraordinary 'ruse,' if you will permit the use of that word for such an act of malice."

Bash suddenly looked awed. "The destruction of Yuttelborough," he said quietly.

Loah-Dath merely gazed at Bash and sipped his coffee.

"And after the success of the *Krixwar* books," Martin added, "you knew what he was up to, and could stop Thomas Graham from having any further attention paid to him."

"It is a sad state of affairs for all concerned," Loah-Dath said. "We have no interest whatsoever in undermining the skill and ability of any entity inhabiting the Multiverse. But there are occasional instances where extreme prejudice is necessary to deter further villainy."

"You kill people if they figure this stuff out and don't join your club?" Bash said sarcastically.

Loah-Dath actually rolled his eyes. "We don't *kill* them," he explained. "Murder is not possible for one of our institution. Deletion of memory is, however, not only possible, but generally advised."

"So what's the catch?" Bash asked wisely.

Loah-Dath grinned as he stood up. "The only 'catch' to your admission is that you must refrain from doing evil of any sort," he said simply.

"How do you define 'doing evil'?" Bash asked, again with his usual keen discretion.

"Our Aristotle decided upon a reasonably good definition of it," Loah-Dath answered. "That which does not venture into the *excessive* or the *deficient*. Balance. Moderation. But, to preclude your next question, we do take this one step further. We insist upon *actively* doing *good works*."

"Which means?" Martin asked, deciding to pre-empt Bash's remark.

"If you come across suffering, do what you can to alleviate it," Loah-Dath responded. "Excesses or deficiencies, left to conclude themselves, will either explode or implode, respectively. If you encounter one or the other, use intelligence and creativity to moderate it. *Extract* from an excess to cure it; *add to* a deficiency to do likewise. This can only be determined with precision and accuracy on an individually contextual basis. The result of moderation is happiness in all respects."

"That's it?" Martin said.

Loah-Dath nodded. "That's it," he said. "You would be astonished—truly astonished—at the number of potential applicants who, upon learning this, attempt in some way to wiggle out of the clause. I can tell you now: your first venture into evil subsequent to acceptance into the Muzzduh-Yassnans will effect your expulsion instantaneously. *You will not remember us.* But if you are sincere—even after such an act, and depending upon its severity—you will gradually come back into contact with us. Hopefully prior to your physical death, which often puts a damper on things."

"Okay," Bash said, looking at Martin. "I suppose that if someone attacks me with intent to kill, then self-defense would be considered 'extraction from an excess'—of force, in this case?"

Loah-Dath grinned widely again. "That is correct," he said. "But be wary of this. One of the original purposes of our discipline—magic—involved the gathering and deflection of vicious energies. Self-defense starts with avoiding conflict, continues with deflating conflicts that have arisen, and ends with *disappearing* from the area where conflict appears unavoidable, along with any innocent entities in the vicinity." He paused momentarily, kneeling down to pet Rowley, who had appeared, cautiously at first, but now seemed positively at ease beside him. "That which alleviates pain *for all* is good. It is unfortunate that many entities think too microscopically in this regard."

"Sounds good to me," Martin said. "Where do I sign?"

THE LIQUID AGENT CANDY Company was the name of one front for the Order, and it was to the nearest offices of this backbone of society that they ventured only minutes later for whatever "official" induction into Loah-Dath's Order would ensue.

The use of magic apparently came with at least one price: it could be *tracked*. And although Bash insisted that he was not a "magical" creature, Loah-Dath made it clear that he was so eminently capable in the arts of sorcery and other magical disciplines as to make practically no difference to one performing a spell of location. One reason for the existence of Liquid Agent involved the movement of merchandise and people *without* extraordinary magical prowess from one location to another; however, another involved maintaining a "map" of magical activity in given areas. Thus had the location of *Occult Architectures of Memory* been tracked following Ward Chapman's presence at the funeral.

"Now, you *did* say 'Candy Company,' correct?" Bash asked from the backseat of Martin's Toyota. Martin glanced at him in the rearview mirror, where Bash sat buckled in, holding tight to Ward Chapman's book. It was the first time since Loah-Dath had arrived that he had a look of hopefulness in his eyes.

"Indeed," Loah-Dath said, seeming incredibly *not* out-of-place in the passenger seat. "Our alchemists required some sort of 'laundering' service for not only their concoctions, but the enormous amounts of gold that one particularly gifted Master of ours produces. Many other uses of the premises have been derived since its origin."

"If I might ask," Martin interrupted, "what 'candies' are actually *alchemical concoctions*?"

"I am not exactly certain," Loah-Dath replied. "Much of the alchemists' lore is hidden even from me. It is not my focus, my primary domain of study. But I *can* say that the way to find out is obvious: if, after consumption, your level of joy inexplicably increases, with no consequent diminishment of energy or focus, you have been blessed by the lucky presence of one of our products!"

Bash nodded enthusiastically. "I could write you a *list* of these!" he exclaimed.

"And I hope that you will," Loah-Dath said. "In the meantime, let us focus first upon your respective initiations, and second upon locating Mr. Ward Chapman and getting him to reconsider his perhaps unintentionally rash actions. The building is up ahead, just beyond Cressida Bridge."

The boulder in the road came out of nowhere.

Martin swerved out of its way only to proceed off the edge of Cressida Bridge itself. The entire situation occurred so quickly that none of them even had a chance to scream or yell with the shock of it.

IT WAS SOMETHING LIKE *sightseeing, except they exchanged bodies.*

Those mountain ranges were heaps of jewels and gold. Those forests were repositories of great wisdom— no tree need be sacrificed to spell it out; one merely rested by the great oaks, for example, and felt their wisdom seep into you, years, decades, centuries of it.

Miraculous gardens, every petal of every flower purposeful and painstakingly cared for; and these an indication of seniority, often, for the children had their own, their miniature plots of land to till, seeds to sow and harvests to reap.

The closest thing to bloodshed: a syrupy mixture extracted from their maple trees and mixed with dough, rolled up in fragrant leaves and even, occasionally, fried up in olive oil, powdered with sugar...

Oh, if you ever wondered what Love is like, you've never been there! For here is Love, oceans of it, and at the center a Fire—please help us, please find me, follow Love, Martin—

THE IMAGE OF EARTH in the midst of outer space—this Martin saw quite clearly in his half-waking reverie. He blinked his eyes and turned his head, which ached. There was a brief flash of pain. He winced, then opened his eyes again, facing the other direction. An image of Bruce Campbell as Ash in *Army of Darkness*. Someone had scrawled "HAZ" in black marker beside Bruce's face, with an arrow pointing at him.

Martin sat up.

He appeared to be in a room, rather large, loaded with artifacts, books, comics—all the representatives of standard nerd culture. He lay on a couch, lightly covered with a cotton sheet, beneath a poster of the solar system.

And there, seated in a large easy chair, was the Nerd Himself. Martin turned toward him.

The Nerd looked up from a gigantic paperback. "Oh my God!" he exclaimed, dropping the book. "You're awake! Guys! Guys! *He's awake!*"

Martin heard scrabbling and running from other areas of the house. The Nerd stood up and rushed half the distance to Martin, at which point he slowed substantially, smiling largely and nervously.

"My name's Haz," he said. "Short for 'Hazzard.' Very embarrassing story about my father's television-watching habits now follows. Okay. Done!"

Martin began to notice a pain on the left side of his face. "Ouch?" he said. Two more nerds entered the room.

"These are my friends Taggart—" he pointed to a tall, skinny kid wearing a Gore Shriek T-shirt "—and Bewley." The latter had long hair and a face full of acne.

"Hello?" Martin wondered if he would ever speak anything but questions again. The two teenagers waved, both smiling inanely.

"You may be wondering why you're in some nerd's room in the middle of the night," Haz said. Martin nodded in agreement, then winced as a sharp pain ran through the back of his neck.

"Dude," Haz turned to Bewley. "Could you grab him some of that ibuprofen? Or stronger stuff." Haz turned back to Martin. "You want something stronger? My mom's got a fucking arsenal."

Martin carefully angled his body into a normal sitting position on the couch. "No," he said. "Ibuprofen's good. I think."

"Right," Haz said. "As I was saying, you may be wondering what you're doing *here*, of all places. And I think you may be astonished—perhaps as astonished as we are pleased—to know that it had *everything* to do with *this*!" Haz held up a typewritten sheet of paper that appeared to have been torn out of a book.

Bewley appeared from out of nowhere and held out a handful of ibuprofen and a can of Coke. Martin accepted both gratefully, taking one pill at a time and tipping his head back as minimally as possible until 800 milligrams had been consumed.

Bewley sat down to his right a few paces off. Taggart had decided to seat himself in a metal folding chair beside Haz, who continued his lecture.

"Now, we don't *typically* make a practice of following suggestions from unknown sources," Haz said, "but boredom invents some drastic resolutions."

Martin's drowsiness began to diminish as Haz spoke. *Wait a minute—*

"My friends?" Martin asked.

Haz looked questioningly at Bewley and Taggart. "Yes, of course," he said slowly. "We are your *friends*. For sure." Taggart was grinning pointedly. Martin heard Bewley chuckle beside him.

"No, no," Martin said. "My *friends*. The two people in the car with me?"

Haz's look became one of genuine concern. "Um," he said. "We only found you. Staggering around in the middle of the street."

"Did you check the car?" Martin asked.

"I checked the car," Taggart said. "But there wasn't anybody else in it. Not that I could see, at least."

"Helluva fall," Bewley added. "Good thing your car hit the far wall of the gorge and didn't tumble down to the river."

"No shit," Taggart said.

"You're *sure* there were two other people with you?" Haz asked. He turned to Taggart. "I *knew* we should have brought him to the fucking hospital. He's probably got a concussion."

"Aren't you supposed to keep people awake if they fall unconscious after a car crash?" Bewley asked.

Haz frowned. "Oh, yeah," he said. "I guess that's true."

"Lucky us," Taggart added. "He's awake."

"Okay, then," Haz said. "Let's take this one step at a time. What's your name?"

"Martin," Martin said. "Martin Ready." He realized a split second after saying it that he really didn't know the agenda of these nerds. What if they were agents of chaos, awaiting an opportunity to destroy Loah-Dath and his Order?

They proceeded to act, at least, like *nerds* of chaos at best, whooping and giving each other high-fives.

"All *right*!" Haz exclaimed. "That basically convinces me."

"Okay—what?" Martin asked. The ibuprofen wasn't doing much, but it appeared as if his adrenaline was kicking in.

"You're *Martin Ready*!" Bewley said. All three of

them were grinning broadly. Turning to Haz, he said, "I think this calls for some of your dad's good stuff!"

"My dad doesn't *have* any 'good stuff,'" Haz replied. "But I guess we could make up for that with some of the Wild Turkey we had last Saturday?"

Taggart cringed. "Barf," he said simply.

"I'll go grab it!" Bewley said.

"Hey, don't make a *racket*, dude!" Haz called after him. He turned to Martin. "My parents are asleep at the other end of the house," he explained. "But that doesn't mean they won't be able to hear him messing around in the kitchen."

Martin sighed, exasperated. "Is anyone going to explain this to me? Why the hell are we celebrating *me*—I mean, other than the fact that I survived driving off a goddamned *bridge*?"

Taggart was opening cabinets on the other side of the room. "Plastic cups in here?" he asked.

Haz ignored him and sat down in the folding chair in front of Martin. "Sorry about all this," he said, "but you've got to understand—up until a couple of hours ago, you were just a myth. And only a few *seconds* ago, you were an incredibly strange coincidence. Now? Jesus *Christ*, man, you're a fucking *legend*!"

Martin glanced about, terribly confused. "I'm still not hearing any explanation," he said.

"How about this?" Haz said, then uttered one word: "*Yuttelborough*."

MARTIN HAD, APPARENTLY, FAINTED. He awoke on the same couch with the same headache. This time, he lay still, becoming dimly aware of the presence of the nerds, still hovering about him.

Martin groaned.

Each of them held clear plastic cups half-filled with the terrible invention retrieved by Bewley and named after hunted fowl. Taggart seemed the first to notice his awakening.

"Guys!" he said. "Check it out! He *is* still alive!"

"Excellent!" Haz said. He gulped down the last of his drink, which made Martin gag subtly. "Oh, shit. Hey, get this man some *water*! Dude, Martin, are you thirsty?"

Martin nodded. "Water would be good," he said, clearing his throat.

"How about food?" Haz asked. "Anything to eat?"

Martin shook his head, instantly feeling the pain in the left side of his neck again. He couldn't wait to see what he looked like in a mirror.

Bewley handed him a plastic cup filled with water. Haz helped him sit up.

"So," Martin said, after taking a few sips, "you were saying something about Yuttelborough?"

Haz leapt up and clapped his hands. "Abso-fucking-lutely, man!" he shouted. "It's time to get packed and head out!"

Martin didn't quite understand. "Head out?"

"Yes! To Yuttelborough!" Haz answered.

"Um," Martin said. He didn't quite know how to tell them that Yuttelborough had been destroyed. "So—ah—tell me. How did you hear about it?"

"The *prophecy*, man!" Haz said.

"Prophecy?" Martin repeated.

"Aw, come on, man," Haz said. "You don't have to be coy with us. Look at it this way: we're on your side. You have all of our resources at your disposal. Taggart here is a pretty good shot"—Taggart waved at him, smiling—"and Bewley's expertise with the crossbow has been demonstrated on numerous occasions." Bewley gave Martin a lazy salute.

In addition to the headache, Martin was now confused. What had happened to Bash? What about Loah-Dath? *Who the hell were these maniacs?*

"Taggart knew the story because Repo-Man told him all about it," Haz said. "That's Kane Jeffries. But everybody calls him Repo-Man."

Martin thought he recognized the name. He didn't bother to ask *why* people called him "Repo-Man," however, fearing that the question might lead once more away from the matter at hand.

"But Repo-Man still thought it was just a *story*, see?" Haz continued. "One of those things handed down from one Dragonlance fan to another on those game nights when everything seems to come to a standstill." Haz tipped the bottle of Wild Turkey into his cup for a refill. "But what me and Bewley and Taggart thought was: *what if it's real?*"

Bewley piped up beside Martin. "I started looking for it," he said. "I was working in the school library because I didn't have a second period. *No one's* in the library during second period, and the librarian usually made some excuse to go take an hour-long cigarette break, or whatever. So I started checking everything—all the books in the science-fiction section, all the fantasy novels. We didn't want to alert anyone to our plans by checking out stacks of books from those sections, and we didn't want to be seen."

"I'd go too, if I had extra time," Taggart said. "We had to be subtle. We couldn't make it look like we were systematically going through every single book."

"Because who knew who would be watching?" Haz continued. "If Repo-Man was right, this was potentially deadly business. But it turned out we didn't *need* to go through every single book," Haz added. "Because there it was, in the G's, under Thomas Graham. The last *Krixwar* novel."

Martin's head reeled. He feared he was going to faint again.

"I remember," Haz said. "I had already read it. I had a copy somewhere. But *this* copy, the one from the school library, had something that no other copy had. And I couldn't believe that I lucked out enough to find it."

"What—" Martin started.

"The note you added at the end of the book," Haz said. "The one behind the flyleaf. Far be it from me to deface a library book, but that's exactly what I did. I tore it out. I figured: fuck it, who reads this guy's stuff now, anyway?"

Haz produced the sheet of paper he had waved in front of Martin originally and handed it to him. On it, someone had typed the date—*today's* date—along with three additional lines. "Cressida Bridge" one line read; then "3 AM" followed by "Martin Ready."

Beneath this, the writing continued:

> The truth about the Land of Promises Kept =
> Yuttelborough. I have been there and returned.
> I fought alongside the Tulku and beat back the
> horde of Black Beetles, whose humming could be
> heard in the forests for miles. They have arrived
> in our world—the dark ships, the flashing lights
> that split and seek to bridge the worlds. They
> leave their messages in our fields and imprinted
> as impossible shapes in our dreaming minds. I

wait with Baevare Baeshazanam in preparation
for our escape.

Martin didn't recall ever having written any such
thing. But its truth was inescapable—it could refer to
no one else.

So who had written it? Even stranger, who had
known what *would* happen to him—and where to place
a message so *infinitely* peculiar that these nerds would
find it and act on it?

"Needless to say," Haz said as Martin handed the
paper back to him, "we kept the place and the time of
your arrival *absolutely private*. Only the people in this
room know about it—for the moment. We all went ahead
and bought what copies of the *Krixwar* books we didn't
already have and read them. Several times, in fact." He
pointed to a shelf beside the couch sporting three thick
paperbacks. One was held together with Scotch tape.

"That was three years ago," Bewley said. "We've been
building up our forces ever since."

"Forces?" Martin croaked out. His cup was empty, his
throat dry.

"Based on what's in those books," Taggart said, "we
were pretty sure that getting back to Yuttelborough was
going to require some actual skills. Like, not just intelligence, but fighting, weaponry, all that."

"So we started to study and practice," Haz said as he
stood up from his seat. "For *this*! This moment! To be
ready—*Martin* Ready, if you catch my drift!"

All three of them stared at him, apparently waiting for
some sort of accession, some sort of battle cry, something
acknowledging their patience and longing. But what to
tell these kids? Who knew if they were part of some ploy

to destroy Loah-Dath's Order—or perhaps this was part of the initiation to ensure his loyalty?

Martin cleared his throat. "Thanks?" he said. When in doubt, it seemed best to simply go along with things and try to escape as soon as possible.

The nerds erupted once again into wild cheering.

"Another round for the Savior of Yuttelborough!" yelled Haz.

LOAH-DATH RESIGNED HIMSELF TO fate. Bash was *literally* like a kid in a candy store.

"No greater charm for the elimination of fog and doubt," Bash said, holding up a Choco-Mountain Pail. This was basically an aluminum cup filled with thick swirled milk- and white-chocolate fudge. Bash proceeded to spoon its contents into his mouth using a Liquid Agent "candy shovel."

Loah-Dath sighed and returned to the hefty tome chained to the lectern in front of him.

The boulder, as far as he could deduce, had been merely the first part of a combination of several sorts of magic. It was an illusion, obviously, having dissipated shortly after appearing, its "goal" apparently to frighten Martin into driving off Cressida Bridge.

But the part that he didn't quite understand yet involved a rather specific teleportation device. Both Loah-Dath and Bash had found themselves transported instantaneously upon impact to a spot in the middle of a nature reserve several miles beyond the Liquid Agent premises, utterly unharmed. It had taken one instance of Bash's clever locator spell to get them out of the wilderness and back to the car—which they found empty of both Martin as well as clues regarding his whereabouts.

Bash had noticed the presence of two sets of sneaker-marks in the ground around the car, but these only served to lead them back to the road.

"I can map possible routes from here," Bash had said, "but something appears to be obscuring Martin's current location."

Loah-Dath had been unable to think of a better plan at the moment than making their way to Liquid Agent, where the resources of the Order would be at their disposal.

Why such a specific teleportation device? And why teleport him and Bash together, but leave Martin behind—or perhaps teleport him elsewhere?

The problem was confusing. There seemed to be no indication regarding who they were dealing with.

Except for the sneaker prints.

Lohim-Yah—dressed convincingly as a night watchman—had welcomed Loah-Dath and the Yuttelboroughian warmly when they had arrived, offering them full use of the facilities. This general index seemed the most likely place to find a cross-referenced spell listing for the combination experienced earlier.

But they had little else...*except for the sneaker prints...*

Bash seemed perfectly content at the moment. He had switched on a television in one corner of the room, where *Tales from the Darkside* now played. Bash had turned the volume down until it was nearly silent. Ward Chapman's all-important book sat innocently beside him.

"Would you perhaps like to—" Loah-Dath started.

"I'm thinking," Bash responded without looking away from the screen. He shoveled some more fudge into his mouth. "Let me finish."

Loah-Dath returned to the fine print of his text. The creature was a strange one, but undeniably capable. *The methods of genius are ingenious so far as they are not constrained by the rules of average minds*, he heard his own Master, Chai-Shadd, direct him from an old lecture. *We would do best to attend to those wiser than ourselves, saving judgment for the times when we foolishly think ourselves the wisest.*

That sentiment had saved Loah-Dath from failure on more occasions than he could count. He lifted his eyes from the text and gazed about the storage room. Bins of candies and chocolates neatly stacked and arranged from floor to ceiling on immaculate shelves ranged the length and breadth of the room. He and Bash were stationed in a sort of breakroom toward the back. This area would be off-limits to the typical visitor—ensured, indeed, by use of a variation on the same illusion spell that must have generated the boulder.

Cantrips, Loah-Dath read as he returned to the index. *See also* allowing, besting, ... The list continued for a paragraph. There was also a list of several hundred variants on "cantrip" spells beneath the entry.

"By the kind of sneaker-print, its size, and the manner of its movement," Bash suddenly said, "I'd say we're dealing with at least two perpetrators, one a teen-aged human. But they did not extract Martin from the car."

"Indeed?" Loah-Dath said, grateful at last for a useful interruption.

"Martin's sneaker-prints show that he was probably injured in the crash," Bash answered.

"How do you know that?" Loah-Dath pressed.

Bash stood up and strode over to a bright-red trash can beside the breakroom table. He tossed the empty fudge pail into it. "Martin's prints stagger from the driver's side of the car, then lead in semi-random fashion back to the street," he responded. "And I'm assuming there were two perpetrators, to answer your hidden question, because of the *other* set of sneaker-prints and the fact that there were no tire marks on the side of the road nearby. Thus, no one *parked* anywhere—they simply pulled up, sent out one of their number to check the vehicle, and left."

Loah-Dath paused. "Your conclusions?"

Bash began riffling through a box of Candy Quakers chocolate bars. Finally, he chose one and tore the aluminum packaging open. "It seems likely that what *we* saw as a boulder in the road was, in fact, merely camouflaging the vehicle," he said. "But this worries me greatly. For it indicates that someone took *specific action* to find us on the road to Liquid Agent at precisely that time and date."

Loah-Dath took a deep breath. "Indeed," he said. "That is worrisome."

"Luckily," Bash said, taking a bite of Candy Quaker and swallowing it whole, "we have a secret weapon."

"What is that?" Loah-Dath asked.

"Me!" Bash laughed. "Do you guys have a map of the city? Really, this barely requires any magic at all to solve!"

MARTIN MADE IT TO a bathroom and cursed their negligence.

The left side of his face, surrounding his eye, was swollen and bruised. He had clearly been knocked out by the crash—the nerds must have thought he'd disappear or be abducted by their enemies if they dropped him off at a hospital.

What had happened to Bash and Loah-Dath?

The thought made Martin anxious as hell. Were they being held captive elsewhere?

Knowing that someone out there had preternatural awareness of his location in spacetime gave him chills. He sat down on the toilet in the immaculate little half-bathroom upstairs.

Walk out, he thought. *I could just walk out of this house...*

And go where? He had no idea where "this house" was in relation to Cressida Bridge. Did he even have his wallet?

Yes, he did. So the nerds hadn't robbed him. They merely kidnapped him and waited for him to *tell* them that he was "the Savior of Yuttelborough."

And unless they were consummate, practiced liars, they seemed to have no idea whatsoever that Yuttelborough had been *destroyed* in the conflagration with the beetle creatures. Haz hadn't mentioned accessing New Yuttelborough at all—besides, no one (meaning neither he nor Bash) seemed to have a clue as to what or where the missing piece required to render New Yuttelborough functional, livable, and accessible *was*.

Martin had to assume that the nerds were genuine... well, *nerds*.

Gods be damned, they were perhaps his "last hope."

Martin sighed and made an attempt to clean himself up somewhat before heading back to Haz's room.

THE GIRL HAD CEASED *to pull at her chains long ago. She felt with her mind again. And again. And again.*

Nothing, as always. For days at a time—nothing.

Wherever they had deposited her, it appeared to be insulated somehow. There was no crack in the walls of the dark chamber, and only the briefest period of light from some indeterminate source, rising and falling in the chamber.

With this light she attempted to count the days since she'd been imprisoned here. Was it one hundred, now? Two hundred?

Her back hurt. Every part of her hurt. Tears still came unbidden to her eyes; she blinked them away, along with the foolish sense that they might somehow still matter.

She felt in her mind for her heart and attempted for the thousandth time to crush it, but some defense mechanism—deeper-rooted than her peculiar powers—stopped her.

The humming began again from above. She closed her eyes. Energy in the form of misty light coursed out of her, toward the sound, like blood from a wound.

PARISA?

Martin had fallen asleep again despite the general clamor and plotting of the nerds. The vividness of the dream had him practically shaking as he awoke, partly out of a peculiar sense of identity with the beautiful, caramel-colored girl.

It was Parisa...

"He's awake," Haz said across the room. "Yo! Marty! The world's waiting, man!"

Martin sat up on the couch. The pain seemed to have lessened somewhat, at last.

"Almost time to head out," Haz said.

"Head out?" Martin repeated.

"Yeah," Haz said. "It would probably be best to make it to the rendezvous point before daybreak."

"How long was I asleep?" Martin asked.

"Dude, you've been asleep *all day*," Haz answered. "We all took naps. But Modafinil does the trick when you've got some serious work to do."

Martin noted Bewley studying some sketches on the large table near the center of the room. "Where's Taggart?" he asked.

"He's setting up the jammer," Haz said. "In the van. I designed the forms—you know, empty parking space, rolling boulder. Et cetera. Can't let those badge-wearing motherfuckers interfere." Haz held up a hand in the sign of the horns and did a brief headbang.

"I'm still a little unsure of what we're supposed to be doing," Martin said.

"Very simple," Haz assured him. "We've alerted our forces to your arrival. We're meeting up with the rest of them at the pre-arranged coordinates in two hours."

Martin grabbed a bottle of Aquafina that someone had kindly placed on the table beside the couch and took a long drink. Haz appeared to notice something across the room and cringe. Martin glanced quickly in the direction he was looking: a hefty, solid-steel safe stood partially covered by a tablecloth in the corner.

"What kind of 'forces' are we talking about here?" Martin asked quickly, pretending not to notice.

"Can't be too careful," Haz said. "Repo-Man—well, he *had* to know, kind of. Without him, we really *never* would have found you. But he's got some reinforcements, just in case the Crazy Eights show up."

Martin simply looked at Haz. "You *do* realize that

none of that was an answer to my question?" he said.

"Sorry," Haz replied. "We just want you to know that you're covered. When we get to Rookville Mall, you just do your thing and leave the rest of it to us."

A flash of insight revealed to Martin that this extraordinary ambiguity may prove his best bet in escaping the clutches of the nerds.

"Then you *also* realize," Martin said, deciding at last to simply act the part they wanted him to play, "that I will need *complete* focus to do this? I must be *totally alone*— no one can be a witness to it."

Haz's eyes grew large. He could not suppress a half-smile. "We'll do our best," he said. "If the Crazy Eights *do* show up, we may have some trouble, of course. But I'm sure we can *silence* them, if you get my drift!" Haz emitted a sinister chuckle.

Martin smiled while inwardly bearing a look of utter, astonished worry. "Whatever you have to do," he said, looking down at his hands for dramatic effect. "Just make sure that I'm alone for at least ten minutes. I will alert you when everything is ready."

At last! Years and years of struggling with the ambiguities of writers, searching for clarity in the midst of sentences made useless with the groping hands of their words, had borne fruit he never could have supposed he'd need.

Just keep them distracted, Martin thought. *Keep them focused the other direction, just long enough.*

"THE MODIFICATION IS SIMPLE," Bash informed Loah-Dath. They both hovered over a map of the city. "I simply alter one formulative logic component of the spell. We're going to try to pinpoint the area of *highest* probability *not* containing Martin!"

Loah-Dath smiled broadly. "And I'm assuming that, once located, you simply—"

"—find the center of mass! Exactly!" Bash finished for him. "The area will almost certainly not resemble a simple circle, so it will require a bit of integration."

Loah-Dath's smile faltered briefly. He would have assumed a Euclidean circle around the point of least probability.

Bash began to chant the usual locator spell with a few minor variants as Loah-Dath spread patented Liquid Agent Emerald 39 dye over the map in thick swathes. The translucent dye began to shimmer with greenish light as the harmonics of Bash's chant activated its magical constituents, forcing the seven-times-distilled molecules to coalesce. Bash held his mind focused on an image of Martin—even more so, on the *feel* of the *being* known as "Martin Ready." The instant Loah-Dath had finished coating the city map in dye, Bash focused with full intensity on the image—and *deleted* it from his mind's eye.

As Bash had predicted, a squiggly area appeared instantaneously on the map. He stopped chanting.

"Okay," Bash said. "We have now located the area where whatever magic is cloaking Martin has its highest effect. If my reasoning is correct, he should be precisely at the point where the spell tells us he has the least probability of being."

Loah-Dath sat down and watched in wonder as the Yuttelboroughian began scribbling away on Liquid Agent stationery, using the closest grid-points on the map as a basis for his calculations.

MARTIN MADE A SHOW of entering a sort of profound trance once seated in the back of Haz's van.

The three nerds took places up front, and maintained a tranquil silence for the sake of Martin's fakery.

Rookville Mall. Why the hell would they want to meet up at Rookville Mall?

Martin decided to close his eyes and begin breathing in a rhythmic fashion. Anything to convince them. Anything to keep them hypnotized while he planned his escape.

Amidst the hypnagogic imagery that floated behind his eyelids, he suddenly remembered Ben Crabbe at the Fall County Jail.

~~~

THREE YEARS AGO

"SOMETHING MIGHT HAPPEN BY chance," Ben Crabbe said as he took Martin's Queen. "Then again, when you set up the conditions for it, 'chance' is what we in the business would call 'not knowing shit.'"

Martin slumped at the table bolted to the floor. He made a tentative reach for a pawn, then thought better of it, and paused.

Ben smiled. He had been here a long time. Armed robbery—supposedly. Martin had to piece together the story from hints that Ben dropped and the absolutely unreliable data provided by other inmates. Possibly the kindest, most put-together person Martin knew. Aggravated assault. Intent to kill—maybe? Married—a wife and two children that he spoke of exactly once in three years' time. Not married any longer. Martin never saw anyone visit him, but he didn't know if this was by his own request.

"You look over *here*," Ben gestured to the Knight placing his second Rook in immediate danger, "while I do the job, over *here*. You know."

Ben hadn't exactly been *caught*. He had been *informed upon*. This was a very different state of affairs. Apparently, when you beat the "CEO of a major corporation" (Jim Staunton from the next cell block described the guy in those words—but how would he know?) nearly to death after robbing him blind, the latter calls in a number of favors on his own behalf. Vengeful bunch, those rich guys. But precisely *who* the hell had Ben robbed?

"But it's not just sleight of hand," Ben continued. He set his hands down on either side of the chessboard. "Most of these guys, they get caught because they get obsessed with the show of it. They get confused."

"Not all of them," Martin said. He moved his remaining Bishop. "Check."

Ben grinned at him. "They don't want what they think they want," he said. He moved a Pawn, blocking Martin's attack and revealing his hidden strategy. "They might as well join a fucking fitness club. Checkmate."

~~~

THE VAN WAS SLOWING to a stop.

Martin kept his eyes closed for a few moments more, then opened them. He decided to make something more of a show.

"This is not the place," Martin said, taking a shot in

the dark. "Where have you brought me?"

Looking up toward the front of the van, he saw the nerds glance hurriedly at each other. Haz smiled broadly and glanced back at Martin. "I've got to take a piss," he said. "We're at a Short Stop. You want anything?"

Martin shook his head slowly and closed his eyes again. Hopefully, they were even more convinced now that he had some sort of magical power. Martin felt particularly lucky that he didn't need to do any more explaining, and inwardly sighed with tremendous relief.

Bewley and Taggart whispered to each other after Haz exited the van. Martin could only catch a few words—"stab that sonofabitch" and "fucking *out* of here!" stood out—but Martin honestly couldn't determine who "that sonofabitch" was. He secretly hoped for a double-cross situation, but he wasn't about to rely on it.

Moments later, Haz returned to the van.

"Guys," he whispered to Bewley and Taggart, "I think we have a little bit of a problem."

"What?" Bewley asked.

"Geordi's out there in the spacemobile," Haz answered.

All three nerds groaned. Martin kept his eyes closed and tried not to act interested.

"This close to a fucking home run?" Taggart said.

"No shit," Bewley said. "Can we lose him?"

"Gonna try," Haz answered, starting the van. "This is just bad *luck*, man."

Martin desperately avoided asking who the fuck "Geordi" was, and even more desperately tried to keep himself from saying "Spacemobile?" aloud. He had never realized the enormous stress of total absurdity before.

They pulled out of the parking lot. They drove smoothly along for about five minutes by Martin's estimation. They rolled to another stop.

They felt the impact of an explosive rocket, which flipped the van like a pancake and sent Martin and the three nerds sprawling.

"SHIELDS UP!"

It was Haz's voice. Martin had had the presence of mind to fling his arms up over his head and pull his body into a tight ball before being rammed into the roof of the van.

Sparks were flying and Martin heard Taggart groaning from up front. Bewley appeared unconscious, a few yards away from Martin.

Haz was hurriedly and frantically hitting buttons on the console that Martin had thought were controls for the radio. Another blast shook the van and skidded it some distance, but the van itself seemed to have been saved by whatever "shields" Haz had managed to raise.

"Taggart! Under the seat!" Haz's voice seemed rather undiminished given the circumstances. Taggart continued to groan inconsolably. "Taggart! Bewley! Oh, Christ!"

Martin felt himself to insure that he had not broken any bones. Haz seemed to have forgotten him completely in his understandable urgency. Martin made his way to the back door of the van and attempted to push, wrench, or coax it open. Nothing worked.

"Marty!" Haz finally yelled. "Are you all right?"

"I'm—fine, I think," Martin responded.

Taggart appeared to have gotten with Haz's program; he was gingerly avoiding shards of glass, climbing through the shattered front windshield.

"Look, just—ah, sit tight for a minute!" Haz yelled back, watching Taggart carefully and turning his head back slightly to address Martin. "Make sure Bewley's all right. We got this under control!"

Martin highly doubted that. "Okay," he said. He turned to the back door of the van again. He focused on it, and noticed a strange twisting or warping sensation occur within his mind. This was accompanied by a visceral sensation in his gut—the same sensation he felt whenever he noticed a misspelling or grammatical error during a copyedit.

That door shouldn't be there, he thought. *That door is a* mistake. *It's in the way. It's an unnecessary word in a sentence...*

Martin "edited" the door.

He gasped as a rush of wind blew through the van, from the new emptiness at one end through the smashed-out windshield on the other. He turned to gaze out the front of the van momentarily, backing slowly toward the exit he had somehow miraculously created.

"YOU WILL HAND OVER the prisoner!" Geordi's high-pitched voice rang out over the parking lot by way of a megaphone affixed to the top of his bright-green Ford Festiva. This attempt at intimidation was further severely compromised by the presence of a horde of teenage dorks whose ranks were split between endo-morphism and frailty, barely organized into a ragged rank-and-file behind the car.

They were matched evenly by a second group who had emerged from their cheap vehicles wearing a profusion of costumes. It looked like a stand-off between two sets of action figures gathered at random from a toy store and forced through some kind of magical rendering machine which granted them a semi-existence, a failed attempt at their prior glory in bodies unfit for service.

No man ought ever witness a rail-thin Viking warrior wearing glasses as thick as his broadsword.

"You will hand over the prisoner!" Geordi repeated, enhancing the irritability of his voice with a nasal twang.

Haz stood in the midst of his troop, Taggart beside him. Not to be outdone, Haz held a megaphone in one hand, which he raised to his lips. In the other hand, he held what appeared to be an Uzi.

"You will *go fuck yourself*!" Haz yelled into the megaphone.

An astonished gasp followed this as Geordi's convention-attendees shuffled anxiously, eyes widened.

Geordi hit his response button a moment too soon. There was a sigh, followed by: "You have chosen your fate, Son of Earth!"

Haz hefted his Uzi, frowned briefly as if considering what to say, then dropped the megaphone and decided to let his weapon do the talking for him.

THE BLOODSHED WAS INCREDIBLE. Martin had never seen so many peculiar weapons simultaneously active in one spot.

There were broadswords and axes, morning stars and spears, borne by those wearing chainmail and horned helmets; there were the expected ballistic missile launchers: the Uzi that started it all, handguns, rifles, shotguns, six-shooters; there was even some sort of phaser gun that apparently had an "annihilate" setting, carried, aimed, and fired quite casually by a thin, bespectacled maniac in a one-piece, silver jump-suit with a large collar.

The results of this latter weapon were viciously glorious, though its wielder demonstrated no sign of emotion in the execution of his duties as High Priest of the Geeks.

Their Ritalin-addled minds kept both groups narrowly bound to the violence at hand. Martin fled through the evaporated back door of the van. He crawled, sprinted, hesitated, and crawled again on his way from the shat-tered wreckage of Haz's van to the drainage ditch at the darkest end of the mall parking lot, but other than what might have been the whizzing of stray bullets and the staccato purr of Uzi-fire, he met with nothing untoward.

He rolled into the ditch and paused momentarily, noticing now the occasional screams and moans of dying nerds. He felt himself once again for broken bones, bruises, cuts—nothing but mud. His glasses could stand to be washed.

An explosion sounded from back in the parking lot, illuminating the night sky. One flaming piece of white van door landed on the grass to Martin's right, just barely missing him.

A long stretch of grass sloped away from the shelf he lay upon, toward a neighborhood at the far end. Martin made a run for it.

He had not gotten twenty yards when a radiant light shone from somewhere above and consumed him.

PART TWO

QUOD EST SUPERIUS

THREE YEARS AGO

T HIS WAS A SKILL of translation.

The year that Martin did for burglary in Fall County Jail taught him a great deal about translation. You might say that he entered prison illiterate and left with a fortune in letters.

"You see that?" Ben Crabbe pointed briefly at a slight figure seated on bleachers. The day threatened rain. They were about to retreat.

"What?" Martin followed Ben's indication. "The Grayson guy?"

"Yes, and no." Ben moved his hand in front of Martin's face. "That."

Martin frowned. "*What?*"

Ben repeated the movement, this time a little slower, and Martin saw it: the slightest crossing of two fingers, the most minute wavering of the path through which the hand ought to fall in space.

"*Any* deviation from the normal is a sign," Ben said. "That one means 'pickup now.'"

"Why are you telling me this?" Martin asked.

"Because you're one of the only other people here

smart enough to play this game," he responded, waving a hand to encompass the courtyard. "If you learn, then it gets better for the rest of us. Especially me. Am I making myself clear?"

Martin nodded.

"If I tell you something—'go ahead and grab one of that'—it means something very specific," Ben continued. "I spoke 'improperly.' The natural laws of grammar, of logic, continue to hold. *But I have told you something new*. I have *changed reality*, at least temporarily."

Martin nodded again.

"Similarly," Ben said, making a nearly imperceptible flutter with his fingers in the air as he adjusted the collar of his shirt, "silence conveys messages. The spaces in the midst of things—what they call 'negative space'—hold all the possibilities. We orchestrate those possibilities in accordance with our wills." He brushed down the front of his shirt with both hands in an unusual rhythm. "But we must be attentive. We can't *ever* lose vigilance. What did Grayson just do?"

Martin blinked. "Um—"

"He just placed his hands in a steeple pattern, with his thumbs crossed," Ben answered for him. "It means the pickup will proceed as planned."

~~~

"PRETTY COOL, HUH?" BASH observed.

Martin had to admit to being impressed when he found himself teleported to something eerily akin to the Enterprise's transporter. *Very* impressed.

"My apologies for the ostentation of our arrival," Loah-Dath said. "Apparently, the only way to arrive quickly enough at your most probable locus required that we borrow one of Liquid Agent's—"

"*Flying saucers*!" Bash interrupted happily.

"Indeed," Loah-Dath said. "Although Bash reminds me that these are often mistaken for extraterrestrial vehicles." He repositioned himself in front of a console with no discernible steering wheel. Martin was pleased to note that it held the expected array of multicolored buttons and electronic displays. "They are indeed terrestrial. The extraterrestrial machines are more beetle-like in shape." Martin noticed Bash's understandable shiver. "Apparently, this has been clearly indicated in reports of unidentified flying objects on Earth, but media representations latched onto alternative descriptions providing for more sensational headlines."

Martin gazed at his surroundings in awe as Bash assisted him in descending from the "transporter" to a comfortable reclining couch secured to the floor in the midst of the room.

"Thanks for the rescue mission," Martin said. "This is incredible! Does anyone know what *happened* back there on the bridge? Or, for that matter, in that *parking lot*?"

Bash shook his head. "Regarding the former, perhaps," he said. "There was an illusion spell of some sort, followed by or in conjunction with a cloaking spell. It is apparently the case—as should be obvious to you now— that *other people* have become aware of your involvement with Yuttelborough."

"This was to be expected," Loah-Dath said, eyes still affixed to a computer screen readout. "With the presence of Ward Chapman, it was only a matter of time before your involvement in the conflagration at Yuttelborough would become more widely recognized."

"Have I got information for *you*," Martin said. "Those nerds down there know *all about* this stuff, apparently. And they got the information from someone who *knew I'd be on that bridge at that time*."

Bash's eyes widened. "How did they—"

"Is there anywhere I can clean up in here?" Martin said, gazing at his dirt-encrusted hands.

"Unfortunately, we only have basic facilities in this vessel," Loah-Dath answered. "But we have arrived at the Liquid Agent premises during our brief discussion. We can continue this inside."

THE FACILITIES TURNED OUT to be rather accommodating. Bash made his typically useful contribution by "speed-cleaning" Martin's clothes for him using a variant on the negentropy spell he used to clean the dishes on occasion.

While freshening up, Martin noticed that the bruise covering the left side of his face was not nearly as bad as he originally thought. Although it was still sensitive and tender, it had already begun to darken a bit. Thankfully, the crick in his neck had also begun to loosen—there didn't seem to be any extant whiplash.

"There's something weird about the 'anti-locator' spell I used to find you," Bash said as soon as Martin came back into the breakroom at Liquid Agent.

"What's that?" Martin asked. Loah-Dath had gone off to some other part of the factory to deliver printouts from the UFO to the lucky guy who dealt with that sort of thing here.

"I didn't *exactly* tell Loah-Dath this," Bash said, "but when I finished my calculations, there were *two* areas that seemed to indicate your location."

"What does that mean?" Martin asked.

"Well, I'm not precisely sure," Bash answered. "I made the assumption—which turned out to be correct—that you were at the area of greatest 'anti-probability.' But there was *another* area indicated by the spell and the calculation—about twenty-three percent less likely to be your location."

Martin grabbed a Coke out of the refrigerator and cracked it open. "Where?" he asked simply.

"Right over Thomas Graham's estate," Bash said.

"Am I supposed to be impressed by that revelation?" Martin said, taking another gulp of Coke. "Because I figured Thomas Graham was kind of the central person in this whole thing."

Bash made a sound of dismissal. "You're probably right," he said. Martin felt sure that Bash had in no way dropped the line of inquiry—not to mention the fact that Bash *never* dropped a line of inquiry. "So what is this about 'somebody' knowing you'd be driving on that bridge tonight?"

Martin's eyes lit up. "Right!" he said excitedly. "Those nerds who kidnapped me—"

"*Kidnapped* you?" Bash interrupted. "Was it really full-scale kidnapping?"

"Well," Martin said, "maybe not *full-scale*. But they did take me from a crash site and *not* bring me to the hospital."

"That could just be stupidity," Bash said.

"True enough," Martin said. "Anyway, they said they found a *prophecy* about my arrival folded into the back of the last *Krixwar* book. And they just assumed that I had written the thing myself."

"Did you?" Bash asked.

"No!" Martin responded. "No, I didn't." He paused for a moment.

"You *were* a little shaky, if I recall—" Bash started.

"No," Martin said. He sighed. "Oh, fine! *Maybe*. But I sure as *hell* didn't put the damned thing in the back of *The Devil Escapes*! I know that's true."

Bash raised his fuzzy eyebrows at Martin, but didn't comment further.

"*Any*way," Martin continued, "the piece of paper was *not* written in my handwriting. But it *was* written in first person. And it basically gives the whole show away."

"Hm," Bash's eyes narrowed. He began to pace. "Who has a vested interest in giving the show away?"

"And why *hide* it 'just enough' to make someone go looking for it?" Martin added.

"It was *pure chance* that those nerds ran across the purported prophecy?" Bash asked.

"Oh, wait," Martin said. "No. No it wasn't. They talked about some guy, some kind of super-nerd. Some guy they called 'Repo-Man.'"

Bash laughed. "Ranked with three out of four stars by Roger Ebert! Did you ever see it?"

"What?" Martin had a confused look on his face.

Bash whistled. "You don't watch enough *television*, Martin!" he said. "Anyway, this guy might know what's up. My guess is that he wrote it himself. And it *is* theoretically possible to deduce facts regarding Yuttelborough from the *Krixwar* saga."

"So what do we do now? Go find this 'Repo-Man' and force him to fess up?" Martin suggested.

"I'm thinking that we have the ultimate tool with which to do such a thing," Bash said. Both he and Martin were thinking along the same lines: *super-nerd...UFO transport...*

SHE HAD BEEN SOMETHING *else.*
  Living, still, yes—but something else completely.
  Words on a page? Words in a book? A book itself?
  Confusion. A focus.
  She felt the traces of it; she felt the love, the reverence,
the admiration. What she was—now vibrations in the air,
in the air, in the air of—of—

MARTIN AWOKE IN THE best of all possible beds.
  And for a moment, she was there with him, living,
breathing, somehow changed, yet precisely the same...
  Gone.
  Loah-Dath had returned earlier that evening with a concoction that tasted like a combination of vanilla Coke and creamy chocolate. The brew had a strange scent that reminded Martin of popcorn at a movie theater—not an unpleasant combination with the taste, oddly. A little on the extra-carbonated side.
  "Occasional disturbances in the perfection of the substance result from phase-shifting on the molecular level," Loah-Dath had explained. "It should take care of the bruising from your crash, at minimum, and alleviate any associated aches and pains. Though you may feel somewhat drowsy."
  It was the typical doctor's "somewhat drowsy" = *fucking comatose.* But after Martin had consumed the alchemical "ibuprofen" (= *heroin*), Loah-Dath led him to a private barracks beneath Liquid Agent and left him to rest while he conferred with Bash regarding their poten-

tial candidate for alien abduction.

The dreams, though. Again. Like he kept switching places with her. *With Parisa...Parisa Par—*

He had almost drifted off again. It seemed as if the potion had worked its magic. Some clever magic had been rigged in the room as well: a sorcerous variant on the "clapper," which altered the level of light in the room based on your brainwave pattern, apparently.

Martin sat up and looked around. The lights flickered into greater intensity accordingly.

He was wrapped in downy blankets, lying in the midst of a bed large enough to fit three of himself. He wore a yellow Liquid Agent T-shirt and flannel pajama bottoms with a selection of Looney Tunes characters imprinted on them.

The little room was mostly bed, although it had a desk built into one wall with writing materials on it. A water jug with conical cups in a dispenser beside it. A few posters and images on the walls, oddly random, as if whomever had set up the place had only a moderate knowledge of what a human might be interested in seeing on a regular basis. Multiplication tables from 0x0 to 9x9. A framed print of a green-feathered duck swimming in a lake—"A man is only as good as his feathers" read the caption below it. What the hell did that mean?

There was also a console by the door that looked like an intercom. A little red light was blinking on it.

Martin approached the panel and noticed a digital readout. "MESSAGE," it read. Martin pressed the button.

"We'll be in the breakroom until noon," Bash's voice announced. "Take the elevator to level minus three."

Martin proceeded to get changed into his freshly laundered clothes and head out of the room into a hallway of similar rooms. At the end of the hall stood the elevator.

"WE TOOK CARE OF work for you," Bash said when Martin sauntered into the breakroom, feeling refreshed and miraculously healed thanks to Loah-Dath's concoction. He sat alone on the floor of the room, the television on as usual, this time tuned to *Tales from the Crypt*. The text of *Occult Architectures of Memory* lay open before him on the surface of a stool he was using for a desk, along with a notepad and pen. "Called in sick. You've even got a doctor's note! Good through Friday."

"I hate to break it to you, Bash, but you sound nothing like me," Martin said.

"Honestly, Martin!" Bash said. Then, in a flawless imitation of Martin's voice, colored with just a touch of the flu, he continued, "Must've been all the stress, recently. Can't barely get up out of bed. I'll see if I can get some of those latest sections done from here."

Martin was impressed. "Nice job," he said. "But we've got to get back to the house and feed Rowley at some point today."

"Already taken care of," Loah-Dath said, striding into the room. "We sent Ling-Watha this morning, before you awoke. She has a certain affinity for Earth-animals, especially felines."

Martin sighed. "Well, I'd like to see the little fur-ball nonetheless," he said. "And soon. So we've got, what, three days to find Repo-Man before coming up with another excuse for Pam? Then what?"

"Then we retrieve the *Gah Quinkwe*," Loah-Dath said.

Martin stopped in his tracks. "Woah," he said. "How do you propose to do *that*?"

"Bash has his suspicions regarding its whereabouts," Loah-Dath said. "But we *do* seem to have located this 'Repo-Man.' It appears that he works in a shop in Rand's Square. A video-store clerk, if I'm not mistaken. His real name is—"

"Kane Jeffries," Martin finished. "I remember now. And I *know* that guy. At least, I've seen him. He's definitely a little weird."

"A little weird?" Bash repeated. "How's that?"

"Oh, starting with the bright-green mohawk," Martin answered, "and continuing with the Old Norse *futhark* tattoos—I'm assuming he's got some interests that probably align with those of Liquid Agent."

"Indeed?" Loah-Dath said, looking pleased. "We usually keep a record of those with interests of that sort. Perhaps we have a file on him?"

Martin noted Bash rolling his eyes at the bureaucratic suggestion.

"Whether you have a file on him or not, I know the place," Martin said. "Corner of Fifth and Main. Quest Video, the one right next to Beta Mart."

"Of course!" Bash said. "Beta Mart! That's where I got that *fantastic* macaroni and cheese that we had last Wednesday!"

KANE "REPO-MAN" JEFFRIES EXITED the premises of Quest Video at approximately 10:30 p.m. that night. He locked the front door and headed to his car, a lone Subaru sporting six bumper stickers and a shattered tail-light.

When the infrared "sentience meter" on one panel of Loah-Dath's interface displayed a single blip—Kane Jeffries—the abduction process was initiated.

"Ben Crabbe."

It was the first thing Kane Jeffries said after Loah-Dath loaded him into the flying saucer via transporter. He looked directly at Martin

"Excuse me?" Martin said. How did he know Ben? And why wasn't he more astonished by his close encounter?

"You're Ben Crabbe's protégé," he explained. "Martin—Martin Ready."

Bash looked from Martin to the abductee and back again. "You didn't tell me—" he started.

"Wait," Martin said. "You know *Ben Crabbe*?"

Kane nodded. "Did time with him," he said simply. "He mentioned you when I told him I went to Rosewood. Your picture was in the college paper that year, if I recall correctly—something about a fellowship?"

"Right," Martin said, perturbed. "Huh."

"Can I sit down?" Kane asked.

"Oh—of course," Martin said, gesturing to one of the several half-eggshell seats bolted to the floor of the vessel.

Kane—his mohawk was now bright blue, but he still resembled a linebacker or Hell's Angel, especially the latter, given the runic inscriptions running up and down both forearms—proceeded to seat himself peacefully in one of the chairs.

"This is about Grajug, isn't it?" he asked.

Bash's astonishment carried him literally into the air about a foot. "Grajug!" he exclaimed.

"Wait—what?" Martin said.

"I know he has been upsetting things lately," Kane said.

"Grajug is *here*?" Bash was ecstatic, hopping about like a mutant rabbit.

"Who is—" Martin started.

"I'm just trying to keep him calm," Kane continued,

lowering his eyes. "He's safe. At least for the moment, ah—I'm sorry, what's your name?"

"Martin calls me 'Bash,' which is sufficient," Bash said.

"Bash. Good." Kane rubbed the bald sides of his head with both hands. "I'm assuming some of the Argonauts must've found *you*—so I don't know how long his safety will last."

"Where is he?" Bash said insistently, puffing himself up beside Kane. He looked like a fluffy stuffed animal beside him. "We can't delay!"

"Hang on!" Martin shouted. "The 'Argonauts'? Who's Grajug?"

"The Argonauts. It's what Hazzard Groschen calls his absurd gang of dorks. Grajug is the Yuttelboroughian," Kane said. "The *other* one, I mean."

HE REMEMBERED THE WORDS of the story being read aloud. They drifted to him from elsewhere. *A wall—a barrier—a limit of any sort...it's just something we invented...*

The City of Kept Promises

THERE IS A STORY told about stories, about creatures dwelling in another world who live because they have been *written of.* This is from a book that no one has ever read—well, *almost* no one, save the Great Priest in his little body.

And it says that there is a City hidden everywhere in plain sight.

Now, there's another story about what *our* world is made of. When a man speaks, his words enter this field of play in a certain shape; when a man listens, he can hear another shape, but this may not always be his free choice.

When a promise is made, it is held in the gentle hands of this Ether, where it is kept, whether or not the promiser himself decides to hold true to it.

One day, it was found, much to the delight of those dwelling there, that a City had been made out of all promises made that had never been brought to fulfillment by those who made them. So although in the world in which those promises were made nothing ever became of them, they called their City one of "Kept Promises," which is one meaning of its Name in their language, which sometimes resembles our own language, and many times does not...

Yuttel-borough.

The Name came to him in his unchosen sleep. It came in the form of a Door.

This was the first time that Martin Translated, although he would not remember it until a while later, when in his cell at Fall County Jail he did it again, in a state of utter despair. He remembered the latter with perfect clarity: he lay in the top bunk, since Ben Crabbe not only deferred to him but preferred the lower one.

He wept, as silently as he could. He thought of the docks at Trevisa Pond, back by his parents' house, what they would look like at this time of night, the scent of the water, which always seemed to him like some thick, living substance, like mercury. Weighty. He felt himself standing there, in the mud warmed by a day's worth of sun, a soft shivering sound, now, the leaves of the oaks and maples behind him.

He held his hands up, they looking black against the indigo night, and Orion's belt, Orion, always clear, always static, then the moon, there, just to the left, a sliver only, now, and...

He breathed deep. The scent of the water, the scent of damp trees.

What in the WORLD?

He looked down. His bare feet were stuck in the mud of Trevisa Pond's bank. His hands, again, he gazed upon: living hands in the living world. The night seemed somewhat blurry, though—he reached up, felt his face. No glasses. He had left his glasses on the shelf back in—in—

Martin blinked.

The ceiling. He was looking at the ceiling of his cell, from his bunk in Fall County Jail.

He sighed. He could still practically *smell* Trevisa Pond—

When he rolled onto his side, he noticed two rather shocking things.

The first was a figure standing in the semi-darkness, gazing at him. Martin flinched and sat up, heart racing—which is when he noticed the *other* thing.

Mud, covering his feet and the lower cuffs of his jumpsuit pants.

The figure was Ben Crabbe.

Martin breathed a sigh of relief, which was immediately replaced by anxiety on remembering the mud in the bed. He had a brief, absurd thought about how he was going to explain it to the guards in the morning. At that moment, Ben spoke up.

"You disappeared," he said simply in a low voice.

"I didn't—I didn't *know*—" Martin tried to explain.

Ben approached the bed. "I got up, just a few minutes ago," he said. "I had to take a piss. And I looked over—and you were *gone*."

Martin placed his hands out in front of him. This—being here, in jail—this felt more like a weird dream than any sort of teleportation act.

My name is Baevare Baeshazanam.

The memory hit him like a howling wind. *Baevare Baeshazanam.* He called him "Bash" because he couldn't precisely replicate the sounds of the name. Bash had laughed about that. *Bash it is, then. Welcome to Yuttelborough—um—what was your name again?*

"Have you ever done this before?" Ben asked. "What's that?"

He had noticed Martin trying to clean off the mud from his feet with one of the thin sheets.

"Um—"

"*Where did you go?*" Ben asked. Martin did not actually detect even a hint of malice from him. There was something else in his voice. It was...envy? Longing.

Martin decided to be straight with him. With Ben Crabbe, anyway, there was no point being anything else.

"I went back home," Martin said. "Back to the pond by my parents' house. I love it there."

He heard something then that he had never heard before: it was Ben, *bursting into muffled tears.*

"I'm sorry," he said, holding his hands up to his face. "I'm—this is very embarrassing."

Martin felt somewhat awkward in the circumstances. Ben Crabbe, who was twice his size, who knew the secret language of the underworld; his teacher, his friend—Ben Crabbe wept. He sat on the edge of his bed and Martin listened to him, half astonished and half guilty, muffling sobs.

In moments, it was over.

"Don't tell anyone about this," Ben whispered from

below. He sounded normal, unaffected. Martin heard him reclining once again in his bunk. A few moments later, he heard Ben breathing regularly, restfully, presumably asleep, as if nothing unusual had happened at all.

Martin spent the next fifteen minutes cleaning up the mud as best he could, rolling up the sheets and realizing that he would have to "admit" to something supremely embarrassing the next day in order to disguise the truth.

But all the while, he was thinking about what Ben had said just before falling asleep. Did he mean the crying jag? Or the teleportation?

"VIC'S CAR? YEAH, THAT was an accident," Kane said. "I mean, it was supposed to be a quick getaway."

"Why Vic?" Martin asked. "It doesn't make—"

"Grajug was mistaken," he answered. "It was obviously supposed to be *you*. But something about your association with Bash here must have messed up his readings."

"He's probably right," Bash said. "Earth has a *lot* of electricity running through it. Since Yuttelborough ran primarily on channeled Ether—we just collected it the way a *siddha* would collect *ojas*, for example—the chaotic vortices generated by so much raw electromagnetic energy *do* seem to interfere with the magic. Sometimes positively!"

Kane was smiling. He appeared perfectly delighted by Bash's presence.

"At any rate, Grajug jimmied his way into the unfortunate Vic Toronto's apartment on several occasions," Kane continued, "but he never found any evidence of trafficking with Yuttelborough."

"So when Vic started talking about seeing a little creature stalking him—" Martin started.

"It was Grajug," Kane said. "Throwing the paint on him was just being a jackass, I think. It was there in the garage."

"But why steal his car?" Martin asked.

"He was checking it out, one final place to look before giving up," Kane said. "He turned on the radio, started flipping through the dials. And he hits an AM station, tons of static, where someone was talking about Yuttelborough."

"Oh, gods no," Martin said.

Bash started laughing. "The *nerds*, man! Ham radio!"

Kane nodded his head. "I would presume so," he said. "I told Grajug about the old legend: that there was some clue hidden in the high school library. One of his divinatory mechanisms confirmed it, and he identified the nature of its surrounding data. Lo and behold—fiction becomes fact."

"So you *did* tell Haz and those guys about the legend," Martin said.

"Of course," Kane said. "But that was long before I met Grajug. Long before I knew it was actually *real*."

Martin shook his head. *Who had placed the message in the book?*

"Why is it taking so long to get back to Liquid Agent?" Martin asked, looking at Bash. They both glanced over toward the control panels.

"My apologies," Loah-Dath said. "And to you, Mr. Jeffries, for not introducing myself."

Kane didn't seem fazed by the lack of etiquette. "I figured with the beard and the cloak that you were busy with important things," he said.

"Indeed," Loah-Dath replied. "We are in orbit around Earth for the time being."

"No shit?" Martin said. "I mean—why?"

"There appeared to be some questionable presences surrounding Liquid Agent," Loah-Dath said. "In the wake of the Rookville Mall massacre—which appears to be all over your Earth news—there is also heightened constabulary activity."

"Best to keep a low profile by staying *far away*, then. Good idea." Bash said. He turned to Kane. "But what about Grajug? Where is he?"

"I have inherited property a few miles outside of town," Kane said. "I told him he could make free use of it—as long as he didn't burn the place down or otherwise draw attention to it."

"The note," Martin said simply and abruptly.

"Excuse me?" Kane said.

"He means the note in the back of the *Krixwar* book," Bash explained.

Kane's eyes widened. "Is that where—"

"Someone, some*how*, managed to add a page to *one single copy* of *The Devil Escapes*," Martin said. "My location at a certain point in spacetime, and a summary confession of my dealings with Yuttelborough."

"That's practically heresy," Kane said.

"Tell me about it," Bash said. "That's why I don't believe he wrote it. At least not physically."

Martin turned to Bash. "Go on?"

"Well, you *have* demonstrated some peculiar abilities, after all," Bash said.

"But I *remember* all those times!" Martin insisted.

"Peculiar abilities?" Kane repeated.

Bash strolled over to a little refrigerator and opened

it. "Hungry, anyone?" he asked.

"Wait, Bash," Martin said. "Seriously. Do you think I could have somehow inserted that message *myself*—unconsciously, maybe?"

"Sure," Bash said. "Not impossible. Especially if you were just coming out of a coma, for instance."

Martin let out a long breath and leaned back in his chair.

"Ben told me about it," Kane said. "The coma, I mean."

"That was just a disaster," Martin said, embarrassed.

"Hey, don't get too down on yourself," Kane said. "Each of us got caught by way of our own respective stupidities."

"I thought I had the whole damned thing plotted out," Martin said, closing his eyes. "Can't believe it. *Still* can't believe it."

"At least you were trying to do something productive," Kane said. "I was too strung out to realize I was in prison until I started to detox."

"How long were you in for?" Martin asked.

"It was supposed to be a year," Kane said. "But an excellent lawyer got me out after six months. With the usual concessions."

"I had just finished my dissertation," Martin said. "Everything looked so goddamned legitimate."

"Think of it this way," Kane attempted, nodding to Bash who held up a bottle of Coca-Cola to him. "You really *did* get away with it. Your plan *worked*! You were in and out with all the cash you needed—not a cent more. And you didn't hurt *anyone*. That's nearly a perfect job."

"But I ran a *red light*!" Martin protested. "I ran a red light, freaked out, turned my head for *one second*—one goddamned second!" He stood up from his chair.

"You still didn't hurt anybody," Kane said. "And I respect the fact that you swerved."

"To avoid a deer! I *had* to swerve—"

"You didn't harm a life," Kane said. "I didn't always respect life. They call me 'Repo-Man' because I used to get in fights a lot when I worked at the salvage yard, paying my way through school. I was a bastard. Someone just said it one day and it stuck. Repo-Man. I was wrong to have done those things." He accepted the Coke from Bash, who hopped into a chair and proceeded to open a bag of Snyder's cheddar pretzels. "You swerved to avoid the deer, I believe, because you didn't want to harm it— not because it might damage your vehicle."

Martin walked over to one wall and leaned against it. Instantly, a viewport that had been seamless and opaque a moment before opened. All three of them looked out— into *space*. The deep blackness of the spaces beyond Earth yawned before them, interspersed with dots of light, sometimes white, sometimes blue. The red eye of Betelgeuse. The blinking radiance of Venus.

The vehicle rotated. Suddenly, breathtakingly, a vision of Martin and Kane's home planet appeared before them.

No one spoke. In the silence, all they could hear was the sound of Bash crunching pretzels by the handful.

SAMANTHA SALIERI WORRIED. NOT only had she been re-assigned the pabulum of Thomas Graham's unconscionable "prose" in the wake of Martin's illness, but Martin himself seemed somehow—what? Inaccessible? No. In trouble? Perhaps. *Lying?*

Yes. Martin was lying.

Any editor worth a quarter of her salt could spot a lie

shimmering in the midst of a story like iron pyrite in the monocle of a seasoned jeweler.

Had Thomas Graham's death *really* affected him *that* badly? He hadn't actually given her much by way of information regarding his meeting the previous Friday night with the old bastard. (Sorry. She meant "dead bastard," there. Sorry! I mean: "old dead guy." Seriously!)

Samantha sat at her desk and spun her chair to gaze out the window.

There sat Rookville in all its glory—or, at least, a flawless representation of it. The brick wall of the Humdinger Building, twenty yards away. Yes, it was called the "Humdinger" building. Shawn "Sharky" Humdinger owned it, and had set its occupants the task of paying exorbitant rent in exchange for being able to practically *see* their places of work here in downtown Rookville.

Ah, where were earthquakes, floods, fires, and general catastrophic destruction when you needed them?

Samantha had memorized every flaw in the masonry. The little crack in the fifth brick from the left, three bricks down. There appeared to be mortar in it. Mortar! She could practically *hear* the story in that every time she regarded it: *Say, Jimmy Bricklayer, look whatcha gone 'n' done! Sorry, Mister Humdinger Sir, I'll try harder. Bricks cost MONEY, ya lazy wage-slave! I know, Sir, sorry, Sir, I'll fix it right on up fer ya, Sir!*

She liked to imagine that this exchange took place between Mr. Humdinger and Mr. Bricklayer as they floated, unwittingly, forty feet in the air.

"Samantha?"

Samantha started, shaken loose from her reverie like a cat from a counterpane. "Bah! Oh, sorry, Pam, I—"

"No, no," Pamela said, stepping into the office. "My apologies. Things can get a bit stifling, sometimes, can't they?"

As usual, it was a little difficult to determine what precisely Pamela referred to as she spoke. Harvard trained. Briefly taught rhetoric at Columbia. Took a bit of time off to polish her tan and model for *Playboy* back in the late '70s. She might be almost fifty now, but time seemed to make daily apologies to her by making sure everyone failed to measure up in some way.

Outstanding material for a manager.

"Any luck with *To My Decent End*?" Pamela asked, sliding black fingernails lightly up and down the edge of the door.

Samantha sighed. "I'm seriously *trying*, Pam, I *am*, but—"

"Why don't you take the rest of the day off?" Pamela suggested.

Samantha had to restrain herself from immediately leaping out of her chair and knocking Pamela over on her way out the door. "Really?" she said meekly instead. "You think so?"

Pamela nodded, stepping back out the door. "The stress—both good and bad—this past weekend has left us all tense and volatile," she said, smiling. Samantha couldn't help feeling like the succubus in Pamela would eat her if it didn't think it would get blood on her five hundred dollar blouse. "Perhaps go check in on Martin for us? Help ensure his recovery?"

Oh, Jesus. Did Pamela think that she had a thing for *Martin Ready*?

Didn't matter. This was her out.

"I think you're probably right," Samantha said. "I think

I'll go do that right now."

Pamela's smile grew a few centimeters before disappearing from view. That sexy goddamned Cheshire cat was up to something, Samantha could plainly tell, but for the moment, getting the hell out of the office and away from Graham's *magnum opus* was enough to let any concern for it slide.

THE HUMMING FROM BENEATH Thomas Graham's basement began again. Frank Fleurety felt, as he typically did, a bit anxious and a bit courageous. He affixed two electrodes to an electric plate in the midst of the central control panel. That substance—he and Thomas had always just called it "candy"—isolated from the Liquid Agent Marshmallow Chew Bars liquefied, simultaneously collapsing into a small, quivering pool, silvery like mercury.

White mist sifted through the small grate in the floor, headed directly for the plate with its "candy" offering.

Frank couldn't help thinking that the pool, once touched lightly by the mist, which it absorbed instantly with a small, silent flash of light, began to look more like tears. It separated into droplets that pointed toward a common center.

But *that* was part of its secret power. The point at which geometry became tangible body—*that* was what they were dealing with. *When nothing becomes something.* Euclid had nailed down a portion of it in his definitions and propositions; the sorcerers that followed him—before science became so ignominiously separated from its identical twin, *magic*—had hammered out, through trial and error, reason and argument, a method of *magnifying thought*, of turning the things within our heads into bodily phenomena without.

The idea was that we did it *all the time*; the secret mechanism by which it functioned remained secret insofar as one could not actually witness its functioning. *Life begins in the dark*.

And even in that strange, dark space within our *crania*, somehow, eyes closed, in blackness, in darkness, *we can see*.

How?

The idea fascinated Frank Fleurety to no end. Here he had been merely a fan, a reader, perhaps the writer of an editorial or two or three of note. Hired into Ever, Nevers, & Co. as a grunting, asserting pencil to be put to use, back in the days when things were a little more tiring, but when you were compensated with actual time off, not just a promise that people would leave you alone.

Along comes Thomas Graham.

They were the same age, approximately, both in their early twenties. Managerial dispensation placed Mr. Graham with Mr. Fleurety, as neither seemed of much particular importance.

But they both had a secret heart, a passion, an uncommon link shared between them. *How badly do you want a new world, Mr. Fleurety?*

That was the first thing Thomas Graham had ever said to him. Walking into his office that day in his threadbare brown suit, white dress shirt missing a button, clearly discernible behind an old black tie that was supposed to cover it up.

How badly do you want a new world, Mr. Fleurety?

The pages he had passed over to him, many of them handwritten in painstakingly precise cursive, proved that Thomas Graham *had* a new world to offer, a world so strangely real and complex, he could barely feel the hours passing in the day as he worked to perfect it—no, as he *bathed in it*, gloriously, unremittingly.

That it would come to *this*.

Sometimes, he wished that Ben Crabbe had killed him after he'd found out. But that would have been too easy, wouldn't it? No, no—if there was anything Frank had learned, it was that *the story would play out*, no matter what.

Every move you made was part of it. The freedom he felt sometimes was entirely the result of realizing that he could never choose and not *be chosen for*.

Frank realized he had been staring into the little reflective droplets for some time. They had hardened into crystals, which he scooped off the metal surface and into a paper cup, to be added to the rest of them.

Soon. There would be enough—very soon.

SAMANTHA THOUGHT ABOUT *To My Decent End* as she drove out of the parking garage onto Trammell Road, took the usual left and then an unusual right on the way to Martin's. There was a little delicatessen off Sligo Street that sold cups of extraordinary chicken noodle soup. She figured that she could increase the guilt quotient with Martin by bringing him something touchingly unnecessary.

Unconsciously, she practiced her frown of disappointment.

Hummingbird Bakery. Dollars & Sense. (Cute.) There. Wednesday's.

She parked the car and headed into the deli. There

was a line—it looked like Pam let her leave right around lunchtime anyway. Good. She'd get a sub. That turkey and avocado one—she got that the last time with Martin, when they came here right after work last Monday.

And he made some weirdo excuse, as usual, and rushed home with the half-eaten sandwich in a box. What had he said?

Gotta check on the laundry! Something like that. Out of the blue.

She got in line. An old lady with frizzy gray hair, three people ahead of her, was commenting on Wednesday's menu not being kosher enough.

Come to think of it, everything had changed at Ever, Nevers, & Co. roughly a month before Vic Toronto "retired" to Glory Days in Perryville. Vic had started talking weird like that, too. Well, weirder, true—but just as abrupt. *Ever seen a rabbit that walks on two legs? But he's got TEETH, man! TEETH—like a dinosaur's! But he's still real small...*

That she *very clearly* remembered. She had been finishing up one of those filler novels they occasionally got—something about a couple of kids who time-warp in the Midwest—and she heard him from the office beside Pam's. Ranting to himself.

Then they came in the next morning, and found that he had plastered pages from one of the *Krixwar* books all over his office. They were connected, here and there, by thick marker lines, occasionally drawn over and through items on shelves. *HERE is where they cross over!* She remembered a small note with an arrow made in red pen, pointing to the spine of *The Going of Jacinta*, which had been torn from the book and stapled to the wall.

Ugh. *To My Decent End.* That is the way the mind

works. Think of a monster and his misbegotten fruit shall appear.

To My Decent End was like a Kerouac novel that tried to be about *something* instead of about nothing. It simply didn't *work*. Even the title seemed to apologize for its having been written.

In short, it was like an autobiography. But Thomas Graham had apparently forgotten how to formulate narrative—or had somehow forgotten how much of his life had actually occurred.

Samantha recalled the passage she had been reading before Pam had saved her from it that morning:

> But my love, my book—*she* didn't know, did she? That was all in the past for her—but being a *book*, she couldn't *possibly* have been a victim, any more than a pulped newspaper bearing nothing more than tomorrow's news could be considered a "victim of the future."
>
> I had to hope that it was all in the past. The mathematics of it made no sense otherwise.

That was how it went—for *pages and pages*.

The best summary she could make of it—and she had already written this in a note to Pamela the week before: "It seems like he's *desperate* to talk about something, to confess to something. Even worse, he's *actually trying to say it*—I mean, *for real*! But no matter how hard he tries, *something else* gets written. He's going on for hundreds of pages, crying out to be heard, unremittingly telling us exactly *nothing* about what he wants to say."

She could glean only one thing—*maybe*—from the wreckage of *To My Decent End*: Thomas Graham had done something *terrible*. But what *was* that terrible thing?

This was what she kept trying to rewrite in a comprehensible fashion. Because it seemed as if Thomas Graham—there was really no way to be *sure* about this, of course—but it *seemed* as if he had *stolen a treasure...* although he kept referring to the robbery of the "book" or the "treasure" as a *kidnapping*.

Why?

HAZZARD GROSCHEN—ONCE *&* FUTURE Nerd King of Rookville—tried to sleep sitting up.

After a brief visit to Jackson Hospital—one of the last stops on the way to Fall County Jail, he thought dismally, though he hadn't *quite* gotten there yet—Haz had been deposited unceremoniously in the holding cell of Rookville Police Precinct 3, ostensibly because he was still a minor and they didn't quite know what to do with him.

His parents hadn't been answering their phone. A visit to their house left the police somewhat concerned, especially given the blood (mostly that of others) covering him when he was found unconscious behind a planter wall in the parking lot of Rookville Mall.

He was waiting, silently. He was a little angry, a little scared, but mostly taking advantage of the fact that the only other occupants of the holding cell were two old drunks, as dead to the world as Haz's unwritten future in the computer gaming industry. The police were waiting for a search warrant, functioning under the perfectly legitimate assumption that Haz—in a *Halo*-induced rage—had murdered his family and called for a geek rumble to live out his ballistic fantasies.

None of that was true. But he knew that keeping his

mouth shut implied total ambiguity—and "shadow of a doubt" was basically all he had.

Were any of the others still living? By the gods, if *Geordi* had lived and *Taggart* or *Bewley* had *died*, he would spend the remainder of his incarceration plotting that motherfucker's extended torture sequence...

And where the *fuck* was Martin Ready?

The fucker was supposed to have saved them *all*! What did it matter if a cumshot like Geordi Space-Race got splattered on the parking lot and washed into the gutter by toddler piss? He and Taggart and Bewley—at least, if not Roly-Poly and Jerry the Squatter and Punk-Rock Mike, Odin rest their souls—were supposed to have made it to Yuttelborough by now.

Had they killed Martin, too?

One of the cops—Haz thought someone had called him Ricky—was unlocking the hall door that led into the holding area. A man who looked elderly, but had the bearing and movements of a spry eighteen-year-old, followed him, holding a briefcase and wearing a suit that looked like it cost as much as the cop made in five years.

"Hazzard," the cop said, unlocking the cell door. Haz gazed steadily at him, eyes hooded. Adrenaline, again. This tiredness was not working for him. "You're outta here. Get up."

Outta here?

The old man with the briefcase smiled gently at Haz, who hesitated to stand. "Good afternoon, Master Groschen," he said in an accent that could have been British. It seemed a little practiced to Haz, though. "My name is Prescott Mayhew. I am your attorney."

He stood there like an expensive statue, or perhaps even a hologram from an expensive virtual-reality device, restful, his briefcase hanging from both hands in front of him. *Aikido expert*, Haz thought instantly. Watch enough Japanese anime and you could write an encyclopedia on it—whether or not Taggart said it was all glorified bullshit.

Haz kept his mouth shut, waited a beat, then glanced over at the two drunks as he stood. He nodded at Prescott Mayhew, then waved a hand over at the two drunks, a peculiar sensation of ecstatic joy suddenly washing over him at his imminent, comic-book-scene freedom. "What of my men?" he said.

Prescott actually chuckled. *Maybe this guy isn't so bad?* Haz thought, and strode through the jail cell door, *almost* deciding to shove the cop out of the way in his happy disregard for the law.

Prescott Mayhew stepped out of his way, and waved one hand in the direction of the exit door. "Your car awaits, sir," he said, still chuckling mildly.

SAMANTHA'S CONFUSION REACHED A new level of potentially homogenizing mass when she reached Martin's duplex.

She pulled up on the other side of the street. Sagrada Circle was a little cul-de-sac tucked into the far end of Hathaway Heights—which had neither a way out nor could be called "high." Rookville looked down on Hathaway Heights, as it did onto the sloping field behind the division, which gave way to Porter River about a quarter of a mile beyond.

And Samantha did see a wondrous thing there—insanely normal, criminally average.

It looked to her like a little old lady—Martin's mom,

perhaps?—was locking the front door of the duplex. She tested the door handle, once, twice, then peeked into one of the windows next to the door, unburdened of a few shade slats due to Rowley's insistent morning prowling.

Samantha continued to watch as the woman, dressed in numerous layers of pleated blue and white cloth that somehow formed a dress of sorts around her squat figure, waddled away from the house and to a brown Pinto parked neatly at the curb. She glanced up at Samantha, winked one of a pair of bright blue eyes at her, and entered her vehicle, which started shortly with a huff and a puff, and chugged away in a cloud of emissions-testing failure.

Samantha blinked.

"Okay," she said aloud. "Okay. Why was that weird?"

Indeed—why was that weird? Was it because Martin had never mentioned nor suggested the existence of ancestry in all her conversations with him? Was it the strange multicolored barrettes in the old woman's hair, each one of which appeared to be correcting the errors of their cohorts?

Or was it simply the fact that something about that woman seemed *not wrong at all*?

Damn! She should have gotten the license plate number...although what a civilian *did* with the license plate number of a vehicle that had done nothing wrong, she couldn't fathom.

Done nothing *wrong*? How could she know that?

Samantha grabbed the little paper bag in the passenger seat labeled *Wednesday's—Every Day!* and exited her vehicle.

"Okay," she said again, under her breath. She proceeded to the front door, exhaust from the Pinto still fresh and lingering in the afternoon air. "I'm just here to check on Martin. Just to check on Martin. That's all."

She knocked, waited, knocked. She looked in the window off to the side of the door, just as the old lady had. Through the broken slats, she saw Rowley, sitting demurely in a small patch of sunlight in the kitchen, gazing back at her expectantly.

"C'mon, Rowley," she whispered. "Go get Martin. Tell him his best buddy's here with *treats*." She tried to emphasize the final word, lengthening the "s" slightly, knowing that this was Martin's own code word for use with the puckish feline. Rowley widened her eyes slightly and twitched her ears, indicating that she had heard and acknowledged Samantha's offer.

Well? She could practically hear Rowley's thoughts. *What are you waiting for? Come in.*

"Oh, fuck this," Samantha whispered to herself. She took three steps back, turned and faced her car. "Fine." She turned around once more and headed for the back gate on Martin's side of the duplex, knowing that there was a good chance a window or even, if she was lucky, the back door would be unlocked.

MARTIN WAS SUPERBLY IMPRESSED by Kane's capacity for focused attentiveness and profoundly reflective questions.

"So the precise mechanism by which a world is annihilated—this appears to boil down to the 'vacuum' principle, if you will," he summarized, having attended to Martin's explanation of the note in the back of *The Devil Escapes* and Bash's summary of *Occult Architectures of Memory*. "These 'beetle' creatures—and they are considered so only as a result of their insectile impedimenta, along with the peculiar buzzing or humming sound asso-ciated with their presence—exist at the farthest reaches of any given existent quantity. They are attracted by *vacua*; they are, in essence, *non-being*."

Shades of Martin's dissertation flashed through his mind. That was the gist of it. *We may thus conclude that a given* n-*dimensional vector may* refer *to magnitudes, without actually representing those magnitudes. Such entities as evinced by, e.g., astrophysical data*—he was referring, here, to black holes, but he didn't want to make the point *too* obvious—*lend intrusive factuality to the mathematical construction delineated on pages 263-307, inclusive...*

Martin sat in a cross-legged wooden chair by one immaculately carven windowsill set into Kane's ancestral home, a few miles outside Rookville. They had arrived hours previously, but hovered invisibly in the midst of a grove of trees on the property, which spanned a square mile and included some of Porter River, effectively linking the estate to the town proper. Loah-Dath had wanted to be utterly certain that there were no untoward entities vying for pouncing rights on the four of them, since his readouts did not detect the presence of Grajug immediately.

"There appears to be a trace of him," he had said. "Only an hour old."

When Martin and Bash had finally convinced Loah-Dath, in the midst of conversation with Kane Jeffries regarding the more abstruse and archaic conditions prevailing, to *go ahead and land, already*, they had discovered Grajug's note stuck to the banister of the stairs with Scotch tape, just inside of the front door.

My good friend Kane, it read, in a peculiar scrawl

showing deep similarities with Bash's own, *I have taken it upon myself to replenish our ever-diminishing stock of viands and hunger-palliatives. In addition to this important task, I will be visiting the locked stacks of nearby Rosewood College, as per your implication that an important clue might well be had amongst the papers and personal effects of the late Mr. Graham. My best to you, as always, GRAJUG.*

P. Scriptum: If you might oblige me, the Crockpot is ready to go. Please set it to a mere 150°F. I have an exceptional dinner in mind for us this evening!

A reasonably warm breeze had picked up during their stay outside of Earth. Even witnessing Earth's rotation for a few hours hadn't been enough to convince the deeper parts of Martin's mind that the whole exquisite display wasn't a complicated stage-show of some sort—like seeing a mountain range against blue sky for the first time: it couldn't be more than a painting, or a photograph at best.

This dwelling in the abstract served to guarantee a minimal level of distraction. Kane's ability to focus seemed to dwarf Martin's own; he had apparently been in the midst of a master's degree in philosophy when circumstances had led him from the simple introspection of hallucinogens to the darker potency of opiates. Having had little experience with the former and none with the latter, Martin merely decided to allow himself to feel abased in the presence of Kane's formidable adaptability.

So, in a word, Martin knew some math, but Kane was fucking smart.

"Those beetle-creatures consume everything in their path," Martin said from his station by the window. Another breeze picked up; he watched leaves and branches quivering in it. "As they get sucked toward the center of whatever world they define the limits of, they *eat*. But they don't even really do that—eating *changes* things from one form to another. These creatures...they *eat form*."

"And when form is gone, what constitutes substance?" Kane said rhetorically.

Martin nodded.

Bash was stirring the Crockpot contents with a big wooden spoon. "Oh, Grajug, you *have* outdone yourself!" he said, gazing merrily into the bubbling stew.

MEANWHILE, WARD CHAPMAN WAS busy building a world.

The Rookville Inn waved at travelers entering off Highway 64 from its location on top of a little hill that sloped off in a flurry of bushes, trees, and lawn. At the moment, three vehicles rested in its parking lot.

One of them, a low-end black BMW, its wheel wells spattered in dried mud, belonged to Ward Chapman, D.Litt., DPhil, FRS, SI, E∴O∴D∴, S∴W∴C∴, etc., etc., etc. He looked terribly good for his age, which according to his latest forged identification gave him as 5'10", 165 lbs.—a well-preserved 48-year-old.

Before him in the dimly lit room, floating above a wooden table set up ostensibly (judging by the marks and notches in it) for the occasional traveler to toss their keys and wallet on, Ward had established a small Door. It appeared to the unpracticed eye to be simply a shimmering globe, about three inches in diameter, sparkling randomly with various colors. To those who knew the magnificent arts practiced—and, in part, developed—by

Ward Chapman, those "random" sparklings were gravid with information: a vector field imparting an enormous amount of data regarding the material phenomena that evolved beyond the Door itself.

Ward appeared to be resting, in fact; he leaned back in his chair, eyes hooded but open, gazing *through* the Door, into the unfinished occult architecture of New Yuttelborough.

There...

The old City of Kept Promises, whose architecture had been established by the *Gah Quinkwe* however many untold millennia ago, had collapsed in the wake of a cosmic theft. But there was just enough left in memory—ironically, as a result of the thief's having profited from Yuttelborough's annihilation—to begin the restoration process, to allow a New Yuttelborough to be established in a spacetime less compromised by cracks in its foundational armor.

Maintaining *balance*, as usual, required absolute focus. In the wake of Thomas Graham's murder—for what *else* could it have been?—this was proving somewhat more trying and exhausting than Ward had initially suspected it would be.

Even demi-gods get tired.

Establishment of an initial *seed-point* from which the City could, fractally, begin to generate itself—in accordance with Martin Ready's unwitting mathematical support by way of an ingenious application of Brouwer's Fixed-Point Theorem—had taken most of Ward's considerable resources. But there was only one other option: omniversal collapse, like one half of a see-saw suddenly evaporating, leaving the fulcrum in a state of confusion and desperation for balance...

It had been just a room.

That was all Ward's imagination could maintain in fending off the mindless Editing of the Children—that, and the sincere belief, milked almost daily over the past several years, in a re-established Yuttelborough, maintained by the most loyal resistance to Fact he could possibly have enlisted: the Nerds of Rookville.

And it had seemed to be proving itself sufficient, despite constant need for maintenance. Although the recent, unexpected consequences of the nerds' fanaticism had proven almost fatal to the project.

The concern was clear: if the *Gah Quinkwe* could not be restored—if the Hesterian Fire remained unlit long enough—there would be no hope.

Martin was certainly *a* key to the mystery of the *Gah Quinkwe*'s whereabouts—but it seemed to Ward Chapman quite clear that he was a loose cannon, capable of far more in the way of sorcerous meddling than anyone seemed to suspect.

Could *he* have been the one? Could Thomas Graham have truly met his end at the hands of the polite and typically unassuming Martin Ready?

Ward removed himself from the Assembler beyond the Door, bringing himself back to Rookville, to the environs of the Inn. He remembered the words of Baevare Baeshazanam, echoing back to him from his brief sojourn in the City so many years ago, under a different name and practically a different face.

"Everything in the universe is merely letters to an Editor," Bash had said. "Things let in. Things eaten."

Ward Chapman heard the words again in his mind, but this time he shuddered with horror.

"THAT WILL BE ALL, Prescott," Pamela Stoyanova said, finalizing her utterance with a lust-imbued once-over of Hazzard Groschen's pathetic physiology. "You may leave us."

Haz knew that the blonde Bathory before him couldn't possibly mean him well—he had given up on any probability of finding comfort in the arms of Earthly women long ago, replacing, as it were, hardware with software.

But there are biological prerogatives that only the stupid or the jaded can ignore, and Haz was neither.

"I'm very thankful to you," he said as she sidled up next to him on the soft couch in the library at Thomas Graham's estate. "For, you know, getting me out of prison."

Pamela gazed at him, her wide blue eyes like oases in a desert of pleasure. There was nothing bad about her body, as far as Haz could tell. There was little enough of it covered by her Victoria's Secret wardrobe, which made the observation trivial. How old was she, anyway?

"Thankful," Pamela repeated. Her lips kissed the word pornographically. Haz experienced a sudden, uncomfortable sensation of blood rushing into his nether-regions. Oddly, the absurd image of a man in Mayflower pilgrim costume giving him a smiling salute passed through his mind. "Yes. Thankful."

Haz tried to smile, but it made him feel like he was committing murder. "Yes," he said, unsure of what else to do. "Um. Thankful."

Pamela reached out one insidious fingernail toward Haz's hand, frozen between them on the couch cushion. When it touched his flesh, light as feather, he became stiff as a board.

"Now, we may come...to some agreement, or other, as

the case may be." How did one lick words? Pamela did so now, coating them in honey, dripping them into the porches of his ears.

Haz was *not* "all ears" at the moment, and despite being all *horns*, Pamela attacked. She fell upon him, an exquisitely schemed air-raid on an ugly city. Barely one wave of minor nukes had passed before a megaton explosion rendered the plundered territory helpless and void of options.

Pamela shifted to the side, one exquisite leg hooked over Haz's very limp, very pale torso. He no longer knew if he was breathing, and he didn't care. Then something spoke: a serpent, its tongue flicking into his ear.

"I want you to tell me" —breath heavy upon him— "everything you know"—and the war waged on—"about Yuttelborough."

SAMANTHA DIDN'T KNOW WHAT she'd stumbled upon, but *in no way* did she like the implications of it.

So she hadn't *exactly* broken in. After knocking repeatedly—front door, side door, back door—she had officially decided that there was reason for worry. The argument was quite simple: if Martin was profoundly asleep, then he wouldn't know that she'd been there OR if Martin was *dead* or *beaten unconscious* (by that little old lady?!?), then she might be able to either (a) get an ambulance in time or (b) call the cops and report a suspicious brown Pinto fleeing Hathaway Heights.

In both cases generated during her anxious fiddling with the back door lock (it wasn't *precisely* breaking and entering if you were concerned about someone's welfare, was it?), she hadn't suspected one of two *other* possible options: no Martin or one weirded-out Martin.

Technically, she found *no* Martin.

Not in his bedroom, kitchen, or living room, at least. The bathroom door was open, and she (hesitatingly, fearing that *here's* where she'd find the body) found no one hidden behind the shower curtain.

There was *one* other possibility...

Rowley followed her at a distance from room to room, and had presently sat before a door that Samantha had *thought* must be a closet.

But it was not: it was a cellar.

And in that cellar was a room.

And that room was *definitely weird*.

There was a selection of colorful blankets and quilts thrust into one corner. Okay, fine. Next to that she found a pile of about thirty paperbacks, mostly old horror novels. A few notebooks. A selection of pens and pencils.

Near the middle of the room sat a cinder block covered in a cloth. An open package of Chips Ahoy! cookies had been torn into and left upon it. An empty bottle of Vanilla Coke. This was interesting: it looked like a big circuit board sporting some sort of equipment with a readout hooked up to it.

On the walls she saw a few interesting items: a large periodic table, with what appeared to be notes scrawled on it in a peculiar, indiscernible script. Several of the chemical elements had been *crossed out*, a few had arrows pointing to other boxes, and a number of *new* boxes had been added to the image, with what appeared to be mathematical formulas appended to them.

Fine. She knew that Martin had degrees in math. Could just be that he got into chemistry.

But why would he be sleeping down here? And what

in the name of all the gods was the purpose of the gigantic *map* covering the far wall of the room? And what the hell was the map *of* anyway? It bore no resemblance to any city, state, or country she recalled from any geography class she'd ever taken.

In front of it was another small table. This one had a little oil lamp in the center of it and a small brazier filled with a handful of astringent incense. There was writing all over the map done in that same immaculate, utterly foreign scrawl she had found on the periodic table. It looked to Samantha like it could have been Arabic, perhaps.

Down in the lower right-hand corner, there *was* something in regular English script, although the handwriting could have used some work.

List for Martin, it read. *Fangoria. New SK book. Hamburger Helper. MOS5175 RF transistors (x6). Foil resistors? Trolli Bright Crawlers.*

Fine. Very good. But either Martin was writing notes to himself *labeled* to himself—*or someone was living in his basement.*

Samantha returned to the heap of blankets in the corner. A small-size lamp on a movable arm was affixed above it, presumably for reading. She switched it on, and looked carefully at the bedding.

On it, she found fur. Lifting up one corner, she shook it out slightly, whereupon the casing of a shed claw, about twice the size of anything Rowley could produce, fell to the floor.

THE TWO YUTTELBOROUGHIANS HAD been yammering in their peculiar, melodic language, back and forth, nonstop for at least forty-five minutes.

Ever since Grajug had appeared in the doorway, bearing several bags of groceries and a few items "borrowed" from Rosewood College's special collections department (for further perusal, of course—he would return them, he swore!), he and Bash had been merrily chatting and singing and dominating the kitchen of Kane's home, preparing a feast that smelled as exquisite as the joy that seemed to be going into its construction.

"Do you understand *any* of that?" Martin asked Kane finally, after their general lack of importance to Bash and Grajug's plans had been made patently obvious.

"Not a word," Kane said, smiling. He and Martin had made their way out to the back porch with a bottle of Bordeaux after leaving Loah-Dath to his "meditations" in the modest library at the other end of the house. The old man had seemed particularly adamant about getting some "quiet time," a point conveyed in his usual overly polite manner. He had also insisted upon sending one of Liquid Agent's stretch of grunt workers out to fetch Kane's car from the parking lot of Quest Video, after Kane explained that this might reflect poorly on his good standing with the community.

"I can explain an absence due to illness," Kane had said. "But probably not why I walked home the night I got sick."

Martin and Kane sat in two wooden deck chairs over-looking the large stretch of forest occupying most of Kane's property. In the midst of the forest was the "flying saucer," cloaked to both Loah-Dath and Bash's satisfaction.

There seemed no good reason to avoid the infectious good cheer of the Yuttelboroughians, who seemed to have no genetic capacity for worry.

"We'll discuss the recapturing of the *Gah Quinkwe*, of course," Grajug had announced. "*After* fortifying ourselves!"

"I'm sure you have thought about it," Kane began, practically ensuring that Martin had, indeed, never come *close* to thinking about whatever he was going to suggest, "but the strangest link in this chain of events seems, to me, our common association with Ben Crabbe."

"I hadn't—yes, of course," Martin said. He actually *had* considered that.

"That the two humans effectively fostering the only two known Yuttelboroughians might share such *specific* causative events in their past..." Kane trailed off and sipped his wine. "I gave up believing in coincidence long ago. It seems like a way of saying 'I don't know' that superficially hides the fact that you don't know."

"That I can agree with," Martin said. "Besides—'coincidence.' What the hell does it actually *mean*, anyway?"

Kane nodded. "*Incidere*—to fall upon or happen to. *Co*—mutually."

Martin smiled. Perhaps it was the wine. Perhaps it was the laughter of the Yuttelboroughians coming from the kitchen, or whatever peaceful meditation Loah-Dath was presently engaged upon in the library. But he felt somehow different in these circumstances—strange or alien, even.

He felt like he had made some friends.

AFTER THE MEAL—ENTIRELY VEGAN, as Kane consumed nothing with a central nervous system (although Martin could swear that the potato stew from the Crockpot tasted,

somehow, like a truly exquisite *boeuf bourguignon*)—
Martin felt himself somewhat dizzy with a pleasant tiredness.

"Get some rest," Kane had insisted, showing him to
a comfortable room upstairs with its own bathroom and
shower. "I'll see if I can find out what Bash and Grajug's
plan consists of, in the main. Whatever it is, I have a
feeling that you are probably central to it."

So Martin had cleaned up a bit and then lay himself
down in the absurdly inviting bed.

He let his mind wander. The first thing he thought of
resulted from an absence: he missed Rowley. Almost
three full days away from her! This was highly unusual.
Martin never actually *left* when he went on vacation. He
would typically buy a stack of paperbacks and retire
to his home, spending most if not all of the time off in
bed, reading something he *chose* rather than something
chosen for him.

Rowley.

He could picture her now: the fluffy white fur and
great, wise, green eyes...the noble bearing...the soft mewl,
even when plaintive, and the feeling of paws landing with
a soft *thud* on the covers...then the inevitable hunt for
exactly the right spot to lay, for the all-important cleaning
session, accompanied by the low rumble of purring...

Martin reached out a hand and petted her, resulting
in louder purrs.

He shifted in his bed.

His bed.

Martin sat up, discombobulating the contented queen
in her ministrations.

He had done it again. *Translated.*

And as relaxing a scene as he was presently experiencing, he noticed the unmistakable sound of *someone* puttering around in his house.

He held up a shushing finger to Rowley, who gazed at him curiously, unaware of why he would be getting up *now*, of all times.

Slowly, carefully, Martin slid out of bed and followed the wall of the room, peeking around the corner past the bedroom door.

Someone was coming up the stairs from the cellar. *Bash's room!*

Martin held his breath as the cellar door opened...

...and Samantha Salieri came out.

"Sammy?" Martin said.

Samantha screamed and almost fell back down the stairs.

"Woah!" Martin shouted, and leapt for her. She had stabilized herself within the doorframe. "What are you *doing* here?"

"Me?" Samantha said, breathing heavily and gazing at him in diminishing terror. "What about *you*?"

"Um, this is my *house*?" Martin suggested.

Samantha extricated herself from the doorframe and Martin closed the door. He stepped back and regarded her. She did likewise.

"But you—you weren't—" she started.

"Calm down, Sammy," he said. "What's going on? Who let you in?"

"Well, I—I kind of—let myself—oh, Christ, whatever," Samantha said, and trudged over to the couch in the living room where she sat down heavily. "I came over here to *check* on you, because *Pamela* suggested it." She thought, perhaps, she could shift some of her own guilt onto a common target.

"She did?" Martin said. "How nice of her," he continued, feigning sentimentality. "What a gal!" He laughed.

Samantha looked up at him, confused. Then she laughed herself. Rowley wandered into the room and looked from Martin to Samantha and then back to Martin. She seemed to shake her head in disbelief, and made her way into the kitchen to get a snack.

HAZ DISGORGED HIMSELF TO Pamela, placing every detail in context as richly and profoundly as he could. He felt like some sort of criminal mastermind—or at least a Dungeon Master with one hell of a campaign in play.

A Dungeon Master who had just gotten *laid*.

It was unreal. Taggart and Bewley would—

And that stopped him in his tracks. They'd what? Continue to rot in their graves?

Pamela had mixed them both drinks after their engagement—something *extremely* alcoholic, but with some sort of added kick to it that made him feel almost hyperactive. He talked—and talked and talked.

Pamela didn't say much. Whenever Haz seemed to stumble over his words, she would give him a playful nip—on the *lips*, no less!—that would remind him of his true purpose in life: to serve her in whatever regard she found useful.

After recounting basically everything he could think of—including the extensive training sessions, money spent on weapons and ammunition, experimental devices ordered from shady organizations with PO Boxes in Utah and Nevada (items that Taggart, with his electronics wizardry, was actually able to get working the way they were supposed to)—Haz understood what he had been working on so passionately over the last few years: an organized *coup* on Reality Itself.

The purpose was, had always been, and continued to be *leaving this world.* Yuttelborough was the big secret—they were Chosen, they *had* to be...

Pamela removed the glass from Haz's unconscious hand and pressed a button beneath the heavy wooden table beside the couch. Moments later, Prescott Mayhew appeared at the door of the library.

"Set him up in one of the cottages outside Rookville," Pamela said as she brushed past Prescott on her way out of the room. "Give him access to the facilities, as well. Make sure any of the official files are purged of his involvement in the massacre."

Prescott bowed obsequiously, still grinning like a wolf carrying off a rabbit.

Pamela paused briefly just outside the door. "And Prescott," she added, "now that I think of it, set someone on that Kane Jeffries fellow. We certainly don't want him meeting up with Martin Ready."

"Consider it done," Prescott responded immediately. He chuckled as Pamela floated off to her chambers. He had been almost certain the day would end miserably—perhaps not even an ounce of bloodletting.

What luck!

LOAH-DATH SAT IN PERFECT calm, unmoving, and shifted his energies into the liminal space of awareness.

I speak to you, Author, he suggested mentally. *I speak to you. It has been given me to understand that I am part of a script, part of a play—and yet this has not clarified my understanding. To what end?*

He felt the subtle stirrings of an answer within him, bubbling up in the form of multivalent geometric forms and images.

He witnessed *The Going of Jacinta.* A thing of great beauty—a book, yet not a book. *Like the philosophers' "stone that is not a stone"... And yet what thing is, indeed, itself, for longer than the refresh rate of experience?*

That villain: Thomas Graham. And yet, from this new perspective, not a villain...*part of a prophecy...for that which is all-powerful requires only our capacity to trust in it...when the world changes, it is our folly that tries to hold it back...*

Free will and determinism. The next moment is certain; before it is written, it is not.

Loah-Dath opened his eyes.

Why *The Going of Jacinta*? That text focused around the book-engine of Yuttelborough—its power-source. As they all knew, when the *Gah Quinkwe* was stolen—why did he want to use the word "abducted"?—non-being consumed the world, its consumption rate increasing exponentially with every component devoured...

Loah-Dath closed his eyes again.

He saw Martin. Bruised, laying in a hospital bed. The coma—the *comma*, to him; the pause-mark... He followed the editorial thread into Martin's mind, and listened.

From somewhere beyond, a voice. *When their backs were turned, gazing in awe at the interesting but unnec-essary spectacle of not only one Comet, but two, now three,* four... It was a woman's voice, coming from the room just beyond Martin's.

And he watched as Martin blinked out of *this* existence, into another. Moments later, he returned—but there was something undeniably *different* about him.

He seemed to have aged.

How long had he been gone, over *there*?

Loah-Dath shifted his perspective to the room beyond Martin's.

"...in an effort to ensure that the joy of his people could endure just a *wee* bit longer, the Great Priest (in his little body) returned to his quarters. He could sense the inevitable, like a mother the loss of her child—but, in his case, as for all those in the City of Kept Promises, it was a child who had lost its mother instead." The woman closed the book briefly and reached over to feel the warmth still emanating, still a bit too strongly, from her daughter's forehead. She brushed the bangs of her child's hair aside lovingly.

Loah-Dath sensed tears brimming up in the woman's eyes. Perhaps in an effort to stay them, she returned to the book and continued to read.

And all the while Martin Ready, preternaturally conscious, though not so in any Earthly sense, lived out the story she told in his own mind, and became a part of it.

IT WAS A STORY that Martin found himself relating, though from a substantially different perspective, to Samantha Salieri in his living room, while (presumably) Kane Jeffries and the Yuttelboroughians generated their (undoubtedly ingenious) scheme for re-acquiring the *Gah Quinkwe*.

"...and I think that brings us pretty much up to speed," Martin concluded. "I mean, with me appearing here in my house, apparently from out of nowhere."

After taking a few moments to compose himself and get properly dressed, he had decided to go for broke and tell her nothing but the truth. It seemed like something Bash would do, at any rate, and *that* guy never really worried about much of anything.

Samantha gazed at him, a forgotten mug of cold coffee sitting on the edge of the table in front of her. Martin had encouraged her to eat the sandwich from Wednesday's, ensuring her that he was, himself, stuffed to the gills. She didn't.

"So what you've spent the last hour explaining to me," she finally commented, after a few moments of silence, "is that you and Vic Toronto should switch places?"

Martin, wide-eyed, worked his mouth silently for a few seconds. Samantha, unable to contain herself, burst out laughing.

Someone knocked on the door.

Immediately, Samantha fell silent, concern spreading over her features.

Martin shrugged. "Delivery man?" he whispered. "Let's wait it out."

The knocking sounded again, somewhat more insistently this time. Rowley trotted out of the kitchen, ears flattened back against her head, and into the bedroom.

"Maybe we should—" Samantha started, before the kitchen door burst inward with a deafening crash.

Samantha screamed. Martin lunged for her in a bid to protect her from whatever missile might be intended for him. Both of them crumpled to the floor.

Dust and debris from the kitchen wafted into the living room. Martin could hear thousands of dollars being flushed down the toilet with every creak and whomp of snapping wood. Finally, when silence had returned, he opened his eyes and turned toward the entryway from the kitchen.

"Greetings, prisoner," the high-pitched voice announced, a note of gloating superiority ringing through it. His eyes could delineate a thin, spacesuit-clad form standing in the doorway, holding what appeared to be some sort of extraterrestrial rifle—looking more like a child's toy than a gun—with hands gloved in shiny, reflective material. "You and the female are commanded to submit yourselves to judgment, as allotted to the Council of Rookville, Terran Quadrant Alpha."

"GENERATING THE SAME SORT of map for the presence of the *Gah Quinkwe*? A thaumaturgical density function, you mean. That would require—oh, please, thank you!"

Bash accepted a refill of his Mountain Dew from a two-liter proffered by Grajug. Kane declined, finding that excessive sugar intake often dulled his focus.

"Where was I? Oh, yes. That would require an initiate of the Higher Orders. Someone who had read it, I'm thinking. The suggestion is a good one, at any rate, if presently unfeasible," Grajug said, seating himself once again at the table. A map of Rookville was laid out in the midst of the grand feast's remains. "And it is indubitably true that we of Yuttelboroughian blood ought to show up with rather *peculiar* signatures. But there is no guarantee that entities with no central nervous system would appear similarly—if at all."

"Assuredly," Bash said. "But I can sense that Mr. Jeffries has already considered this."

Kane smiled, leaning back in his chair and gazing at the twinkling lights of the chandelier. They seemed unwilling to call him by his first name—something about his physical aspect, perhaps? "I suspect that there may be elemental *quanta* of Yuttelboroughian provenance which exceed the parameters assumed to the elements of Earth. It's just a guess, really—but this nonsense that *intelligence* and *life* are somehow distinct events has always baffled me."

Both Bash and Grajug began knocking repeatedly on the table, the classic applause of a scholar in one of their academies. Kane responded with a mock bow of his head.

"It deserves a try, certainly," Grajug said. "I wonder if Loah-Dath has come up with anything during his meditation?"

"And we should certainly check with Martin," Bash said. "The man has dreams that often crack codes. At oddly relevant times too!"

A slightly troubled look suddenly darkened Kane's face.

"Kane?" Bash asked. "Is there something else?"

Kane shook his head. "Something I started to talk to Martin about," he said. "About Ben Crabbe—the man at Fall County Jail whom we both 'happened' to fall in with."

"Certainly," Bash said. "That is peculiar. Yet what *is* coincidence, anyway—"

"Yes, of course," Kane said, cutting him off. "There is a peculiar characteristic of individuals here on Earth that Yuttelboroughians may not fully understand." He leaned forward again and gazed at the two fascinating creatures. Grajug was helping himself to another serving of apple pie. Bash waited patiently for Kane to continue.

"Persona," Kane finally said. "The word means, basically, *a mask*. The original sense was 'that which one is not.' Amongst humans, we value those whose *masks* most closely approximate the underlying truth of their being."

Bash was nodding his head. "I understand," he said.

Grajug looked up as well, swallowing a bite of apple pie. "Of course," he said. "What kind of pie is it that provides merely a veil of nourishment—and yields nought but sawdust when sliced by those who would enjoy it?"

Kane nodded. "That's exactly right," Kane said. "Again, amongst humans, we often find ourselves wary. What does this person *really* want from me? Why is this person being nice? Most humans have utterly forgotten one of their most formidable powers."

Bash and Grajug both looked at him, their wide eyes intent. "And that is?" Bash urged.

"Kindness," Kane said. "In other words, our ability to *choose*. No matter what happens, I can always *consciously choose* to do that which engenders the greatest possible degree of happiness. Forgetfulness of this fact—the true power-source of humanity—leads to all villainies and viciousness. It leads to all sense of weakness—both in oneself and in others. In short, it leads to pain."

Bash smiled, as did Grajug, who decided to finish the remainder of the pie.

"A fine argument—nearly perfect!" Bash said.

"Nearly?" Kane felt a rise of pridefulness that made him want to argue, which he urgently quashed.

"Yes, nearly," Bash repeated. "In Yuttelborough, we have a saying that translates roughly as: 'A fool forgives all and fears nothing; a wise man loves fools.' The sense is that to be *wise* is to be capable of the 'foolishness' that forgives all and fears nothing—a capacity that requires *forgetfulness*. But the wise man is known for remembering that he is being foolish. He loves peace, and creates intricate, peaceful lessons for those who would harm the fools. These latter often become wise men as a result!"

Kane was deeply pensive. "Huh," he said finally.

"You make a fine brother to us, Mr. Jeffries!" Grajug said, chuckling.

FRANK FLEURETY EXITED THE basement of Thomas Graham's mansion feeling weary.

It was a weariness brought on by guilt, plain and simple.

But there was really no other way, was there?

He made his way to the central stairs and up to the master bedroom. Pamela already lay there, asleep, breathing softly. He lay down as quietly as he could beside her and closed his eyes...

There was really no other way, was there?

He thought again of how Tom had done it—the absurd combination and the unusual skill. Only Tom's poverty would have led him to consume all that damned sugar for dinner—Broom Zoom and Sugar Triggers. That was funny, because it had been Halloween night, and the Broom Zoom had been an afterthought, really—dropped in the street outside the door to the Rookville slum he called home and eagerly snatched up as if it had been a twenty dollar bill.

Although Tom hinted that there was more to it than that. Something about Ellington Mayhew...?

I saw the strangest sigil in a dream last night...

And he saw it again, on the Door to his rickety old room, after eating sugar for dinner and making his escape into a waking dream.

He found himself there—Thomas Graham, accepted, gazed warily at by the High Priest, but not knowing why. In their libraries, reading and absorbing all manner of "myth and legend," until that Day when the strange Star shone forth in the sky.

It corresponded with a Vision of the Yuzzutahs; the Priest left his confines to witness it, to bathe in the intoxicating rainbow of lights streaming down from it...

The Book—the Heart and Soul of Yuttelborough— had called to him, then.

No obstructions; no locks or barriers.

As the Yuttelboroughians sat in awestruck wonder just outside the confines of the Temple, Thomas Graham opened the Book...

It was like a great pressure, massing in my skull, Tom told him, years later. *I thought that this was it! Finally, I was to die—malnourishment, or whatever. But no... instead, I wrote...*

He wrote—and every black mark on the page was a Beetle inching toward the central Soul of Yuttelborough.

He wrote continuously—page after page—and the World that once was became, gradually, a fiction in his own.

"LOOK, MAN, THIS IS a *major* mistake—" Samantha started to yell. A lurching halt followed by sudden acceleration stopped her from continuing, not that the maniac up front could necessarily hear her anyway through the sheet of metal separating them from the cab.

She and Martin were handcuffed to an inner wall in the back of what appeared to be a converted FedEx truck. Geordi "Space-Race" Mifflin sat up front, shooting around curves and corners with no apparent regard for his own safety, much less that of his "prisoners."

Geordi remained silent, occasionally coughing and grimacing from various pains inflicted by his mortal enemies during the rumble at Rookville Mall. A cracked rib, possibly? He hoped that he could hold out for long enough to get to the rendezvous point.

"I don't think"—Martin braced himself as the truck shot over yet another pothole—"he's listening, Sammy."

"I *know* that!" Samantha said. The sudden tones of Clara Rockmore playing a theremin emanated from high-treble speakers in the truck's front cab. "Oh, Jesus. Martin, who the fuck *is* this weirdo?"

"I'm just guessing," Martin answered, "but I think his name is Geordi."

"Geordi?" Samantha said.

"Yeah, like—oh, man," Martin became suddenly aware of the potential *Star Trek: The Next Generation* reference and cringed.

"Okay, well does your buddy Geordi know not to *kill people* yet?" Samantha said, eyes wide.

"Frankly, I have no idea," Martin said. "I don't really know what all this is about—"

"Oh, let me *guess*," Samantha cut in. "Maybe it's about that damned alien refugee you've been harboring in your basement?"

Martin nodded. "Well, obviously," he said, resigned. "But *other* than that, I mean."

Samantha growled and pulled once more at her hand-cuff with a futile effort. "We probably should have run when he corralled us in here," she said.

"Survival instinct," Martin said. "We didn't want to end up like the kitchen door."

"Where the hell's the rescue squad?" Samantha asked. "Shouldn't there be someone rescuing us by now? I mean, even the fucking *cops*, for example?"

Martin shook his head. "Don't know," he said. "Haz used some kind of signal blocker in his van. Maybe this guy's got something like that?" Martin paused for a moment. "I hope Rowley's okay," he added somberly.

"Yeah, no shit," Samantha said. "Ring-a-ling better be on the fucking ball."

"Ling-Watha," Martin said, genuine concern in his voice. "And yes. She'd better."

"Sorry," Samantha said. "The neighbors have definitely called the cops—"

They were skidding to a halt. Martin and Samantha fell quiet. Up front they could hear Geordi clambering out of the vehicle, then trudging around the side. Low voices followed.

"Well," Martin whispered. "Guess we find out what kind of trouble we're in now."

Samantha stared at him, wide-eyed. "How can you be so fucking *calm* right now?" she said. "If I wasn't a girl, I'd be shitting my *pants*—"

The metal doors at the back of the truck creaked open.

Martin gasped.

"Hello, Martin," Haz said simply. He stood, arms crossed, grinning evilly against the backdrop of an unassuming little house that looked like it was in the middle of nowhere. "We keep finding ourselves in this *weird* situation!" he continued sarcastically. "I wonder what the hell it means?"

"Wait a minute!" Martin said. He noticed that Samantha had a look of terrific confusion on her face. "I thought Geordi was your *enemy*—"

"Old disagreement, based on a misunderstanding," Haz explained as Geordi sidled up next to him, still dressed in his absurd spacesuit and bearing his high-tech blaster gun. "Geordi's in on the game, now."

Martin tugged on his handcuff. "Is this really necessary? I mean, I thought you and I were friends—"

"Certain facts have come to light, Martin Ready," Haz explained. "I'm afraid that you and the girl will be getting used to those chains until we can be assured safe passage to Yuttelborough."

"I don't know how to *get* to Yuttelborough—" Martin started.

"Calm!" Haz said. "Calm, Martin. No need to get evasive. How about we show you to your quarters and let you think about things for a little while?"

Geordi entered the back of the truck with something that looked like a P.K.E. meter from *Ghostbusters.*

"Woah—wait a minute—" Samantha said as he shined a light from it into her eyes. She fell instantly to sleep.

Martin resigned himself. "Do whatever you have to do, I guess," he said. "You'll find out soon enough that I—"

He slept.

THERE WAS A WEAKENING.

If only it had been of the bonds! But no—it was of this substance, this "flesh" of which she was composed. She narrowed her focus again; like any book, the next page, though it is, *though it* exists, *is unknown until read.*

And she felt it—a Door. Not close—but near enough.

She reached *for it—every ounce of her strength, every ounce of her* being *reached, stretched, groped, cast about for it, a light in the dark—*

Martin snapped awake.

It was cold. A pale light shone through the small room. *Oh, gods, no, not* again—

A cell.

He recognized it: the uncomfortable "mattress," the cold, the bare, blank walls. He looked up and around. Sink, toilet with no seat, light coming in through iron-grey bars.

But he seemed to be alone.

Martin lay his head back down upon the thin pillow and groaned, covering his eyes with the crook of one elbow.

~~~

THREE YEARS AGO

THERE WERE RULES, AND there were rules.

Martin lay flat on his back in his cell, hoping against hope that the throbbing pain in his lower left side did *not* indicate a hemorrhaging kidney. That was the worst part. Doc Sibley assured him that he was fine—because he had been a grunt in Vietnam, if your guts weren't hanging out all over the place or your face was in (roughly) the right spot, to him, you were fine.

And just when the *last* black eye had started to thin out, too—now he had a pair of them. He looked like a fucking raccoon.

"How you holding up?" Ben asked.

Martin considered his words carefully. "Like Atlas," he answered.

Ben chuckled. "Smart-ass," he said. "I *told* you what was gonna happen if you shot off your mouth again to those pricks."

"It's like I can't control it," Martin said. "Like there's a certain degree of ignorance that I actually cannot exist in the same environment with."

"No wonder you're in here," Ben said.

"What do you mean?" Martin asked.

"You might as well be," Ben said, "since you just described any person with an ounce of brains on planet Earth."

Martin risked a laugh. Streaks of pain shot through his ribs. He stopped.

"Why didn't you fight?" Martin asked.

Ben knew what he was talking about.

"I didn't need to," he said.

"Didn't need to?" Martin said. "What about—"

"No one needed me to," Ben answered simply. Martin heard him roll onto his side in the bunk below. "It's better, when you're beat, to let those who count believe what they need to believe. You gotta get out of your own way so that you can do what you need to do."

Ben paused for a moment. The world "out there" was just a big prison, anyway. The lines were invisible; the bars were atmospheric, chemical. But there were consequences for crossing the ones you could cross, and insurmountable barriers when you tried to get past the others.

Ben sighed. "Besides, there are rules, and there are rules."

Martin knew what he was talking about.

~~~

"MARTIN?"

It was Samantha's voice, coming from the cell right next to his.

"Martin? Are you awake?"

Martin opened his eyes again and shifted into a sitting position, his back against the cold stone wall. About two feet of cinder block separated the cells. The place was clinical, at least; it smelled like more like residual ammonia and not at all like a sewer. Unlike some places he'd been. "I'm awake," he said.

"Jesus, Martin, where the hell *are* we?" Samantha asked. Her voice was low, just on the verge of tremulous.

"We're in a jail of some sort," he said.

"Well *that's* fucking obvious," Samantha said. She paused momentarily. "I'm sorry."

"No," Martin said, "*I'm* sorry. This is all my fault."

"You seriously don't know what you're mixed up in?" Samantha asked.

"I guess I do, kind of," Martin said. He stood up from the bed and strolled over to the bars at the front of the cell. "Not really, actually. I need to talk to Bash."

"Well, *can* you?" she asked, having shifted to the spot closest to him at the front of the cell.

"Maybe," Martin answered.

"Have you ever tried to do any of that stuff"— Samantha hesitated—"you know, that stuff that you've done before, you know, on *purpose*?"

Martin thought about it. "No," he answered finally. "It always seems like it just happens *to* me."

"But it happens to you when you're either really relaxed or really desperate?"

"Yeah," Martin said. "I get the same sensation as when I look at a page and I *know* that there's something wrong with it before I even start reading it. Something in my gut tells me. Spelling error. Grammatical issue. Something."

"What do you do differently?" Samantha asked. He could tell what she was doing. He hoped that it worked.

"I—" Martin thought about it. What *did* he do differently? He looked at a page, in his mind. There it was: orthographical nightmare. He felt the sensation again: something in his gut, physical, kinesthetic. Like he'd just been punched—physically offended in some manner. "I fight back?" he suggested.

Samantha was silent for a moment. "Could you do it now?" she asked.

Martin wondered. Why didn't he feel like fighting? "Maybe," he said. He didn't really know; he didn't feel like he *wanted* to. A terrifying sensation gripped him: that he felt *safer here, behind bars* than he did out there, in the world...

"I can try," he said.

"What do you need me to do?" Samantha asked.

"I need you to..." Martin paused again. What could she do? Piss him off, maybe?

She waits in the cold, in the darkness, in chains...

"Samantha?" he said. "This is going to sound completely crazy."

Samantha managed a laugh. "I *promise* you that, given the circumstances, it absolutely *will not*."

"All right, then," Martin said. "Sing for me."

"What?"

"Like I said: crazy," Martin replied. "Sing me a song—but make sure that it's one you don't know very well."

"Martin, I can't sing worth a damn," Samantha said.

"And you know it."

"Sure I do," he said. "Now, *sing me a fucking song*."

Samantha huffed and puffed for a moment. "What—I don't know what song to sing."

"Okay, okay," Martin said. "Try a poem, then. Just think of any poem and start singing it out."

Again, Samantha went silent for a few moments. Then Martin heard a quiet, almost ghostly little voice, wavering and out of tune, emanating from her cell.

> "He fond yn the pavyloun
> The kynges doughter of Olyroun,
> Dame Tryamour that hyghte;
> Her fadyr was kyng of Fayrye..."

Martin's stomach began to rumble and quake. *Dear* God *what is she* saying*?!?* His mind ached with the effort of visualizing the words—*almost* English, not *quite*, just *not clear enough*—

> "Of Occient, fer and nyghe,
> A man of mochell myghte.
> In the pavyloun he fond a bed of prys
> Yheled wyth purpur bys,
> That semyle was of syghte..."

Martin felt the volcanic uproar in his guts spread; to his veins, to his nerves—every fiber and molecule of his being pulsed with the desire to *fix* what she was forcing him to visualize. He shut his eyes tightly; tears streamed forth from behind the lids. He wrenched the words into channels in his mind—*this way, this way,* this way*, goddamnit*—

He pounded his fists against the wall between them, but refused to speak. He *would not* tell her to stop—he would *fix* the words, for love of all the *gods* he would—

Something snapped in his mind. He fell forward and landed on concrete with a thud. Opening his eyes, he leapt up at once and launched himself at Samantha, who stood there before him, eyes closed, still warbling the poisonous evocation of his latent powers.

> "Therinne lay that lady gent
> That after Syr Launfal hedde ysent
> That lefsom lemede bryght—"

Martin kissed her. Samantha's arms wrapped about him and held him tightly to her, returning the kiss, fiercely, fulsomely, flagrantly. They fell onto the mattress at the other side of her cell, moaning and groping. At some indefinable spatiotemporal point, they were less than two people; then many more in colorful condition than could be said for one; and finally they were nothing, spent, done for, exhausted, out of breath.

Martin could not get the taste of her out of his mouth. He had no desire to taste anything else, ever.

Her breathing slowed and they fell asunder, her hair still knotted in one of his hands, his wrist still clutched in one of hers.

"What the hell *was* that?" Martin finally asked.

Samantha took a deep breath, held it for a moment, and then burst out laughing. "I did my thesis at Rosewood on Middle English poetry," she said.

Martin smiled, forgetting for a moment their predicament. "It was like—a nightmare, or something," he finally said.

Samantha laughed aloud again. "Wait a second," she breathed, shifting and gazing across the room. "So much for the wall... But. Hey. Look!" They both glanced up at the empty space between the two cells. Everything that could possibly indicate the previous existence of a wall separating the two cells had evaporated, including the bed on Martin's side.

There was something else: moonlight, coming from a two-foot ridge running between the back wall of the two cells, where the separating wall had once adjoined them. A light breeze picked up, wafting into the room the scent of pine and spruce trees. It appeared as if whomever had constructed the prison had done so *one cell at a time*, rather than as a large warehouse-type room divided into individual cells. It also appeared that they were on a ground floor.

"Quick!" Samantha said. "Pull your pants up! *Let's go!*"

"MAGICAL THINGS HAVE A tendency of finding each other," Bash explained. "Kind of like magnets. And on much the same principle!"

Grajug sat beside a credenza in the dining room, alternately toggling switches on an oscilloscope that rested upon it and touching electrodes to one of Bash's absurdly complex circuit board arrangements. What had once been a feast was now a Faustian amalgam of diabolical wiring schemes laid out with abandon on the dining room table.

"All we need to do is zoom the signals appropriately," Bash continued. "That's what this is for." He indicated one particular circuit board with a peculiarly ornate arrangement of transistors and resistors embedded into it. A soldering iron emanated what was certainly some toxic gas into the air from an old coil of half-melted lead—it was the best they could get on short notice from the supplies (extensive, but admittedly twenty years old) in Kane's basement.

"And this is all based on Hermetic principles!" Loah-Dath exclaimed. "Ingenious! One merely miniaturizes the conditions."

"Same thing in any physical system," Kane added, marveling no less than Loah-Dath. "Like when car companies realized you could test the mechanical efficiency of a system by simply making an electrical circuit that modeled the classical interactions."

"It's exactly why we assume a unified set of energetic fields!" Bash said. "And, incidentally, why thoughts are like 'non-magnified' physical phenomena. We add density to them by thinking them repeatedly, or with great emotional investment."

Loah-Dath nodded, grinning. This was exactly the system taught in his Order, modified to accord with a means of "forcing" energies—the blessing and the curse of modern scientific methodology.

Kane and Bash followed a trail of zip-corded wiring into the next room, where they had shifted a replica of Rodin's *Paolo and Francesca* into a corner to make way for the spiraling and strange Hieronymus machine that Bash and Grajug had etched into the floorboards in chalk.

"This is where it will happen," Bash said, pointing to the inscribed collection of squiggles and zig-zags and curlicues running rampant over the floor. "That triangular image over there will function in almost precisely the same fashion as a medieval 'Triangle of Manifestation.' The basic trigger for manifestation should, theoretically, be blood or some encapsulation of genetic data. And this is where we hope that our guess is correct. I will go awaken our hero and ask for a lock of his hair."

Kane laughed. Loah-Dath glanced up briefly from a sketchpad he had produced, on which he was rapidly making notes as he analyzed the setup.

"This is one *hell* of an assumption," Kane said. "Let me get this straight. Your original 'anti-location' spell distinguished *two* sources where Martin would *not* be. And you're guessing that the *other* source must somehow be of particular significance to locating the *Gah Quinkwe*—"

"Indeed," Loah-Dath interrupted. Bash nodded at him and disappeared into the recesses of the house to awaken Martin. "Not the most untoward advance in logic. From what we can tell, it was Martin's arrival in Yuttelborough that directly aligned with the final destructive sequence of the Dark Children. His return was occasioned by the simultaneous return of Bash, obviously, but *also* the unwitting return of Grajug. It is hence possible that his practical role as the only likely Savior of Yuttelborough found some—perhaps many—additional links in the chain of coincidence."

"Might as well give it a shot," Kane said. They both turned toward the room's entrance as Bash came sprinting back in.

"Martin's gone!" he cried out.

Kane shot up and ran toward the guest bedroom on the other side of the house without a word. Loah-Dath, Bash, and Grajug followed suit.

An empty bed, looking like it had been slept in for no more than a few minutes. That was all.

Bash spoke up. "Hang on!" He ran into the bathroom and returned moments later bearing a hairbrush. "Thank the *gods* for human grooming habits!" he said, typically undaunted. "This ought to be enough to proceed as planned."

SAMANTHA AND MARTIN SQUEEZED through the space in the back wall, each of them silently thanking the gods for fast metabolisms and irregular eating habits. They found themselves in a band of tall grass about five yards wide that stretched along the outside back wall of the prison and backed up to a dense, dark forest.

"Into the woods?" Martin suggested.

Samantha shrugged. "Is that the first place they'll check?"

"Probably," Martin said. "We can try running out front...?"

Samantha nudged past Martin and entered the forest of trees. Only a meager light shone from the moon, barely useful in lighting their way. There was, at least, a single concession from Mother Nature: clearly enough space to walk without having to hack through brush to get anywhere.

Ten minutes after making their way into the forest, Martin and Samantha were utterly lost.

"I can't even see the fucking jail from here," Samantha said.

"Are we still going in a straight line?" Martin asked. "I wasn't really paying attention."

"What forest could this possibly be?" Samantha asked. "We didn't drive far enough from your place for it to be Wendigo National."

Martin thought for a moment. "No," he said. "But we *did* drive just long enough to get to Eastland."

Samantha let out a breath. "So *that's* where they took us—"

"Frinkley's property," Martin said, referring to an ancient plot of woodland outside Rookville proper. Bram Frinkley had provided for its upkeep for the next two

hundred years, supposedly, damning the excessive defor-
estation that he thought was ruining the world. "Rural
Route 12 ought to be somewhere out here. And there's
the old mall."

Samantha grabbed Martin's shirt and pulled him along.
"I know where we're going," she said.

Martin followed without complaint.

Five minutes later they thought they saw Rural Route
12 ahead of them. They also heard the unmistakable
sound of helicopter blades approaching. Fast.

SPRINTING IN A DARK forest on questionable terrain was
not a good idea.

A split second after he started for the road, Martin had
collapsed in a heap, tripping over a patch of tangled roots
and somersaulting once before coming to a stop.

"Marty!" Samantha yelled, turning back.

"No!" Martin yelled back. "Run! I'll catch up!"

He pushed himself back up into a standing position.
He took one step and winced as a sharp pain flared up
from his right ankle. Samantha had become a dark patch
up ahead. He glanced in the direction from which the
helicopter was driving down upon them.

No spotlight. What did that mean? Infrared sensors?

He took another few limping steps.

"God*damn*it!" he yelled out. He couldn't see Samantha
in the darkness. He hoped that she had not done something stupid like turn around—

Rapid footsteps approached, trudging through the
leaves. "Marty! I thought you said you would keep up!"

Damn it.

"Sammy, you need to *get the fuck out of here*," Martin

said.

"No, I need to *help* you." She grabbed his right arm and placed it around her shoulders. "Come on. Like this. Nice and easy."

They limped along at about a quarter of their original speed. The helicopter approached and paused above them.

"I think they've got some kind of infrared sensor in that thing—" Martin started.

A Dopplerized siren wail resounded from up ahead, rapidly approaching on Rural Route 12.

"Cops?" Samantha said. "Marty, we've got to get to the road!"

They hopped, skipped, and jumped like a pair of blindfolded, drunken Siamese twins through the last stretch of forest.

The helicopter, perhaps sensing defeat, retreated back the direction it had come.

Red-and-blue lights began flashing at the top of the hill that descended to their location. Martin would never have believed that he'd feel elation at the sight of a cop, but there it was, rising within him, hopeful sap in a blooming tree.

Samantha deposited Martin on the shoulder of the road and began waving her arms crazily, standing in the middle of the road. Martin breathed the night-forest air deeply, leaning back on his hands. The police car approached rapidly, turned on its brights, and slowed to a stop.

"Wounded man!" Samantha yelled. "Wounded man!"

Wisely, she didn't run at the cop car. After a few beats (probably calling for backup, Martin assumed), the police officer exited his vehicle. Martin could barely make out his shape against the blinding lights.

The officer approached, one hand at the ready on his gun, the other holding yet another flashlight up. "Ma'am," he said. "We got calls about a disturbance in the woods. That you?"

"That's us," Samantha lied. "My friend and I got lost out here. I think he sprained his ankle."

The cop, still keeping his distance, shined his flashlight on Martin, who grinned at him and waved.

"Can you get him up?" he asked.

"I think so," Samantha said. "Yeah. Sure." She walked back over to Martin and lifted him.

"Okay," the cop said. "You guys been drinking? What the hell are you doing out here at this time of night? You know that forest is private property?"

"It was an accident," Samantha said. Martin stood next to her, leaning against her slightly. "We were supposed to meet some people nearby earlier, and we took a walk. It got dark. We got lost."

The cop nodded. "Fair enough," he said. "Whyn'tcha get in the car. I'll give you a ride back." He motioned them over, switching off his flashlight.

MARTIN'S ANXIETY AT BEING in the back of a police car was only slightly offset by Samantha's fawning over him, trying to make sure that he was comfortable.

But something about the situation didn't seem right at all.

"You can just drop us off at the bus station, I guess," Martin said. "Isn't that up ahead?"

The cop didn't answer.

"Yeah," Samantha said, sensing the problem immediately. "Bus station's fine. Or wherever."

The cop hesitated just a *bit* too long for Martin's liking before answering. "Prob'ly get him to the minor emergency at Rookville General," he said. "Get that ankle looked at."

Martin nodded. "Right," he said. "Good idea."

Samantha was nudging Martin in the ribs. He nudged her back to indicate his wariness of the situation.

The cop slowed his vehicle as they approached a private drive that appeared to cut back into the forest they had exited.

"Hey," Martin said nervously. "You're not—"

"Don't worry," the cop said. "I just gotta make a quick pit stop."

Samantha and Martin turned to each other, wide-eyed. The car rolled to a stop on the shoulder of the road. The cop got out and walked off into the forest.

"Um," Samantha said. "Maybe he had to pee?"

Martin was shaking his head. "I don't fucking believe this," he said. "Getting into a cop car is *never* a good idea! *Never*!"

Samantha was patting down the door on her side of the back seat.

"You can't get out, Sammy," Martin said. "They're built that way."

"Oh, come *on*, Martin!" Samantha exclaimed. "We can't have made it *this* far only to get bumped off or whatever by some backwoods—"

A large truck rumbled into view from the private drive. A converted FedEx truck.

"*Fucking Christ!*" Samantha yelled. "Goddamn *fucking* shit *fuck goddamnit*—"

"Woah!" Martin said. "Woah. Calm. Down." He

grabbed her by the shoulders and looked into her eyes. She was tearing up. "Okay. Whenever they open the doors, I will cause a huge distraction. I'll grab the cop's gun, or something. You *run for it*—run into the forest."

"What if they start *shooting* at me?" Samantha asked reasonably.

"They won't," Martin said. "At least, I'm pretty sure they won't. Think about it. They put us in holding cells. They didn't beat us or torture us. They located us easily enough in the helicopter, but they didn't rain bullets down on us. The worst that can happen is they catch you and bring you back. But now is our only chance. You have to try to get back to town. And you have to try to get help."

"Who do I get to help?" Samantha was frantic. "I can't get the cops—"

"Kane Jeffries," Martin said. "You know the name? Kane Jeffries. Quest Video. *Find Bash if you can.* Liquid Agent. *Anybody*. We have friends! Remember—"

Martin's side door opened. Hazzard Groschen peered in.

"Martin Ready! How exciting!" he said, sneering. "And is that you're little lovebunny, too? Oh, this is just *too much*!" He started laughing.

Martin lunged at him, ignoring the pain in his leg. He punched—once, twice, three times. It was as easy and as difficult as he remembered from the few fights he'd been in at Fall County Jail. *Just hit them as hard as you can as many times as you can.* Thanks, Ben. It works.

Someone was dragging him off. Martin realized that he had shut his eyes tightly while wailing on the nerd. He heard groans and coughing. He felt, despite the circumstances, a few degrees better than he had the moment before.

"Let's save cage-fighting for the main event, buddy," the cop said as he restrained Martin and slammed him against the back of the car. Martin glanced up. Samantha was being led to the FedEx truck by Geordi.

"Goddamnit!" Martin shouted toward Haz's prostrate form. "What do you *want* from us, you little mother-fucker?"

Coughing, sputtering—then chuckling. "Everything, Martin Ready," he breathed out. "Everything."

It was the last thing Martin heard before blinking out of existence.

WARD CHAPMAN'S MIND WAS a congeries of images.

Reality had ceased to generate distinctions between "waking" and "dreaming" for him over a hundred years ago. Instead, the underlying quantum eigenstates informing that false distinction became untangled; certain occult disciplines referred to the type of discrimination mastered as *viveka*. Others referred to a special form of it as *mahasatthipatthana*.

He preferred to think of it as *caution*.

One never assumes that the experience presented exists as a phenomena distinct from one's perception of it. Von Neumann's simple proof at the conclusion of *Die Grundlagen* demonstrated this easily enough. This does not mean that it does not exist distinct from you—only that the form energy takes depends upon your interaction with it, your role in the show, your part in the game.

Ward allowed his perception to begin to coalesce centripetally, spinning and condensing until it formulated itself into a massless, partless point. Simultaneously, he generated a stream of energy that fed into the matrix of

New Yuttelborough.

Suddenly, a burst of energy, like a nova or a volcanic eruption, shattered the stream and flung him back to his corporeal substrate lying on the hard bed at the Rookville Inn.

Ward's eyes snapped open. He gasped for breath.

Sitting up rapidly proved to be a poor decision. Blood streamed out of his nostrils in two thick rivulets onto the front of his black dress shirt

"Bah!" Ward cried out, then calmed himself, and lay back down. He slowed his heartbeat, breathing gently through his mouth. Two minutes later, the blood flow had ceased. He sat up slowly again.

"What on Earth...?" he said aloud. Something potent enough to divert *that* much energy from a concentrated, insulated stream? Who in Rookville was generating *that* kind of sorcery—

An image of Bash flitted through his mind. *What was the Yuttelboroughian up to?*

There wasn't much point in any further functional-izing of New Yuttelborough's architecture, it seemed, without locating the *Gah Quinkwe*—not if sorceries *that* powerful were operating within reach of it. That must be what Bash and Grajug were working on; it was the only logical move at this point. It was the primary piece of the puzzle left. Without it, New Yuttelborough would remain a ghostly figment of Ward Chapman's imagination.

And the *Gah Quinkwe* itself was here in Rookville. Right here in the city. *Somewhere*.

Ward Chapman lifted himself off the bed and changed his shirt for a clean one after mopping up the blood from his face with a handkerchief. Whether the City of *Remembered* Promises would hold or not appeared, now, to be a matter for the future to judge. He would have to locate the *Gah Quinkwe* himself, if the Yuttelboroughians hadn't already done so.

MORE COUGHING, MORE SPUTTERING—DUST clouds and the scent of burning plastic.

Martin felt around himself. He could see nothing but white smoke surrounding him. A second later, his hand felt a body beside his, which reacted by grappling him.

"Martin?"

Samantha's voice.

"Sammy?" Martin responded. The smoke began to clear at the same time a sound, like that of a large vacuum cleaner, erupted from somewhere outside the cloud.

"I think we've succeeded!" That was Bash. That was Bash's voice!

Martin stood up rapidly and immediately winced in pain. Samantha pulled herself up beside him.

"Bash?" Martin called out. "Bash is that you?"

"Marty!" It *was* Bash! "Marty! How extraordinary! I think we just nailed some *brand-new* principles of thaumaturgical mechanics!"

"What the—where the fuck are we, Marty?" Samantha said. Martin looked down at her; she was wide-eyed, still seeming moderately and understandably terrified.

The smoke cleared.

Martin and Samantha, coated lightly in white dust, stood in the midst of a Hieronymus machine etched onto the floor at Kane Jeffries's mansion. Kane stood just outside the confines of the markings, holding what appeared to be a large vacuum cleaner with which he was sucking dust and debris out of the air.

"Martin!" Kane said, switching off the machine. "Great to see you, man! I have to admit, I didn't know if this particular setup would work—"

"Marty!" Bash leapt into the midst of the Hieronymus machine. Martin squatted down, beaming, and the two friends embraced, patting each other on the back vigorously. "This is a *wonderful* occasion! A splendid, magnificent success!"

Samantha stood, staring speechlessly at the pair before her, unconsciously staggering back a few paces. "Ah—what did we—um—" she started, and almost tripped over a thick length of wire running just outside the etchings.

"Pardon, m'lady," Grajug placed a hand gently on the back of her thigh. "Lots of electricity running through that!"

Samantha shrieked and fell backward anyway.

"Did I do something wrong?" Grajug said, concern overcoming his features as he descended upon Samantha in a flurry.

"Ah!" Samantha shouted again, flinging out her arms instinctively. "I mean—" she propped herself up on her elbows and glanced at Martin and Bash, who had separated and turned toward her. "Sorry. This is—? Um—*who* again?"

"Oh, God, sorry," Martin said, standing up again gingerly and limping over to her. Kane appeared beside her and extended his hand, which she took. "Bash, Grajug. Kane Jeffries," Martin said, nodding to the three of them as he spoke. "Oh, Loah-Dath. I didn't see you over there."

Loah-Dath stood witnessing the spectacle from the far corner of the room, fiercely scribbling in a leather bound notebook with a fountain pen. "Apologies, Martin!" he said. "This is a truly singular event! Best time to document the proceedings, you know."

"Of course," Martin said. "Hey, Kane, can I get some ice?"

Kane had stabilized Samantha in the midst of them. "My apologies to you, ma'am," Kane said softly to Samantha, who finally seemed to notice him. "I didn't mean to imply that you couldn't get up on your own. I just thought you seemed a bit unsteady. Please forgive me."

"No, that's fine," she said, starting to breathe regularly again. "I'm just not used to—"

"Yeah, we had a bit of a scrap," Martin said.

"Undoubtedly!" Bash said. "I'd love to hear all about it!"

Martin turned to Loah-Dath. "How often does Ling-Watha visit Rowley? Because there was a *bit* of a situation—"

"How long ago was this?" Loah-Dath asked.

"I don't know," Martin said. "Maybe—"

"Half a day, at least," Samantha said. "We were in the jail for at *least* that long, right?"

"I will ensure its containment," Loah-Dath said. Rather than getting up to make a phone call, he remained seated, returning his gaze to the notebook open before him.

"Jail?" Kane inquired.

Martin nodded. "I can't seem to stay away from the place," he said.

Kane chuckled. "You'll have to tell me about it."

Bash knelt down and checked a few of the patternings drawn on the floor. "It is *most* peculiar though," he announced.

"Why is that?" Martin asked. "I mean, I'm not exactly up to speed with whatever it is that you guys did here, but—"

Kane led Samantha to a chair at one side of the room next to Loah-Dath, who barely glanced at her. She looked tinier than usual, and huddled into herself as Kane stepped away from her.

"Well—genetic material," Bash said. "We got yours from the hairbrush you used upstairs."

"Prime locator media!" Grajug said. "Did you say you needed ice?"

Martin limped to another chair on the opposite side of the room from Samantha and sat down heavily. He knocked his thigh. "Sprained my ankle," he said.

Kane nodded to him and stepped out of the room in the direction of the kitchen.

"But why is your co-worker with you?" Bash asked.

"How did you—oh, yeah. The funeral," Martin said.

There was a sharp intake of breath from Samantha. "You were at the *funeral*—" she started.

"Only the wake, really," Bash explained. "But I'm baffled, still. You're not related to her, are you?"

"No-o..." Martin said, trailing off. Then: "Oh. Right." He looked up at Samantha, who returned his gaze, questioningly at first, then suddenly understanding.

"Oh," she said. "Gulp. Yeah, I guess that makes sense." Bash glanced at both of them, a look of mild confusion still in his eyes.

"I'm guessing this is an issue we can overlook for the present," Grajug said. "Chalk it up to *tangential tantra*. At any rate, whatever happened is clearly the result of great good luck!"

Bash brightened immediately. "Indeed it is!" he exclaimed. "This calls for at least a bottle of decent brandy! I wonder if Kane would mind if I fetch another from the cellar?"

The doorbell rang.

Everyone froze.

Kane stood in the doorway, an icepack in one hand, and shifted uncomfortably. The bell rang again.

"I'll...go get that?" he finally said uncertainly. "Maybe you guys want to—?"

"Right," Bash said.

"Good idea," Martin added.

"Are you sure you should?" Samantha inquired.

Loah-Dath shut his book and looked up. "What are we discussing?" he asked.

"I'll just go take a look," Kane said. He handed the icepack to Martin.

"Do you want me to—" Martin started.

"No," Kane said, turning from the group. "Just see if you can keep this stuff under wraps. I'll be right back."

The remainder of the group shifted materials and chairs around enough to close the doors and listen as Kane headed to the foyer at the front of the house.

"Who could that be?" Grajug asked.

"I'm assuming it's trouble," Samantha said.

Martin nodded. "I *guarantee* you it's trouble," he agreed.

Martin glanced at Bash. They both looked over at Grajug and Loah-Dath. Samantha closed her eyes tightly.

"Backup plan?" Martin asked generally.

Bash shook his head. "Humans typically use the default plan entitled 'run' when things 'go south,' as they say."

"Should we wait for the signal?" Grajug asked.

"Signal?" Martin repeated.

"You know," he said. "Yelling, screaming. General

chaos."

Martin feigned a grin.

Loah-Dath's eyes were closed gently. "I'm not sensing—" he started as Kane rushed back into the room.

"*Technically* it's just one guy," Kane said. "But there's something very strange about him."

"*Technically* 'one guy'?" Martin said. "What the hell does *that* mean?"

"It means one guy standing there, ringing the door-bell," Kane answered, "with the bodies of two *other* guys laying in the dirt next to him."

PART THREE

AD PERPETRANDA MIRACULA REI UNIUS

*F*IRE.

And then nothing, darkness.

But I know where the Light has gone.

I am Parisa Parviz. I know myself. I know myself! I am—

FRANK POURED THE LAST of the condensed diamonds into a glass jar and waited.

This was the point he never knew what to do with. When you're done, when you're ready to go—well, it's like death, isn't it? Do you choose it or does it choose you?

Frank stood and exited the room swiftly. No need to delay inevitabilities. He carried the jar with its precious contents to the blank wall at the other end of the room and placed his hand against an image of Botticelli's Venus.

The wall slid open, revealing the best-kept secret in Rookville.

Well, perhaps the *second* best-kept secret.

This was the way.

Thomas may have descended into madness, yes— but the vehicle within the walls of this room was built according to the *Krixwar* plans, the code within the code. Frank lifted an apparently seamless sheet of light metal siding and gently coaxed the glass cylinder into the last remaining slot. As if acquiescing to its destiny, the entire wall of extraterrestrial batteries glowed a brief, brilliant white, then settled down into a low hum.

Frank replaced the metal covering and stepped back. It may not have looked like much, but *this* was the key, this was the way—the way back to Yuttelborough.

He wouldn't be waiting very long, now. Merely take care of those few loose ends. He would be back for Pamela, who would inevitably want to pack things, although it wouldn't matter very much. In the City of Kept Promises, the last thing you needed to concern yourself with was whether you'd brought a change of clothes.

How Tom had raved about it! On and on he went, and Frank had begun to hear the hints in the midst of his rambling (especially when he insisted on pouring Tom a third or fourth glass of Oban).

Curious, how anticlimactic things seemed at this point. He stepped back through the false doorway and allowed it to slide shut behind him. He would freshen up a bit. He would alert Pamela to the Operation, functionally at an end. Then he would set out.

Tonight. He would set out tonight.

The telephone rang upstairs.

Frank sighed, knowing that—at this time of night—it could only be one of two or three people calling, none of whom he wanted to hear from. He heard old, reliable Joseph scurrying toward the phone from his sitting room, then muffled voices.

A few moments later, the intercom near the cellar stairs buzzed. Frank made his way over to it and hit the "answer" button.

"Sir, many apologies for the interruption," Joseph announced. "Prescott Mayhew is on the line. He insists that his call is urgent."

Frank closed his eyes. *Not now.* "Yes, Joseph. Thank you. I'll take it down here."

He gazed over at the hulking black shape of the old telephone seated on a bare wooden desk at the edge of the staircase. A red light blinked on it. He lifted the receiver from the cradle.

"Prescott?"

"Mr. Fleurety," Prescott's voice, which had never once sounded tired to him—a professional secret, Frank was sure—came through, cool, calm, collected, and criminally focused. "There is an issue at the Jeffries residence. Would you like to authorize nullification?"

Frank shook his head. *Why now?* "Standard," he replied.

"Mr. Fleurety," Prescott continued (he'd known him for years, why didn't he ever call him "Frank"?), "I cannot ensure, given the circumstances, a complete enclosure—"

"Standard, Prescott," Frank said. "Good night." He hung up.

Martin accompanied Kane back to the front of the house. They peeked through a side window. Martin gasped when he saw the man standing there.

"It's *Ward Chapman*!" he whispered harshly. "I don't know how Loah-Dath is going to feel about this—"

"Is there any *particular* reason to consider him felonious, Martin?" Kane asked. "Or even *dangerous*?"

"Loah-Dath said—"

"Loah-Dath doesn't like the fact that Ward Chapman defected from his Order," Kane said clearly. "Do we know *why* Ward Chapman left? Perhaps because they decided to become a *candy company*?"

Martin thought for a moment. "Okay, that's possible," he said finally. "But shouldn't we let Loah-Dath know?"

Kane shook his head. "We actually have a potentially objective factor in this set of circumstances," Kane said. "It fell in our lap just now. Given what we know about him, Ward Chapman appears to be interested in helping *you,* at least. The Order is typically bureaucratic. But *neither* entity needs to be considered villainous."

"Then who are those two dead guys?" Martin asked reasonably.

"They're not dead," came a voice from behind them. "They're unconscious, and perfectly safe."

Martin and Kane both froze briefly, stared out the window at the spot where Ward Chapman had been only seconds before, and then turned to face him, behind them, inside the house.

"Time is actually of the essence, gentlemen," Ward said. "I couldn't wait out there all day. But please note that I attempted to play the game according to the usual rules."

Kane nodded to him. "Noted," he said. "Kane Jeffries." He held out his hand.

Ward Chapman smiled and took the proffered hand in his own. "Ward Chapman, Protector of the Point-Source of Yuttelborough," he said. "Very much at your service, sir. Now: will you grant me a place to comfortably hide those two fellows from the eagle eyes of our enemies, perhaps?"

THEY HAD PLACED THE two sleeping spies—assured by Ward Chapman that they would not awaken for, perhaps, a day or more—side-by-side in the coat room by the entrance hall. Martin had suggested they tie them up, but neither Kane nor Ward agreed that the move would be either necessary or proper.

"Mere pawns," Ward had said. "Not guilty. They will awaken refreshed and unharmed, prepared to do good in the world."

Loah-Dath's face fell dramatically and awkwardly when Ward Chapman walked into the room with Kane and Martin.

Samantha sat cross-legged on the floor with Bash and Grajug, who had been attempting to explain the workings of the thaumaturgical mechanics used to transport her and Martin to the Jeffries residence without the usual requirement of traversing any intervening space. To her own astonishment, she was actually understanding the clear and joke-laden lecture.

"It's that *guy*!" Samantha exclaimed. "The one with the book!"

"Right," Martin said. In an attempt to disperse the anxiety that suddenly appeared, threatening to choke the life out of their operation, he added: "Everyone, this is Loah-Dath's best friend, Ward Chapman." Ward started to chuckle at that, which immediately placed him in Martin's "must be decent" category.

Bash and Grajug both gazed wide-eyed at Ward Chapman. Martin glanced from Ward and then back to the two Yuttelboroughians, trying to see whatever it is that *they* saw.

Grajug turned to Bash and whispered something in one furry, pointy ear. Bash nodded in response.

"Baeshazanam," Ward said, nodding to Bash. "And Anaghra-Jogg. May I congratulate you both on your escape from the Children! I give good tidings to you, in the Name of the Fire of Wisdom—"

"She is *living*?" Bash interrupted excitedly.

Ward nodded. "As we speak, yes. Here, in Rookville. Though I fear there is a terrible mistake being made."

"Mistake?" Kane said.

Loah-Dath was downcast. "They have it, don't they?"

"Have *what*?" Martin asked, frustrated.

"They have cloaked Her well," Ward said. "But I am confident that Her bindings are weakening. Unfortunately, that implies that *She* weakens as well—"

"Hang on," Martin said. "Just stop. One second." He stood in the midst of the party, and took a breath. "*Who exactly* are we talking about?"

"The 'who' that was, in Yuttelborough, a 'what,'" Loah-Dath said.

"Indeed," Ward continued for him. "The *Gah Quinkwe*."

The Yuttelboroughians whooped with joy and began scuttling about, gathering equipment together and proceeding to ignore the remainder of the conversation.

Ward smiled at them, then turned back to face Martin. "You know Her under a different Name," he said.

"I do?" Martin said. Then it hit him. "I *do*."

"Who is it?" Samantha and Kane asked simultaneously. The effect was somewhat jarring.

"*Parisa*," Martin said.

Ward nodded. Samantha looked confused. Kane's eyes shifted pensively.

Loah-Dath produced a canvas sack into which he placed his notebook and writing instruments. "I must contact the Order at once," he said.

"How *did* you find us?" Kane asked Ward.

"That last burst of sorcerous energy was impossible to ignore," Ward said, waving his hand at the markings on the floor.

"Why didn't you stick around?" Martin asked him. "At the funeral, I mean? We could certainly have used a heads-up."

"Enemy territory," Ward said. "Sometimes situations are best handled simply. I needed to ensure that Loah-Dath and the Muzzduh-Yassnans became privy to our situation. Outside of that immediate concern, I needed to see that Thomas Graham was, in fact, truly deceased."

"Makes sense to me," Martin said. He nodded at Bash and Grajug who were carefully placing bottles filled with colorful liquids into a case, muttering and commenting the while. "But you knew about them already."

"Every effect has a cause," Ward Chapman spoke gravely. "It is the collection of circumstances, though, that functions as that cause—not the immediate or spatially convenient appearance of them. Sometimes, even, there are threats that one presumes are invitations to collaboration—"

~~~

Two Years Ago

"Sometimes there are threats that one presumes are invitations to collaboration," Ben Crabbe said. "This whole time I've been telling you, Martin, that the basic rule in life is: *things are not what they seem*."

Martin lay in his cell at Fall County Jail on the last night of his incarceration. Other than the usual probationary period, he was effectively done with his term.

But the county had taught him nothing. It was an accident of the state that had amounted to his real survival here: a chance association with a chance individual.

Not in a thousand years would he have thought that he didn't want to leave.

"Things are not what they seem," Martin repeated.

"Sometimes that means that things *are* exactly what they seem," Ben said. "But you couldn't have known that unless you first assumed the opposite."

He seemed tired today. "Never think what they think you'll think," he continued. "Never do what they think you'll do. Sometimes that will appear *exactly* the way they thought or wished. That doesn't matter. Sometimes, circumstances conspire against a man, and that may make it appear as if you have no options. But look again." Martin heard Ben shift in his bunk as he lay down flat. "If that happens, just look again."

"Walls are made to keep people in or out," Martin said. He knew he probably shouldn't bring it up, but what the hell? It was his last night here. He wanted to know. Even if Ben just told him to keep thinking about it on his own. "What if you're surrounded by them? What if there are no windows?"

Martin heard nothing for a few moments. Then: "Walls are *made*, Martin. Anything made can be unmade."

And that was that. Martin was processed and out before sunrise the next morning, while Ben Crabbe lay breathing evenly, unwaking, asleep.

~~~

HAZZARD GROSCHEN HAD ABSOLUTELY *no* fucking interest in tolerating Geordi—but he was going to do it anyway.

The little shitbag spent half his time whining and half his time criticizing everybody. Haz felt pretty goddamned sure that the sole reason Geordi had been able to amass the number of acolytes he had—most of whom had been severely creamed by the Argonauts, thank the gods—lay in his weird, almost supernatural insight when it came to tinkering with electronic equipment.

For example, the weapon that Haz now held in his hands had apparently taken Geordi slightly less than six hours to build *from scratch*, using scrap metal and old parts found basically under a kitchen sink.

And the motherfucker could melt *steel*.

Its only drawback? A high-pitched shriek that it emitted when you depressed the trigger for more than five seconds.

Geordi had the shriek down to a low hum in thirty minutes, and had somehow managed to *increase* the burn ratio while fixing it.

Haz wasn't going to admit it openly, but Taggart's weaponizing powers were no match for old Space-Race.

Oh, right. Taggart. R.I.P.

Haz set the strange, toylike pistol down on the table in front of him.

Martin Ready. How do you catch that slippery fuck? They *had* him—him and his little girlfriend. Had them *both*—but how do you hold someone who can just *evaporate* at will?

And take other people *with* him?

Haz was more than frustrated. He kept thinking about Pamela. Couldn't get his mind off of her. And the more frustrated he got, the more intense and distracting the images of her became.

He had no idea what she had done to entice Geordi, though. For some reason, Haz didn't think mere physical seduction would work on the guy. I mean, come on: he was *still* wearing that fucking ridiculous silver spacesuit!

So what?

So Prescott told Haz that they had twenty-four hours to find Martin Ready and neutralize him. But they weren't supposed to kill him and they weren't supposed to maim or mutilate him.

Prescott had *also* made it pretty fucking clear that if they *didn't* find Martin Ready, then he and Geordi would be dropped off at the local jail with a note attached. "OOPS! These guys really *are* guilty!"

Haz picked up the pistol again instinctively. When he realized he was holding it, he pointed it out the kitchen window of the cottage and aimed at a carrion bird circling some distance away.

"Master Groschen?"

Haz jumped while hitting the trigger and succeeded in evaporating a forty-five degree slice of one window pane.

"Impressive, Master Groschen," Prescott Mayhew said. "Have you conferred with your cohort *in re* the matter of Kane Jeffries?"

Haz turned to face the pristine old bastard. "I have."

"Good! Then we must make all haste," Prescott said. He stood there in his unwrinkled, tailored suit, holding a thousand-dollar briefcase and a five-hundred dollar folded umbrella. "We have provided a driver. You know the rules. Chop, chop!"

Prescott turned on a heel and strode out of the room. Haz cursed him under his breath, took aim at his back, and wondered why he couldn't pull the trigger.

Because you're a damned slave and a fanboy, a voice spoke within his head. *Because you're nothing like the heroes you read about or see in the movies...because you're nothing like Martin Ready.*

He knew that voice well. It had been installed in him by his father at an early age, when the old man discovered to his horror that his son had no interest in sports or cars or—*gasp!*—getting a job, having a family, etc., etc. He hated that voice, fought it, pushed it aside.

Haz experienced a moment of panic as he thought an unspeakable thing: *What would Geordi do?*

Geordi might have been the worst person Haz had ever encountered, but at least the motherfucker had a superpower.

Haz, for all his wishing, for all the promises made by all those damned books and movies, had none.

He lowered the pistol, grabbed his supply bag, and headed out the door.

"MARTIN?"

It was Samantha.

Martin lay in a warm, comfortable bed upstairs. He felt a soft, cool hand against his forehead.

"Martin? Are you awake?"

He opened his eyes. Samantha gazed down at him, a look of light concern on her face.

"Is it over?" Martin asked groggily. "Did we win?"

Samantha shushed him and put one of her cool little fingers on his lips. "You fainted," she said.

"Yeah," he said. "I tend to do that. Probably something with the concussion, you know? Like, it never healed, or whatever?"

"You really need to get that checked out," she said. "Anyway, Loah-Dath said it was the stress of the teleportation. And I mentioned that you did some pretty hardcore stuff at the jail."

"You *told* them about that?" Martin sat up slightly.

"Well, what was I *supposed* to do?" Samantha said. "You made a fucking *wall* disappear!"

"Oh," Martin lay back down and closed his eyes. "I thought you meant that *other* stuff." He chuckled. "The *actual* hardcore stuff."

Samantha slapped him lightly on one shoulder.

"Hey! I'm a wounded man!" Martin protested.

"Yeah, I'll be sure to tell your *girlfriend* that," Samantha said.

"My *girlfriend*? Who—" Martin started.

"*Parisa*," Samantha said, and huffed. "What is she, some exotic Middle Eastern princess that you met at a singles bar?"

Martin laughed out loud. "No, she's—" He stopped. "Wait a second." He sat up straight. "I know where she is." He threw the blankets off. "Or, at least, I know who can tell us!"

"What? Where?" Samantha stood up from the bed as Martin stumbled out of it in a rush.

"*Ready my transport and look to the skies, O Love!*" he shouted. Samantha watched as he flung open the door and heard a crash moments later, presumably the flower vase that always seemed to sit precariously at the edge of the staircase, its life as an ornament finally ended.

THE NEXT DAY WAS beautiful.

Around sunrise, Martin and Kane dressed responsibly in work clothes discovered at the backs of wardrobes in several of the rooms. Their sizes were "shaped" by a quick visit to Bash, who laughed as he tailored the suits magically, and made a comment about the usefulness of fur. After this, Martin shaved. Kane shaved as well, but he also rinsed the gel out of his mohawk and combed it neatly back. It astonished Martin to see the true man transformed into this counterfeit version of himself; it astonished him even further to note that the transformation, even the black suit and tie, appeared utterly convincing.

Loah-Dath took them out in the Liquid Agent Candy Company flying saucer, invisible to the myriad mortal eyes of men. They gazed at the scenery as it unfolded about them: Rookville in all its glory. There, at one end of town, the majestic palatial spectacle of Thomas Graham's estate; at the other end of town, the little circle where Martin lived, squatting like a duplicitous cycle of complexes in a boring mind.

Martin was relieved to know that Ling-Watha had collected Rowley and brought her to a sort of kennel on one of the Liquid Agent sub-levels. He was also relieved to find out that their agents had successfully contained any record of Geordi's destructive activities, and had used one of those incredibly handy negentropic spells to repair the front door and the kitchen.

Ah! There sat Rosewood College! Martin and Kane both silently reflected on its importance to their own respective pasts. Martin wondered briefly if Professor Wronski sat in his office—*there*—grading papers or writing one himself, perhaps indulging a moment of confident reflection in which he *does* confirm the Riemann hypothesis...

Kane thought back to Harpy (well, that's what she called herself, anyway) and all the times they had fallen asleep together in each other's arms—*there*—after talking themselves into a heated frenzy about Plotinus and Porphyry and, oh, *wonderful*, Iamblichus the *Mystes*, when the hardest drug they did was just a little weed that grew anywhere you let it...

And there, only half an hour's drive from Forty Winks, the large, white, plain building with the big fence around it, and a few little droplets of life staggering like staccato notes around the grounds.

Vic Toronto was in Room 208. Sign in here. Yes he seems calm today.

"But you've gotta *tell* 'em, Marty!" Vic was looking pretty pathetic. If he hadn't been crazy before, whatever drugs they'd been shooting him up with had now damaged the rational centers of his brain. Perhaps a life of contemplation and raw foods would repair the damage?

"Calm *down*, Vic!" Martin said. Kane stood by the window of the room, a plain sheet of unopenable, shatterproof glass that looked out onto the big lawn at the front of the building somehow dampening the light in the room. "We're going to take care of this for you. I promise. But the only way I can do *anything* is if you tell me what *they've* been telling you to stop saying."

Vic actually seemed to calm down momentarily. He pointed at Kane. "Who's he, again?"

"Kane Jeffries," Kane strode over to him and held out his hand. "I'm here to make sure Martin keeps his word."

Martin glanced at Kane, then back at Vic. *Please believe it, Victor Toronto, we practiced this over and over again...*

"Aren't you the video store guy?" Vic asked.

"Yes," Kane said. "And no." He gave Vic what he hoped looked like the convincing facial equivalent of "I know something you don't know."

"Well," Vic removed his hand from Kane's and shoved it into the pocket of his white jumpsuit. *They treat them a little like prisoners here, too, I guess*, Martin thought. "I mean, it's easy. After that little fucker stole my car, I *knew* that what I'd been hearing on the radio must've been for *real*. Kept hearing it. Like a girl calling out to me: 'Free me! Free me! More light!' Stuff like that."

Vic patted his jumpsuit. "You guys want to take a walk? And buy me a pack of cigarettes downstairs?"

"Sure," Martin said. Moments later, they were seated in white plastic lawn chairs in a little courtyard outside. Martin watched as a couple of unsteady fellows attempted to toss a large plastic ball to one another and failed repeatedly.

"So, anyway," Vic said. "I got to thinking about it. Why me? You know? Why drag me into all this? I mean, I'm senior guy at Ever, Nevers. Check. I'm about to retire—well, give it another year or so, maybe. Check. Oh, yeah, that's right—*I'm working on those fucking Thomas Graham books*."

Martin nodded encouragement. Kane leaned over, gazing intently at Vic, elbows resting on his knees, hands folded together neatly.

"Thomas...Graham," Vic took a drag off of his cigarette and sent a plume of smoke through the unkempt bangs of his hair. "Sonofabitch was telling the *truth!*

So I started thinking about it, more and more. I started mapping it out. I realized that the hints were given in the books themselves—maybe even in the *words*, maybe even in the *pictures on the covers*. Oh, but that's when it got really creepy."

Martin glanced over at the woods behind Glory Days Sanatorium. Just beyond that clump of trees, a UFO sat hovering invisibly, patiently awaiting the return of the *non-crazy* people...

"Because *who was it* that was *publishing* these books?" Vic continued. "*Who was it* that was saying 'yes' or 'no' to every decision made? Who hired the artist? Who had dinner with Thomas Graham almost every night?"

Vic dragged impatiently on his cigarette and glared at Martin. It was a moment before Martin realized that he was supposed to suggest an answer.

"Oh! Um—" Martin started. "It was—Frank. Frank Fleurety."

Vic clapped his hands together and smiled broadly, then reached to the sky and gazed heavenward. *Maybe this guy really* is *loony*, Martin thought. Kane seemed typically unfazed.

"You got it!" Vic announced. "Franklin Fleurety! The *reason* for the success of the *Krixwar* books! He'd been behind it all along! Do you know"—here Vic stamped out his cigarette, only to begin the process of replacing it with another—"when Pamela Stoyanova came to work for us?"

It was sad to hear Vic refer to his old firm as "us" when it was practically a guarantee that he'd never return.

Martin shook his head.

"It was *right after* the second *Jacinta* hit the news-stands," Vic said. "And, boy! Wow! What a *looker*, huh? I mean, *none* of us guys questioned having her in the office, I can tell you that much!"

He took a pull from his second cigarette and blew a cloud of smoke into the midst of the three of them. He gazed into it as it dissipated, like a skrying crystal made of exhaust fumes.

"Man," he said, his eyes glazing over as he watched the smoke dissipate. "Pam Stoyanova. Wow. Can't say I blame the man for making a deal with the Devil."

Kane and Martin both glanced at each other. *Devil?* Kane mouthed.

"And it's not like she was a *consolation* prize, either," Vic continued. "She was just the *promise of things to come.*" Vic started laughing, revealing a few blackened molars.

He stopped suddenly. "Frank's leaving this world," he said. "He's heading back to the City of Kept Promises."

"Exactly *how* is he going to do *that*?" Martin asked.

"You gotta get me out of here," Vic said in a hushed whisper, ignoring the question and leaning his upper body in towards Martin and Kane.

Martin patted him on the shoulder, then tried to act like touching Vic didn't totally gross him out. "Vic, come on, now," he said. "You know we'll do what we can. But we can't *guarantee* anything until we know where—"

"She's under Thomas's mansion," Vic said. "In a basement. Kind of."

"'Kind of'?" Kane repeated.

Vic started glancing around the area, looking behind Martin and Kane. The two guys who had been playing "catch" were both standing on either side of the beach ball now, gazing placidly down at it, unmoving. "Yeah," Vic said excitedly. He stabbed out his cigarette on the concrete. "Yeah, that's right. Pam was the trade-off. I think it was because Frank didn't take Tom seriously at first. He just said: 'Yeah, yeah. And I want to sleep with a Playboy Playmate!'" Vic started laughing again. "If only it were *always* that easy, you know? Am I right?" He was nodding vigorously.

Martin nodded back. Kane smiled with his usual supernatural calm.

Vic became suddenly quiet and serious again. "But Tom had those new powers, you know," he explained. "From the City. The one in the books. He got those powers and he said to him: 'Sure, thing, Frankie! Wish granted!' Or however they do that." He scratched his head. "How *do* they do that?"

"It's—" Martin glanced again at Kane, who merely raised his eyebrows. "Complicated. We'll let you in on everything. In the meantime, here's what I need you to do: stay calm, stay cool. We'll send someone to collect you shortly, but you've *got* to keep your mouth shut about this. I'm *serious*. Do you understand me?"

Vic stared directly into Martin's eyes, then placed his hand over his heart. "Silence," was all he said.

Martin and Kane both stood up. Martin dusted some errant cigarette ash off his black suit pants. "Very soon," Martin assured Vic. The two of them strode off.

"Don't forget me," Vic said in a small voice behind them.

Martin cringed, turned slightly, and nodded. He didn't want to look at Vic's tired, haggard face. The simple statement had been the first truly sane thing the man had said all morning.

LOAH-DATH WAS SWEATING WHEN they got back to the flying saucer.

"What's up with you?" Martin said.

"We've encountered some issues," Loah-Dath said. "Marlowe—I mean, Ward is attempting to generate a protocol map at the Jeffries residence."

"Trouble?" Kane said. He sat down calmly in his usual half-eggshell seat and folded his hands in his lap.

"There are some—well, some *anomalies* that have become apparent," Loah-Dath responded, typing quickly on a flat panel. The saucer lifted rapidly and shot off toward Kane's place. "They are...not good."

"Out with it," Martin said. He was leaning against the viewscreen wall. It looked to Kane as if he was on a Hollywood sound stage of some sort, with a crazed projectionist firing images out of the sprawling city behind him.

"We've encountered the Children," Loah-Dath said simply. "You call them 'beetles.' We call them the Editors."

Martin did a doubletake. "What? How?"

Kane's eyes showed an usual degree of alert concern—possibly the closest thing to panic Martin had ever seen on his features.

"Something has been taken from the world," Loah-Dath said.

"I thought we already knew that," Kane said. "We know where the *Gah Quinkwe* is, now, though. We can restore it. Her. It."

"Not Yuttelborough," Loah-Dath affirmed. "*This* world. *This* planet. The Editors have awakened at the edges of this universe. *Someone has stolen the point-source of our world.*"

Martin was speechless. "I—ah—" he attempted.

"This is—" Kane started.

"Like a punch in the face?" Martin said. "Like: 'Oh, shit, Bash, we're *so* sorry that your universe got destroyed.' And now: 'Woah. Wait just a *fucking* second here! This is *my* world we're talking about—'"

"Your collective concern is perfectly appropriate," Loah-Dath said as he began the saucer's descent. "Hopefully, Ward Chapman has gathered more data on the circumstances. I'm certain that someone of his caliber has—"

"—NO *FUCKING* IDEA WHAT they're *doing* AT ALL!"

Haz stared into Geordi's dead, shark-like eyes. What he wouldn't give to cut out his heart and feed it to pigs.

"You are to proceed as commanded," Geordi spoke. It was even more awful than usual: he had built some sort of vocalic distorting unit which fit into the folds of his shiny, aluminum neckbrace. Now, instead of just sounding like an asshole, he sounded like an asshole trying to take a shit.

"You *do* realize that, as far as we know, we're the *only* survivors of the mall gig?" Haz said, giving up. What was the use of trying to fight? Just let them fail in their stupid mission. He'd duck out when the massacre hit Rookville Mall levels...*after* cutting off Geordi's head himself. "Even Slick Dave is dead. What're you gonna do about next month's comic books, Geordi? And what about the next Star Trek convention? No attendees. Not even *Shatner* will be there!"

Geordi, with his usual flat affect, began to leave the room.

"Oh, wait a second—Geordi?" Haz said. Geordi turned to see Haz extending his middle finger. "Fuck you. I hope you fucking choke on Martian cock."

Geordi gazed at him passively for a moment. Was that the hint of a smile playing around his features? Then he turned once more and left without further comment.

Every man for himself—that's what it was going to have to be. Haz seemed to be the only person realizing that Martin Ready was *not* going to be caught. Even if he *was* caught, so what? It wasn't like you could *hold* him...

Or *could* you? Was *that* what was going on here?

Wait a second...

Jacinta. The story came back into Haz's mind in a flood of imagery and excitement. *The Going of Jacinta*.

> *And they chained the Queen of Heaven beneath the New Prophet's church. In preparation for the going, they exchanged spirit for matter... The Thief wept, wracked with guilt... Knowing what he had done—this formed the worst part of his imprisonment...knowing what he had become was worse than the cage they placed him in...*

BEN CRABBE KNEW, IN his heart, what would become of him if he remained.

He felt her loss, like the last breath of a greatest love, whom he could never be apart from, no matter the distance.

Sacrifice, sacrifice, sacrifice. This was his story; this was his part in the scheme of things. What the humans never quite understood, here—when one's sacrifice *was* the reward, the purpose and the goal.

Stupid. At least they could still think for themselves.

He thought this was stupid.

Decades in a cage—for what? To become the new fuel for a new world?

Ben lifted up his hands before him and gazed at them. Calloused, scarred—yet finely wrought. He could still practically feel Frank Fleurety's bones breaking beneath his knuckles.

Please! I'll give you ANYTHING—

Bring her back. Undo it.

I CAN'T! Thomas has made AGREEMENTS—

Ben had forgotten for how long he beat Frank Fleurety. He only knew that, later, when they had come for him at his home, he wondered why he hadn't killed him.

It was because—because Parisa would have wept for it...

And so he stayed here, in his cage, with his curse. The Great Translator: Benjamin Crabbe, Thief. Waiting for the story to play itself out.

Waiting. Until Martin went to see Thomas Graham not too long ago. That was the signal.

It was the first time he had *translated* in what seemed like ages. And he wasn't sure what was expected of him, or what was supposed to happen. Just a burst of magical energy: into the mansion after Tom's supper with Martin.

Resulting, unintentionally, in it becoming Thomas's *last* supper, ironically, as the jolt of energy caused a *single* temporal flux; literally, Thomas's heart skipped a beat—then basically said to hell with it and quit its job.

Not Ben's least favorite act, honestly. He had to admit to having chuckled when he found out about it which, as he should have guessed, led him to *translate* to the church service and the wake as a way to make up for the disrespect. *Only because Parisa would have frowned on it.*

Even the death of the Ungruh-Mainyoosh! Parisa had no program for hatred, and none for death—which latter fact gave him a surge of hope. For had he not felt her, that night at the mansion? Had he not almost blown his cover and gone searching for her, letting the threads of the story be damned?

Dear Martin Ready and Kane Jeffries. That Ward had actually been able to deliver them seemed astonishing to him. *It must seem natural*, he remembered Ward saying clearly. *We cannot alert the Order before the Time. I make my promise to you, Benjamin Crabbe...*

But how much of *that* promise had been kept?

There was another way. He felt her loss. Ben *knew*. But there was another way...

Ben felt the old sensation stirring within him. He held up his hands before him once again. *Slowly, slowly...*

The world began to change.

"ALL RIGHT," MARTIN SAID to Ward Chapman, knowing that Loah-Dath would take too long to get to the heart of the problem. "How fucked are we?"

"I must admit that this was...unexpected," Ward replied, scribbling calculations on a sheet of graph paper. "The point-source of your world has been somehow compromised."

"Let's get this straight," Martin said again before Kane could speak up. "Right off the bat. *What* or *who* is the 'point-source' *here*?"

Ward looked up at him, then glanced to Kane, who stood with folded arms beside Martin. Loah-Dath had removed himself to the kitchen where, incredibly, in the midst of the revelation, Martin could hear him opening a can of Coke. Somewhere else in the house, the chittering of Bash and Grajug could be heard, along with occasional whoops of laughter from Samantha. *Showing her some cool tricks, no doubt*, Martin thought.

"You know him as Benjamin Crabbe," Ward said.

Martin continued to stare at Ward, his eyes beginning to water with nervous anxiety. He felt a similar reaction occurring beside him as it resonated from Kane. Neither of them had expected the response.

"Ben Crabbe?" Martin said. "But Ben never—"

"He dropped hints," Kane said, slumping down into a chair. "And there *were*, in fact, a few instances that I had always thought—"

"Benjamin Crabbe was placed in safety, in the Fall County Jail, subsequent to an unfortunate event," Ward Chapman explained. "It was the simplest possible route whereby to ensure the proper confluence of events. You both were to be brought into contact with him and taught—subtly, subliminally, even—the various methods whereby your unique potencies could be actualized."

"The story that *is* to be told *will* be told, whether one likes it or not," Kane said. "Who would have thought that the *errors* were so seminal to the unfolding plotline?"

Martin still stood. He folded his arms over his chest. He unfolded his arms. He began to remember. Things began to make sense.

"But what about Kane's 'potencies'?" Martin said. "I know what *I'm* supposed to be able to do. But Kane? What about you?"

Kane's eyes shifted to the ceiling for a few moments. Ward gazed at him.

"It's what I'm *not* supposed to do," he finally said. "In a sense."

"What the hell does that mean?" Martin asked.

"I'm *not* supposed to stop Frank Fleurety from making his attempt to leave this world," he said. "And, in a strange way, that ensures the destruction of the *Gah Quinkwe*."

"*What*?" Martin exploded.

Ward turned his gaze to Martin. A strange sense of calm suddenly enveloped Martin, seeming to come in waves from Ward's relaxed stare.

"Peace, Martin," Ward said. "The story will unfold."

"I'm not—" Martin started. He shook his head. "I can't let anything happen to her."

"It's already done," Ward said. "There's nothing left to do but return the Yuttelboroughians to their world and hope that somehow this re-installs our point-source here."

"I need this to be clear," Martin said. "I am to attempt to rescue Parisa—who has been destroyed—in an attempt to thwart Frank Fleurety—which is destined to fail."

Kane and Ward both nodded.

Martin threw up his hands and stood. "Well, then," he said. "Let's get this party started, I guess."

"So WE SHOULD BE able to get in and out, no problem," Martin said confidently to the small group of hopeful world saviors in the living room of Kane's house that evening. When no one responded, he added, with just a tincture of worry: "Right? Ward? Loah-Dath?"

"I will be right there with you, Martin," Bash announced from his perch by the window. "Grajug and I will ensure that any untoward forces are neutralized *well* before you would ever need to deal with them."

Grajug nodded. "In sooth!" he said. "There's no

greater reason to feast than success!"

"We will be physically present, of course, Martin," Ward said. "But the extraction itself—even if we stand in the very midst of the place with you—can only be done by one with the natural ability to Edit. I will aid the Yuttelboroughians and assist in the transport of the *Gah Quinkwe* once you have extracted her."

Martin slumped a bit. "What does that even *mean*?" he said. Samantha looked at him curiously, and he shrugged, unsure whether or not he ought to try and explain how he was to rescue an unrescuable thing. He turned to Ward and Loah-Dath. "I still don't *quite* know how to make things happen whenever I want them to—" He glanced nervously over at Samantha again, who was now frowning.

"Being in the Presence of the *Gah Quinkwe* ought to change all that," Loah-Dath said. Ward nodded.

"And if it doesn't?" Samantha asked. Martin felt instantly grateful for her company, even if it was only in deference to his insecurity.

"Then I will ensure your safe escape," Ward said. "With my life, if need be."

Kane looked at Loah-Dath, who seemed somewhat nervous, and then at Ward Chapman, who seemed preternaturally confident.

"Tell me, again, why *you*"—Kane said, indicating Ward with a wave of his hand—"were kicked out of *his* Order?"

Loah-Dath came close to cringing. Ward paused momentarily, seeming to carefully consider his words before answering. "There are deeper Orders," Ward said. "The *assumption* of obedience is only required by those without direct access to the Source of All Power."

"So..." Kane said, thinking. He brightened suddenly. "You mean that *getting kicked out* is how you *go deeper*?"

"Perhaps we might continue this discussion at a later time?" Loah-Dath said, heading for the door. "I will prepare the vessel—"

"Ward Chapman *outranks* you," Martin said in a burst of revelation. Kane was nodding vigorously. "The obedient ones are only following rules because they actually *don't know how* to be good without guidelines—"

"It makes perfect sense!" Kane said. The Yuttelboroughians had scuttled off toward the door, seeming uninterested in the exchange. Samantha followed the discussion with one ear as she stood.

"You get offered a chance to be in the Order," Kane was explaining as he and Martin followed the party out the door. "Then, if you are *prime* material—the best of the best—your 'final exam,' if you will, involves *getting kicked out*!"

"Perfect system," Martin said, thoughts of his own compromised doctoral degree not far from his mind. "Rebellion is the final stage in the evolution of intelligent life to the next level."

Ward appeared, somehow, *behind* the two stragglers. "That man over there," he said, "is a superb thinker and an outstanding magician. Be careful when estimating people based on a new pet theory." He strode past them and caught up with Loah-Dath, whom he patted on the shoulder.

"Well," Martin said, "Ward definitely dresses better."

Samantha laughed beside him. "I disagree," she said. "More robes! More beards!"

NIGHT.

There was hardly a hint of light in the sky. Dim stars hid behind a smoky veil of clouds. A slight breeze ruffled the feathers of the Earth. Frank stood in a small, circular room at the topmost turret of Graham's mansion—*his* mansion, soon to be *Pamela's* mansion—and took a deep breath, letting the scent of pine from the forest surrounding the estate fill him.

His last breath here, perhaps.

Down below, the machine he and Thomas had constructed according to the keys provided by Martin Ready's mathematical results applied to the *Krixwar* texts hummed with purpose. Final distillations of strange chemicals extracted from the corporeal form of the *Gah Quinkwe*—the Queen of the Hesterian Fire, Parisa Parviz, literal Soul of Yuttelborough—sputtered and spat through twists and turns of absurdly complicated laboratory equipment.

Franklin Fleurety gazed out one final time on the fields and forests. What could be better than this world he had created for himself?

A world where the promise of life was a promise kept forever. A world where every moment was pure novelty of a higher and better and happier order. A world where—

He noticed something in the distance.

A new star?

Brightly it shone; he remembered a passage from *The Devil Escapes*.

> *For the Believer had betrayed himself in betraying his enemies. In conspiring with the Ungruh-Main-yoosh, his sinister plan kept only the promises entailing disaster for the City. The Believer now*

> *bore the mantle of his terrible fate like fallow*
> *fields.*
>   *The Hesterian Fire, once burning brightly,*
> *extinguishes with a sigh...until the new star shines*
> *forth, when the essence of the City is distilled,*
> *when the Children are sated at last, at long last...*

The star seemed to shine more brightly, now.

Frank took one more look into the sky. Then he descended.

"INCREDIBLE," LOAH-DATH SAID AS they descended toward the forest behind Thomas Graham's mansion. "The readings, here! Hark!" He pointed at a dense readout of alphanumeric symbols, waving excitedly to Ward Chapman as he did so.

Martin took a brief look at the display. Hexadecimal code, perhaps? He had neither the time nor the inclination to attempt to determine its meaning. Looking back around the room, he saw Bash tapping some sort of control panel beside the transport device. When Bash noticed Martin looking, he winked at him briefly, then returned to his tapping.

"Give me about two minutes," Kane said to Martin. "Once we're down there, just *assume* Bash and Grajug will have the energy field in place. Don't waste any time getting nervous about whether it will happen or not."

"I'm too sick to feel nervous," Martin said. "That's my new plan, in fact. I'm just going to barf all over Frank if I see him."

Kane chuckled. "That's the spirit, man!" he said. "Barf will save the world!"

"So disgusting," Samantha said. She had been gazing

in sheer astonishment out the transparent wall of the saucer. "How do we stay invisible to people, again?"

"We don't," Grajug said, striding back into the room from the engine port. "Not entirely, at least. Really, it depends on the direction of travel more than anything else. Depending upon whether we're spinning, or how quickly we spin, the silvering—if you can call it that—on the chassis of this vessel potentiates a quantum annulment of—"

"Are we excited, yet?" Bash announced, apparently finished with his "work."

"Martin's like a little kid on his birthday," Samantha said. "After too much cake."

Bash looked offended. "I've never *heard* of such a thing!" he exclaimed. "*Too much* cake?"

"Fabulous idea!" Grajug said. "Let's give it a try when we get back to Kane's!"

Martin smiled. "How am I supposed to feel scared when you guys act like this?"

Bash and Grajug both grinned at him. "I have absolutely no idea," Bash said. "A great question! Is it possible we've presented you with an insoluble problem?"

"Is it possible that insoluble problems *themselves* could be what we're looking for?" Grajug asked.

Kane began laughing again. "That's *incredible*!" he said. "That's possibly the greatest method of dealing with metaphysics since Husserl."

Martin began to laugh himself. "I wish we could take a picture of this—"

"Martin? Kane? Are you quite ready?" Ward had turned to the chuckling group, a grin on his own face.

"Sure," Martin said. "Why the fuck not?"

Kane patted him on the back. Bash and Grajug began

to sing a low, melodic, curious tune in Yuttelboroughian and clap slowly.

"What's that?" Martin asked, looking at his two friends.

"I believe I have heard this once before," Ward said. "It is like a call to arms in Yuttelboroughian."

"Well, then," Martin said, and started toward the transport area, Kane preceding him.

Samantha took several quick steps toward him and grabbed his arm.

"Be—" she said. "Be careful." She gazed into his eyes. "Please."

Martin smiled broadly. "Why should I do that?"

Samantha frowned, then smiled, then frowned again. "Because—"

Martin kissed her, briefly, lightly, and honestly. The Yuttelboroughians began to cheer.

"The transport is prepared, Martin," Loah-Dath said. "Best of luck."

"Technically," Kane said from his position on the transport platform, "we *could* say that we're on our way *back*, already. Who decides where the starting point really is?"

Bash was nodding vigorously. "I've tried to explain that to Martin before!" he said. "About causation and how your Aristotle was—"

"Make it fast," Samantha said. "I'm serious."

Martin stepped onto the platform beside him. "Technically," Martin said, "we could also say that we're not in any danger whatsoever. Depending on how you define 'we' and 'danger.'"

Kane laughed.

The incredible burst of electric power that shattered one quarter of the saucer and sent it spinning out of control was really a tremendous surprise to them all.

Satisfaction to the Great Wise One!
Scorn to those hostile to It!
The sacred ground is made of sacred words.
The One is made of sacred words.
These protect when arrows would harm.
Nothing can penetrate the shield of words.
Nothing can Edit an Editor.

— Scorn to the Hostile Ones
Promises of the Krixwar[1]

MARTIN'S VIEW WAS COMPROMISED, he thought, by the blood running down into his eyes from a gash in his forehead.

He blinked several times.

No, not the blood—though sharp pains coming from the proper location indicated its presence.

Darkness.

He pulled in a breath. There was something here in this darkness with him.

Martin reached out—

Immediately, a pale burst of light erupted beneath the palm of his hand. Waves of warm love washed through

---

[1] Rough Translation from the Yuttelboroughian by Ward Chapman.

him and over him. His eyes brimmed over with tears of joy.

"Martan."

The pronunciation gave it away. It was Parisa—her voice, her sweet, singing voice that molded syllables like candies. Martin reached out his other hand.

"*Parisa*," he said. He pulled himself up. The light in the dark room increased, extended, emanating from her. "Parisa. What can I do?"

Her wide, almond-shaped eyes gazed into his. "I knew you would come." She rattled the manacles on her wrists that chained her to a blunt, brown rock jutting up into the center of the room.

"How do I—"

"Kees may, Martan," she said softly. Like magnets they connected. His hands caressed her, following the length of her arms to the manacles at her wrists, which instantly vaporized at his touch.

Moments later, they were entwined together—*like in the dream...* She pressed and prodded him, punishing diversions from her need, handling him like clay, like unkempt earth. He was hers to command, hers to manipulate, hers to suck dry.

And the light glowed, more potently, more vibrantly, consuming them both...

THE FOUR OF THEM—BASH and Grajug, Ward and Loah-Dath—had spent several timeless moments floating in mid-air, sucked out of the suddenly evaporated side of the Liquid Agent Candy Company's flying saucer. Ward had enough time to collect those closest to him—those not blocked by the still-functioning shields of the saucer (who would have thought *those* could cause a problem?)—into a zero-gravity sphere.

The disorientation had been rather staggering. Yuttelboroughians and humans spun and bumped into each other, quite helpless to re-negotiate their course for several precious moments. By the time Ward had determined what had happened and thought he knew the best way to neutralize any ill effects, they had been suddenly sent packing earthward.

Although the zero-g sphere had worked just fine and taken the brunt of their fall, it had burst like an airbag in the process, leaving them strewn about behind Thomas Graham's mansion, the contents of a sorcerous piñata from outer space.

"Loah-Dath!" Ward saw the familiar bunch of robes laying on its side and called to him cautiously.

Bash and Grajug were already standing, brushing themselves off and looking around, amazed. Ward turned to them as he stood, waving toward Loah-Dath's prostrate form.

The latter moaned loudly and began to sit up as they approached.

"Are you all right?" Grajug asked first. Ward was scanning him psychically. Other than a few comic books hidden in his robes, he identified nothing more brutal than an upset stomach.

"Give him a few moments," Ward said, turning back to the Yuttelboroughians. "Do you sense it as I do?"

Bash and Grajug both nodded. "She is *here*!" Bash said. "Right beneath us, as promised!"

Grajug patted Bash on the shoulder. They both stepped aside and began chanting in Yuttelboroughian.

Loah-Dath reached a hand up and was able to lurch to

his feet with Ward's assistance. He was breathing heavily. "There's something *wrong* here—" he started.

"I know," Ward said. "She has—*split*? Spread out? Why is the point-source so diffuse?"

Bash looked up at Ward and Loah-Dath, pausing in his chant. "It seems to be getting stronger over there." He indicated the lower levels of the mansion. "But right where we're standing—"

"Something is stealing her essence!" Loah-Dath said. Ward nodded.

"We must counter it," Ward said simply. "Bash, Grajug: use the Stabular Melody. Loah-Dath: you and I must form the barrier and shunt it all back to her."

Loah-Dath nodded. The four magicians set to work.

HAZ LEVELED HIS WEAPON at the bodies sprawled about the forest.

This was just like in *Predator*. The night-vision goggles Geordi had supplied for him had an infrared function. He could see whatever was living.

That flying saucer battle could have lasted a bit longer, he thought. But Geordi, as usual, was all fucking "get the ball in the goal and to hell with the game." So instead of the extended chase scene that Haz would have preferred, Geordi basically just pulled the trigger, and now here they were, cleaning up whatever was left.

He saw a couple of shapes out there. One crawling, slowly, presumably with the assumption that it couldn't be seen.

A second, off to the left, hanging in a tree. Unmoving.

Third one—

Wait. There *had* been a third one, right?

Haz's face smacked into the trunk of the tree he had been attempting to hide behind, not *quite* knocking him unconscious. He felt himself disarmed, trussed, and gagged in the few seconds it took him to recover his senses. Not only that, but this guy had the nerve to remove Haz's night-vision goggles.

"*whHGHGfHG!*" he uttered through the gag.

"Shhh," the voice came, whispering. Male. It sounded gentle, but that could simply have been in contrast with the violence of seconds ago. "Please remain silent. I apologize for the painful blow. I will not hurt you further as long as you remain silent."

Haz silenced. His head ached where it had impacted the tree. A rather *precise* hit, he had to say—just the right degree of force to render him senseless without undue damage. Professional. Impressive. He decided to remain silent, and simply wait.

That way, he wouldn't have to bother with the rest of Geordi's stupid plan.

The figure came into view as a large, dark shadow. As Haz's eyes adjusted to the darkness, he realized that he recognized him.

That's Repo-Man! What the hell is he *doing here?*

Kane had placed the night-vision goggles on and scanned the forest. He was instantly impressed with their construction—shockingly clear infrared images glared back at him.

There—the remains of the saucer, burning a dull orange near the center. Looks like they'd have to call a cab to get home.

And who—in the tree? That's one. No sign of Bash or Grajug; no sign of Ward or Loah-Dath.

Could be in the saucer, still? Let's assume that they've

managed to get to safety—that means either Martin or Samantha—

Kane heard a single twig crack behind him. He dropped flat to the ground as *something* smacked into the tree he had been peeking around, leveling it and taking down several other trees in the process.

Kane rolled to his right three times in rapid succession, predicting a second blast, which resulted in a man-sized crater in the ground precisely where he had been mere seconds ago.

Haz began a muffled chorus of yells. *Sorry, kid*, Kane thought. *I'd untie you, but—*

Kane barely had a chance to leap forward and to the side before another blast pulsed through the forest. On pure instinct, he shifted, rolled, took a breath, and *lunged* at the figure that suddenly appeared before him, huddled behind a bush.

Two quick punches to the face—left, right—grapple the left arm—upend, pull to the side—

Geordi lay face down beneath Kane, who held both his arms pulled backward and up, right at the breaking point. *Still, calm.* Kane lowered the arms and listened, slowing his breathing, slowing his heart rate the way Ben had taught him.

The infrared goggles had become dislodged during the fray. Kane glanced around without much hope of finding them, only to realize that the pair Geordi had been wearing sat lodged in the ground right beside him. He put them on.

The kid was out cold. Kane attempted to check him for a pulse, only to encounter Geordi's peculiar electronic neckbrace. He leaned his ear closer to Geordi's face, and listened. *Breathing. Good.*

Kane had used his belt to immobilize Haz and an errant handkerchief to gag him. *Everything's got more than one use*—he could still hear Ben saying it. Around Geordi's waist he found a utility belt with all sorts of weird items linked to it. A pocket filled with zip ties served his purpose. He had Geordi functionally harmless a few seconds later—as far as he could tell, at least; the kid seemed pretty goddamned clever.

Kane took a sweeping look around the forest in an attempt to avoid any further surprises. He couldn't identify whatever weapon Geordi had been using; he saw nothing approaching the shape of a weapon emanating any heat. He heard Haz grunting from his position by the crater. Suddenly, he heard the equivalent of a gagged yell. Glancing over at him, he saw Haz's body shift as it began to sink into the crater meant for Kane.

Kane sprinted back to him and pulled him out.

"Will you be silent if I remove this?" Kane said, indicating the gag with one hand.

Haz made a noise of assent and nodded. Kane untied the gag.

"Be very quiet," Kane said. Haz nodded. Kane returned to Geordi and settled him on his side, then gagged him with the old handkerchief. It was gross, but it seemed necessary, given that Geordi seemed to have the most violent motives of the two captives. "I will be back to untie you—*if* you remain silent."

Kane had every intention of speaking with Haz further, but the safety of the remainder of his party was paramount. He headed for the infrared blob emanating from the tree branches.

When he got there, he discovered Samantha, quite unconscious, hanging limply from a small web of branches. He was able to gently bend the branches down and extract her.

"Samantha?" he whispered to her. Pulse normal. Breathing normal. Rapid exterior body check indicated no obviously broken bones, although it seemed probable that she would be badly bruised.

He needed to get her to a hospital. Where was Bash? Grajug? Where were Ward and Loah-Dath?

Where was Martin?

A brilliant, flaming, fiery light burst forth from the Graham residence at that moment, forcing Kane to pull off the night-vision goggles—but not before he caught a glimpse of four figures, two tall, two short, standing some distance away, near the back of the mansion.

The earth began to tremble, then shake.

Oh, no...they can't...

Kane set Samantha down as gently as he could, fighting the urge to simply drop her and sprint over to the figures. Something beat against the back of his mind, impelling him toward them.

He ran, making a beeline for them. As he ran, he heard a sort of chant or humming noise emanating from the Yuttelboroughians. A rapid calculation ran through his head instinctively—like an encryption, a linguistic lock burst forth from his lungs right as he entered earshot, and caught the dazed, entranced look of Loah-Dath, whose eyes began to widen.

Instantly, the four figures blipped out of existence.

Kane stopped short.

What had he done?

A *second* brilliant flash of light now came—this one from a vehicle, more triangular than saucerian, exiting a hitherto invisible escape hatch from somewhere beneath and behind Thomas Graham's mansion, right beside the spot where Ward Chapman, Loah-Dath, Bash, and Grajug had stood moments before.

Truly like a flash of lightning, it zipped into the sky, soundlessly, leaving only a creeping sense of dread and the all-too-familiar sensation that he was too late, or had arrived seconds behind schedule, *if only he'd known ahead of time...*

That latter was from a different part of his mind—the part that had not shouted those peculiar words he knew not the meaning of.

BUT THERE WAS NO need to keep *all* one's promises when stationed on Planet Earth, here in one mere solar system at the edge of one mere galaxy among billions and billions of them.

The churning had begun at the outermost pylons of Martin Ready's universe. Instantly, upon Ben Crabbe's translation to New Yuttelborough, in his honest attempt to ensure that the City of Kept Promises was re-instituted and re-invigorated despite the loss of Parisa Parviz, the Children—also known as the Editors, whose peculiar dark DNA criss-crossed the hominid currents in Martin's veins as well—began their infiltration.

All that was energy, all that was matter—all that was *light*—they ate, consumed, metabolized into *nothingness*.

A number of galaxies too distant to be perceived, whose reality could only be implied by logic, had been devoured utterly by the time Parisa had extracted the strange drugs composed by Martin's system. Most of the quasars at the outer reaches of our cosmos followed shortly. Time existed only as a measurement in *front* of their feast; behind it—well, that could not be construed. "Behind" is a metaphor of things that *could* be—and what the Editors left in their wake *couldn't.*

Erase the canvas upon which an erasure had occurred—that might approximate some idea of their advance.

To Earth, to one seemingly negligible spot, where humans put their living "refuse": in this case, a now-empty cell at Fall County Jail outside the similarly negligible city of Rookville.

Remove a single piece of reality, and it all comes crashing down...

Really, it was basic physics: the conservation laws. That was how Martin had first conceived of the notion that (almost) got him his PhD; that was what Thomas Graham and Franklin Fleurety had slaved over for years and years, as the verses of the *Gah Quinkwe* became not only fiction in the minds of the people of *this* universe, but a crystalline molecule capable of *bending the substance of reality* past a certain acute angle when in the presence of sufficient gravitational force...

Messier 87, in the Virgo cluster. That's what they had chosen—it seemed like a good bet, at least.

Franklin guided the spacecraft through the unreal distances between astral matter, half-unbelieving what his perceptions told him *must* be true, *had* to be true. Whirling gases and brilliantly flaming gaseous orbs—*organized matter*, therefore, *intelligent...*

Beyond the event horizon—into the mad, whirling vortex, with every ounce of faith placed in the shield formed of the substance of the *Gah Quinkwe*—

"YOU HAVE DONE IT, Ward!"

Bash danced about the little room ecstatically. Grajug marveled at the details of the window itself before he gazed out of it, and marveled still further at the sprawling cityscape unfolding beyond.

As far as anyone could deduce, they had been transported—or, rather, *translated*—here: into the occult architecture of New Yuttelborough, designed (if not precisely altogether conceived) by Ward Chapman, who had literally written the book on how to do it.

"I have *started* it, Baeshazanam," Ward Chapman corrected him, still reeling from the unexpected transfer. Bash didn't seem to notice.

"It *is* remarkable," Loah-Dath said, running one hand along the brick of a fireplace. "All this is—"

"Unfinished, as I indicated," Ward said. "But something has stabilized it. Already, within the last few moments, the details you perceive out that window"—he waved a hand toward Grajug's perch—"have multiplied tenfold, a hundredfold, even."

"Where are the others?" Loah-Dath asked. "I make the presumption that our conjuration must have resulted in the cancellation of Franklin Fleurety's plans—"

"They are fighting our battle for us," Ward Chapman answered. He sighed. "And Franklin has not been thwarted in his endeavors. Rather, he has *succeeded*."

Loah-Dath was taken aback. "Who—"

"It was Kane Jeffries," Ward asserted before he could finish. "This is the part I have never enjoyed. Sometimes, healing a wound is the most painful aspect of it."

Bash and Grajug were conversing by the window, giggling and patting each other on the back. They seemed utterly unaffected by the potentially devastating news.

Loah-Dath glanced at them, then turned back to Ward. "But what, then, is our function here?" he asked.

Ward paced the room momentarily. "To take a cue from our Yuttelboroughian friends," he said, waving at them. "Perhaps I should amend that: our *New* Yuttelboroughian friends."

Grajug suddenly turned to Ward. "They must prevail, then? We would not be here if they did not."

Ward furrowed his brow. "I only know that the *Gah Quinkwe*—our Queen, Parisa Parviz—has removed us from harm's way for the time being. Once again, as with countless times before, she has ensured the continuation of the Story. Kane has fulfilled his function. In this, we ought to rejoice, as it could never have occurred if Our Lady had not intervened."

"Which *is* exceedingly good, I should say," Loah-Dath added. "As it indicates she has not perished utterly. The Hesterian Fire has been rekindled!"

"There is nothing we can do from here?" Bash asked suddenly. Ward could see a brief glimmer of concern on his face for the welfare of Martin Ready and his new human friends.

"Indeed," Loah-Dath said. "There is that slight issue of the Children presently consuming Martin's universe."

"What's that?" Grajug asked, pointing out the window.

Ward and Loah-Dath approached the window. All four gazed at the peculiar *black light* that somehow radiated by *not* radiating in the slightest—making its appearance utterly conspicuous by the fact of its apparently utter *vacuousness*.

Ward gasped. "I think I know now why we are here," he said, turning to Loah-Dath. "By all the *yuzzutahs*! He's trying to *seed* New Yuttelborough!"

Loah-Dath's face went from consternation to astonishment. "The point-source—"

"Has assumed the destruction of the *Gah Quinkwe*!" Ward finished for him. "Our own Benjamin Crabbe has left his post!"

THERE WAS A DEGREE of stupidity—or at least willful ignorance—inherent in almost every act of courage.

Kane considered himself somewhat more insightful, in that he did not actually believe courage invented or engendered luck along with its application to circumstance. Instead, as he headed back to find Samantha, repositioning the night-vision goggles, he reflected upon the strange, impulsive action he had just taken—one which appeared to have "evaporated" his friends.

A sensation which at first seemed to contradict his immediate perceptions greeted him upon inquiry: *accomplishment*. Not remorse; not guilt.

He hefted Samantha as gently as he could, and headed back toward Haz. If there was truly great danger imminent, he couldn't leave those two tied up and incapable of fending for themselves.

He would have to trust them, as difficult as that would be.

Samantha needed a hospital visit, that was for certain.

The clouds previously darkening the night parted enough to allow some moonlight and starlight to begin clarifying the surrounds somewhat. Kane removed the night-vision goggles, but kept them around his neck in case the situation threatened to go south again—perhaps Antarctically so. Samantha seemed to come awake somewhat as Kane carried her back to Haz's resting area.

"Took you long enough," Haz said.

"I'm sorry," Kane said, leaning Samantha against the trunk of a tree. She moaned—Kane considered that a good sign.

"Look, I don't know what you're here for—" Haz started.

"I'm going to cut you loose, and ask that you leave," Kane said simply and clearly.

Haz fashioned a doubletake despite his bindings. "What?"

Kane had already undone the belt loop and pulled the remarkably sturdy knot free. "You may go," he said.

Haz rolled to a seated position, wincing and rubbing his wrists. He stretched out his legs. "What the *fuck* are you up to, man?" he said. "Don't you know what they're trying to do?"

"Yes," Kane said. "And they've done it, I think. My recommendation is that you find your way back to town as quickly and simply as possible. Avoid main roads. Sneak back into your house. Clean up and pretend this never happened."

"Pretend this never—? Wait a minute! This is *my* story, too!" Haz exclaimed. His desire to quit the circumstances had suddenly given way to a deeper desire: that of *actually finding out* whether Yuttelborough was still attainable. *They had to be close—*

"You wish to help?" Kane said.

Haz nodded, wincing again as he attempted to stand up. "You bet your *ass* I do!" he said. "With that fuckstain out of the way?" Haz gestured toward Geordi's unconscious form, lying a few yards away from them.

"My conditions would be that you get that 'fuckstain' to safety," Kane said. "Along with my friend here."

Haz literally stamped his foot in defiance. "You don't know what I'm capable of!" he said.

Exactly one second later he was lifting himself up off the ground again and spitting out a mouthful of dirt. "You're wrong about which one of us is ignorant of the circumstances," Kane said, and reached out a hand to help him up. Haz paused on all fours, grimacing with both metaphorical and actual distaste for his dilemma. Stay, possibly make it to Yuttelborough, and—gods be damned—*help* Geordi? Or leave now and cancel all future plans to do much more than build video game settings for a living and wait for the next Trek Expo?

"Fine," he said at last, and took Kane's hand. "Fine. What do you want me to do?"

"There's a vehicle out front," Kane said. "I'm going to try to steal it for our temporary use. You will bring these people to a hospital, and ideally get checked out yourself. Make up a story. Obviously, don't mention this place." Kane strode over to Geordi and undid his bindings. Although the weapon he had been using was nowhere to be seen, Kane checked instinctively to ensure that he was unarmed.

"All right," Haz said unenthusiastically. "Then what? What do I get out of this?"

"When this is all over," Kane said, "come find me at the video store. I usually work evenings. This Friday night should be good."

Something in Kane's voice convinced him that there would be sufficient repayment. The man seemed honest enough, after all, and Haz was tired of having to guess three steps ahead of everyone, and failing to predict accurately, in any event.

"How will I know when it's over?" Haz asked.

"I'll try to make sure that it's obvious," Kane said, that same peculiar sense of *certainty* bubbling up from within, adding the authority of *knowing* to his assertion. "Now, *go!*"

"WE CAN'T CONTAIN IT!" Loah-Dath yelled. A whirling vortex of magical energy swooped down from the dark, ever-widening *locus* hovering thousands of feet above them. He had been muttering the standard Seals with perfect composure for the last several minutes to no effect.

"*We* must *contain it!*" Ward Chapman yelled back over the vast, electric hum. The energy had begun manifesting shortly after Grajug noticed the celestial anomaly. Now, it had begun interacting with the partial blueprints of New Yuttelborough almost randomly.

Bricks were becoming flowers; flowers becoming long-snouted, miniature elephants; and had there been elephants (there were not), they would find themselves such no longer. What *might* happen *was going to* happen. Slim probability was the rule. It was like showing *The Shining* to a classroom of second-graders...who knew what potentially disastrous effects might result?

Additionally, it was like putting the wrong disk in the right disk drive—*something* was happening, but who knew what?

Bash and Grajug had decided on a worst-case scenario approach (since this seemed like the choice even an idiot could properly make in these circumstances): they would combine their efforts and attempt an escape.

At the moment, it didn't seem to be working.

"Every time I try to get the *spin* right, it changes *color!*"

Grajug shouted. A small ocean of shimmering aethyr hovered in the air between him and Bash. The smile on the latter's face had actually slipped a few centimeters—that was how dire the situation seemed.

Bash closed his eyes. *How to control what cannot be controlled?* he thought to himself. Now, *this* was a logical puzzle! Every time you attempted a specific approach, the context within which that approach would work altered—seemingly irrevocably.

But was not that simple fact *itself* reliable and predictable?

Bash's grin widened once again. "It's adapting to our *uncertainty*!" he exclaimed. "We're *part* of the experiment! We're *part* of the system that's *changing*!"

Grajug chanced a look at Bash. His eyes widened, and his own grin returned in full force.

What *felt* like a slow, gradual, and predictable change then occurred in the construction of their escape hatch. (It really only took about a second or two.) Bash and Grajug began to laugh wildly, the perfect expectation of their success *one of the possibilities that could manifest, so it did.*

Ward Chapman—now floating in the air on top of a sixteen-foot wide umbrella that had suddenly unfurled beneath him—happened to notice (because he *could* notice it, and because both Bash and Grajug thought that might be helpful) the previously unforeseen success of the two Yuttelboroughians, and began to wonder how and why such a thing could happen...

"Loah-Dath!" Ward suddenly shouted through a clear tunnel in the chaos which carried his voice in pristine clarity to the mage.

Loah-Dath blinked in confusion. He had been utterly

surrounded by prismatic soap-bubbles shining in millions of colors only a split second before.

"We're *part* of the conditions!" Ward announced happily, sliding neatly to the ground off of the umbrella and walking easily over to Loah-Dath's side. Chaos seemed to collapse into usefulness all around him. "We don't even need the *spells* here, Loah-Dath! They're only necessary where identities have become solid and are believed!"

Loah-Dath smiled with understanding—also partially a result of Ward's intent that he *should* completely understand. The uninvited point-source still appeared to rage above them, but now it seemed more like the transparent skull of someone sleeping, through which their dreams shone like images in a crystal ball.

"It wasn't the *point-source*," Loah-Dath said. "It was *us*."

"Indeed!" Ward Chapman said. "Although the point-source *itself* may, in fact, be in grave danger of imminent collapse." He turned to the Yuttelboroughians, who grinned and waved at him from either side of their "escape hatch." It now appeared as a simple door of fine, solid craftsmanship standing upright in the middle of the street.

"Ready when you are!" Bash announced.

The quiet was refreshing. Loah-Dath approached the door and placed a cautious hand on the knob.

"We're certain that this—" he started.

"Not sure exactly *where* this ends up," Grajug said. "Although it ought to conform to the general *locus* of Earth, in some habitable area."

"How reassuring," Loah-Dath said dryly.

Ward Chapman chuckled behind him. "I'll go first—"

"No," Loah-Dath said quickly. "No need."

He turned the handle and pushed the door open. A fresh breeze wafted through, smelling oddly of—

"McDonald's?" Bash said.

Suddenly, he looked as if he would leap in front of Loah-Dath. Through the door appeared a meeting room of some sort. White walls set with a number of bulletin boards, a long wooden table taking up most of the center of the room, and, indeed, a wide array of leftover McDonald's fast food choices laid out invitingly in heaps along the center of the table.

Loah-Dath stepped through...

...into the central meeting room of Ever, Nevers, & Co. in Rookville. As Ward and Grajug came through the door, an immediate sense of relief washed over him.

This they could handle! This would be—

The door slammed shut, evaporating as it did so.

Instead of Bash the Yuttelboroughian, Pamela Stoyanova stood in its place, looking decidedly less human than the last time we encountered her—though, oddly, not less attractive for it. A rather large pair of curling ram's horns jutted out of her forehead, accenting and bringing out a rather lovely pair of pitch-black ocular orbs. Her skin appeared somewhat darker in shade, as if she'd just returned from a beach, or perhaps from Hell. It did appear as if her fingernails had become something more akin to sharp, black talons—but her tight-fitting black dress and vast cataract of blonde curls still indicated the Stoyanova brand name and trademark.

It was Pam, all right. But this was the Pam that every one of her old boyfriends had always *assumed* must be the case.

"Bash!" Grajug shouted. Ward and Loah-Dath seemed

rooted to their spots.

Pam chuckled. "No need to shout, little friend," she said villainously. "He can't hear you. He won't ever hear you again, in fact." She paused for a beat, then stomped one devilish foot. "And *goddamn* that custodial crew! This mess was supposed to be cleaned up *hours* ago!"

TO SAY THAT MARTIN Ready was in a state of extraordinary bliss would fail to incorporate the recognition, gnawing at the back of his awareness—although, admittedly, *way, way* back there, somewhere—of a sense of guilt.

It was the plain, old fear felt by every nerd who managed to land a good lay, then rode the waves of its ensuing confidence-level into *another* miraculous fleshly encounter in short order.

As most of us know, waves crash, and nerds, being often skilled in logic, attempt to short-circuit such crashings by getting poetically prophetic about it. Kind of like Nostradamus, without the Earth-shattering bits.

To put it quite simply, Martin lay there, empty of everything except thoughts of Samantha Salieri.

Parisa Parviz lay atop him, still clutching him, and *glowed*. Literally. The intoxicating scent of her sweat felt like a quilt of pleasant dreams wrapped about him. A peculiar understanding had dawned in Martin's mind during the consummation of his Chymical Wedding. The Hesterian Fire—the energetic, aethyric *cittam* that powers worlds—had been officially rekindled. It had taken the "blood" (let's remain poetic here, for the moment) of an Editor, but one of a very special type: a hybrid, a mutant whose genetic data incorporated the atavistic potencies of the Children (whose sole function was Editing). In Martin's case it had acted like a vaccine to the leeching of Parisa's essence by Franklin Fleurety and Thomas Graham's insidious machine...but...

"Somesing iss—*wrung*, Martan." Parisa's voice trembled in the stillness. Martin recalled its likeness: as if the buzzing of electrical wires in high traffic had become a low melody sung by one's high-school crush.

"I know," Martin said, mentally preparing a run-through of his confession. "I *know*. I'm so sorry—"

Parisa sat up suddenly, eyes wide. She looked like a frightened animal, startled as it foraged in its favorite woods.

"Zay haff zuh *wrung Star*!" she exclaimed.

"What? I'm—"

Parisa placed a hand on his mouth. "You are forgiffing may," she said. "You are tranz*layteeng* uss." She stood up, his Queen, commanding. "You are *now* tranzlayteeng *uss*!"

"Parisa! I'm not sure how—"

She reached a hand out to him.

"Shouldn't we get dressed first?" Martin said lamely, taking her hand in his. It was warm, soft. He could only ever do what she commanded.

Instantly, they were both standing on the pleasant beach of a calm ocean. Parisa smiled at Martin from beneath the diaphanous veil of a wildly extravagant wedding dress that appeared to be constructed wholly of exotic flowers. She held a bouquet of crystalline roses about which three hummingbirds hovered, merrily extracting bright red nectar that rested like miniature pools of blood in the center of each flower. He looked down at himself to discover a tuxedo made of shimmering, silvery silk—and a pair of green suede shoes.

"Huh," he said. "All right. Interesting choice of shoes—"

Parisa, now impishly grinning and peeking out from behind her bouquet, reached out a hand and caressed Martin's cheek, turning the gesture into a means of getting him to look out across the ocean and then up...

...at a pitch-black, roiling slime-ball writhing in the clear blue sky.

"What in the hell is *that*?" Martin exclaimed. He could practically *feel* the *wrongness* of it.

"Zat iss zee *wrung Star*!" Parisa said or buzzed.

Oddly, she continued to grin. Martin felt his attention suddenly drawn into its center. In a heartbeat, he exchanged places with it.

FRANK FLEURETY HELD HIS course.

The vehicle—as predicted, as *promised*—maintained its stability. It held true through the crushing gravitational winds of the singularity. It countered the molecular warpage that disintegrated all the materials surrounding them, turning matter into energy. It barely shuddered as it exited, clean and unharmed, through the center-most point of the impossible—

—into the old possibility of Yuttelborough where, for precisely the Planck time necessary for the Children of Nothingness to recognize and locate it (not too difficult of a task, given that it was the only thing there that could be considered a "thing" at all), Frank Fleurety delivered himself into the hands of a long-awaited destiny.

As Old Yuttelborough now was, in truth, merely the fiction of his own world—a fiction he had helped to create and bring into being—so Frank Fleurety became.

Or, rather, *un*became.

The Editors had forgotten him, their unwitting repast, almost as quickly as he had arrived.

AH, BUT THIEVERY IS a lovely sort of trade—it is the riding of a two-wheeled bicycle, and though the first attempt may be unusual terrain, the principles remain identical.

When you boil it down, the only difference between what we call a "thief" and what we call an "honest man" is the directness of the action. In this respect, Kane Jeffries was a true man and an honest thief.

The car—a Rolls Royce—sat in the dim light of Graham's circular driveway. Thankfully, Kane's very slight moral dilemma regarding the theft was alleviated somewhat by the fact that it was unlocked, with the keys in the ignition. Haz was behind the wheel with his two companions (one unconscious, one nearly so) in short order, and Kane watched as the gates swung outward automatically at the car's approach.

Kane's instructions to Haz had been to drive the car out to Kane's property outside Rookville and switch it out for the Subaru, then drop off Geordi and Samantha somewhere near Rookville General and make an anonymous call about them to the hospital.

At minimum, the plan was stupid. It would, however, accomplish its primary result: to get Geordi and Samantha whatever medical attention they required.

Meanwhile, Kane would be able to—

"Stop right where you are."

The voice was proper, a lightly accented male. British,

certainly. It came from behind him, somewhere near the stairs leading up to the mansion's front doors.

Kane froze, then relaxed, having some experience with this sort of thing.

"You have committed a felony offense," the voice stated flatly and simply. "But as I am a reasonable man, I will allow you to make a choice."

Kane heard steps coming toward him. *How far? Six yards, five, four—*

Kane ducked, spun around on one heel, and lunged toward where he estimated the knees of the speaker would be.

Old man? Jesus, had to be an old man—

Shots rang out. Whoever it was had been pointing a *pistol* of some sort at Kane. In short order, the old man had the wind knocked out of him and was on his stomach. Kane tore the weapon free from the man's hand and wrenched his arms back.

The man groaned.

"I do not want to hurt you," Kane said very clearly.

The man took a deep breath, paused, and then began to chuckle. The sound sent chills through Kane.

"Have I hurt you?" Kane asked cautiously, lessening the pressure somewhat. Perhaps he had inadvertently caused the man to have a stroke?

The man laughed a bit harder. "Oh, no, not in the slightest!" the man said. "Not even a *little* bit!"

The man's response was proving to be genuinely disconcerting. Kane glanced around the courtyard for any evidence of additional persons, hidden, maybe even aiming other weapons at him.

"I merely wanted to get my friends to safety—" Kane started.

"And you have *failed*, Kane Jeffries," the man said, and chuckled some more.

"Who are you?" Kane asked.

"Let me up and I'll tell you," the man said. "On my word as an Attorney at Law, I will let you in on all you need to know."

So it was that Kane Jeffries was introduced to the venerable Prescott Mayhew, Esquire, who proceeded to inform him that his friends were all either dead or about to be that way.

Would he like to discuss the matter further over a glass of Scotch?

Martin had always considered island paradises absurd.

First of all, they weren't fucking "paradises." They were just expensive. Second, sand is what remains after a world is leveled. And third, basically, if you want a nice breeze, why not save some money and open a fucking window?

(I know! There he is, ignoring smog and the thousand-and-one hellish olfactory insults of the average city! One suspects something else is going on, deeper in Martin's beetle-human hybrid mind.)

These thoughts, dear Reader, may seem arbitrary as all hell, but Martin's predicament had chosen them carefully and placed them very centrally in his mind, when he found himself suddenly, perplexingly resting on a beach towel in said tropical haven.

"What in the *fuck* is going on?" he said aloud. Hawaiian hula music—for the first time sounding like the essence of some plague-ridden horror or creeping death— emanated eerily from roughly nowhere. A "sun" rested in the form of a fat egg-yolk (and, indeed, lopsided?) in a sky blue as sapphires, and Martin shielded his eyes as they lifted toward it.

He leaned up on his elbows.

Further down the beach could be seen the invigorating forms of a decad of curvy supermodels, known by that appellation due to their ability to excite interest in other- wise useless things.

(Okay, what's going on here? I keep trying to tell you about what's happening in Martin's immediate sphere, and *someone* keeps inserting his or her opinions as I do it. Many apologies!)

Several of the hopefuls turned their eyes toward him and batted long lashes like whips at his heart and mind. Martin courageously turned away to survey the remainder of his environment. The usual thatched hut...yet who, there, seemed to be acting as *king* of said thatched hut...?

The man bore an unintended resemblance to Martin *himself*, of course, pouring drinks for a few expensively dressed young ladies. But it could *not*, in fact, be Martin Ready, *not* because of the wonderful things he does, no, but as a direct consequence of the fact that he—

(—gods, no, you're going to make me *say* it? I'm so sorry—)

—wore a Hawaiian T-shirt, two sizes too big, printed with the usual pattern of multiple palm trees, as might be construed by a lobotomized, bored, and stupid Escher.

Okay, all right. If this was *really* what was going on, then Martin knew, potentially, a quick way out of this mess.

He got up, dusted the uncomfortable grit from his

silvery suit, and began to walk over to the little cocktail bar.

How did he do it?

Preston Mayhew did not have a "way with words"— no, that would be like saying "the sun has a way with heat and light" or "Thor has a way with a hammer." Words were an epiphenomenon of Preston Mayhew—that would be the simplest way to put it.

Kane and Preston clinked glasses.

They sat in a small meeting room in the midst of the Graham residence, both covered in dirt and grime, both with blood of various genetic signatures adorning their rumpled and torn clothing (though let it be said that all of the dark stains on Preston's once-unblemished suit derived from his own palette). The much-needed relax-ation Kane felt throughout his whole body had kicked in shortly after he had met Preston Mayhew's eyes; any lingering doubts or concerns regarding Preston's sincerity had utterly evaporated upon sublingual contact with a dram of this singular, expensive Ardbegh.

"Somehow, I *knew* you'd come to see this whole little nothing in a clear and unbiased manner," Preston said. You or I would be able to see the forked tongue sprouting forth with every word.

Kane, oblivious, merely held up the glass of old Scotch toward Preston in a gesture of apology. "They didn't quite know what they were getting into, did they?" he said, and took a generous sip.

Preston's eyes widened in sympathy and under-standing. "Indeed," he said, slithering. "You mustn't blame them in the slightest. You have done everything in your power to ensure that the best possible outcome ought to occur." Preston set down his glass. "Now, you may simply relax. Enjoy yourself! You've earned it!"

Kane smiled. The man—Preston Mayhew, Counselor of the Oppressed—ought to win a medal for compassion (though Kane knew he would never accept it).

A sudden loud banging noise erupted from the back of the house, like someone had thrown a tree at the door instead of knocking on it.

Kane looked up in surprise. Preston briefly added a "non-" to his plussed manner, but repaired the issue before Kane could notice.

"Please forgive me," Preston said, standing up. "Continue to enjoy your surrounds, by all means. I shall return forthwith."

PAMELA HAD WARD, LOAH-DATH, and Grajug rounded up like taquitos.

"I *warned* Frank about this," she said, then added, calmly: "You meddling bastards."

The three protagonists sat in three reasonably comfortable office chairs, enchanted by a spell of magical paralysis that had passed through the still strangely inviting lips of their demonic captor.

Grajug was experiencing one of the strangest sensations of his life. You or I would have called it "worry," but we must forgive him his lapsarian attitude, as such a phenomenon was normally inconceivable to Yuttelboroughians. Loah-Dath's attempt to chant spells under his breath ended with Pamela waving a hand at him—he had been fast asleep ever since, lightly snoring into his beard. Ward seemed the least concerned of them all.

"And you—'Ward Chapman.' Ha!" Pamela chuckled. "It *is* astonishing to think how many people you've fooled with that absurd pen name."

Ward gazed at her, the unnerving twinkle in his eye indicating—

"There's something you know that I don't, isn't there?" Pamela said. You didn't get to be the head of a company like Ever, Nevers, & Co. without *some* degree of objective capability—supernatural lineage notwithstanding. "Although it *could* be that cleverness you've always exhibited. I let you speak—you cast one of those trademark mirroring spells and, *voilà*! I *do* marvel at your maneuvers during the old days. Someone's paying the price for that still, you know."

Something about Ward's demeanor indicated a shrugging of shoulders.

He was pissing Pamela off further with every passing moment. When was Frank going to send word from Yuttelborough? She'd actually have to entertain these nuisances until the messages started coming through.

Oh, but it *was* going to be delightful, wasn't it! *All those years* in the service of humans...and Frank—glorious, cunning, deliciously venomous Franklin Fleurety—had formulated with her a plan and an agreement that would make the humans little more than a moderately useful collection of insects.

She had been gloating over what to do with them for years, now. She and Frank had thought to get a few years' more work out of Thomas, certainly—the latter, being just another human, had, of course, quailed and begun to regret and, finally, lost his mind in the process of trying to cope.

Destruction of worlds always seemed to take its toll

on these little glorified apes.

A phone began to ring from elsewhere in the offices. *Her* phone.

That's *not* how Frank was supposed to—

The ringing stopped. Then it started again.

"Oh, for Christ's sake!" Pam spouted, and stormed out of the room. The ringing stopped once again, then started once again as she entered her office and angrily lifted the receiver from its cradle.

"*What* do you *want*?" she practically shouted.

A small chuckle greeted her. "Many apologies, Madame Stoyanova!" It was Prescott. "I have been cornered into something of an unforeseen set of circumstances—"

"Get to the *fucking point*, Prescott! I've got *guests*, you know!"

"Yes, well," Prescott said, attempting to consolidate his words and isolate the essential ones in the proper order. "You're apparently missing one."

Pam, about to shout a randomly chosen expletive and hang up the phone, stopped herself accordingly. "Missing?" she said, an unintended ounce of fear creeping into her voice.

That goddamned chuckle again. "The young master Baevare Baeshazanam would like to speak with you regarding the new conditions of our arrangement," he said. "He has told me to inform you that they are not in any way negotiable, in order to save us all time and energy in unnecessary debate."

Martin glanced back once at his grinning "bride," who waved in encouragement, then held out his hand to the bartender.

"Martin Ready," he said by way of introduction.

"Good to meet you, Marty!" the bartender said, ignoring the proffered hand. "What can I get for you? Cocktail?" He eyed Martin briefly, then smiled broadly as he looked from Martin to a martini glass. "*Martini*?" He chuckled.

Martin looked briefly at the Barbie dolls sitting on stools to either side of him, sipping elaborate, fruity mixed drinks. "I'll take..." he trailed off for a moment. The bartender's face began to shift and warp as he gazed back at him. There was something *so familiar* about that face; it *had* and *did* look very much like Martin himself. But the man also looked like—

"*Ben*?" Martin said aloud.

The Barbie dolls froze, mid-drink. The bartender's grin faded.

"I'm—" he started. "Not sure? Did you say you wanted your Macallan neat?"

Martin leaned against the bar, trying to keep his focus directly in the bartender's eyes. *Yes, there it was. That look—something in there—just like Ben—*

"Benjamin Crabbe?" Martin said simply, forcing himself to remain focused on that weirdly shifting collage of features.

The bartender picked up a Scotch tumbler and promptly dropped it on the floor.

He gasped, then chuckled. "Will you *look* at *that*!" he said, indicating the shattered glass on his side of the bar.

Martin did his best to ignore it, keeping his gaze as steady and focused as he could on the bartender's—*Ben's*—face. "Ben," he said again. "It's *me*. It's *Martin*."

Ben began to tremble slightly. "You—" he started.

"You wanted a beer? Budweiser?"

The words came suddenly into Martin's mind, from a distance—from just down the beach, where Parisa Parviz leaned back in the sand and watched the tide begin to encroach upon her.

"*In the beginning*," Martin said, echoing the words in his mind, "*countenance beheld not countenance.*"

Something *else* shattered.

The Barbie dolls had disappeared, leaving their drinks to hover momentarily in mid-air, then plummet to the ground in unison.

Ben stared Martin directly in the eyes.

"I'm..." he began.

Martin held out his hand. "Martin Ready," he said again, repeating his introduction.

Ben shifted his glance down to Martin's outstretched hand, then reached for it with his own.

"I'm...Ben," he said, taking hold of Martin's hand. "Benjamin Crabbe."

A burst of light followed, which is exactly what ought to happen when a countable infinity of quantum particles all breathe a sigh of relief and let themselves relax into a lower energetic state, comfortably closer to the nuclear hearth of their point-like home.

KANE AWOKE IN A sitting room in Thomas Graham's mansion, sweating fiercely.

He was alone.

There *had* been a banging noise, of some sort, coming from elsewhere in the house. But how had he gotten *here*? And why was he obviously very drunk, his body a new bottle for the old whisky that sat innocently on a lacquered table beside him?

He staggered on his way up and out of the seat. *Damn.* What on *earth* possessed him to get *drunk*—now, of all times?

Kane took several deep breaths and ran a hand through the mop of hair hanging over one eye, pushing it back behind an ear. *Okay*, he thought to himself. *Try to focus. Where are we? Graham's mansion. Okay. What do we need to do?*

Memories of earlier in the evening flooded through him—he saw Haz's inadvertent grin as he drove the Rolls Royce containing Samantha and Geordi. (Who could blame him? Driving a Rolls Royce was basically as strange and rare an event as any standard close encounter or leap into a parallel universe he could imagine.) But after that?

He heard a voice coming from a room nearby, very faint—like someone on a phone.

"...told me to inform you that they are not in any way negotiable..."

Something very familiar about that voice. He tried to listen for more details, but the phone call ended before he could isolate them.

Then he heard another voice.

"Excellent work, Prescott!"

That was *Bash*!

Kane headed in the direction of the voice, stumbling a bit here and there. "Bash?" he said, and coughed. His throat was a mass of irritation. "*Bash*?"

"Kane! You're awake!" the Yuttelboroughian said as Kane chanced upon and opened the door to a lavish dining hall.

Kane was forced to actually *stop* himself from inad-

vertently grabbing a hamburger when he saw the exquisite panorama of fast food laid out on the vast mahogany
dining table. The kith and kin of every possible wax-paper
and aluminum-wrapped offering from at least five, six—
eight? ten?!?—fast food restaurants posed invitingly in
an artistic display of raw, gluttonous abandon.

Bash sat at the head of the table, grinning from ear
to ear, one hand being rapidly divested of a dripping
Whopper as the other shoveled French fries in bunches
into his mouth following every bite. Prescott Mayhew sat
with the bearing of a schoolboy unable to divest himself
of the rules of etiquette—though still decidedly unkempt
from his earlier tussle with Kane—and chuckled occasionally as he used knife and fork to make short work of
a sequence of chicken McNuggets.

"Help yourself!" Bash insisted.

Kane smiled, shaking his head. "You know that I
won't consume animal products—"

Bash and Prescott both glanced at each other before
bursting into laughter.

"What?" Kane said. He felt guilty—drunkenness
combined with exhaustion from the night's activities were *almost* driving him to doubt his conviction
against any degree of animal exploitation. "Why are you
laughing? And Bash—*who the hell is this guy*?" Kane
tried to deflect his gnawing hunger by channeling it into
solving a problem—*any* other problem. He pointed at
Prescott.

Bash stopped laughing, though his grin remained.
"This is Prescott Mayhew, our new lawyer!" Bash
exclaimed excitedly. "And *all* of this food you are seeing
has been prepared with *plant-based substitutes*! I thought
up a modification of one of Liquid Agent's dairy-reduc-

tion formulas—the one they use for their 'diet' candies. Though who would *ever* bother with a diet when they could just eat candy is a strange thought. I figured you would be hungry, and I couldn't bear to think of your moral dilemma discouraging you—"

Kane dove in, starting on a double quarter-pounder with cheese. He didn't quite recall what meat was supposed to taste like, but he imagined that this was better.

Bash and Prescott laughed again. It was several glorious, heavenly moments before Kane returned to his senses and prepared to ask the question that had been on his mind since his second helping of Frito chili pie.

He took a breath, a few sips of Coke, and leaned back. "I thank you for this, Bash," he said. Bash lifted another handful of fries in acknowledgment of Kane's toast and tossed them back into his mouth. "But you said something a moment ago—about this man here." He indicated Prescott. "Our 'new lawyer,' I think it was?"

Bash nodded his head vigorously. "One of the best, I think!" he said. Prescott bowed his head modestly at the appraisal.

"What—ah—" Kane tried to formulate the question as simply as possible. "What do we need a lawyer for, again?" He could think of several possible reasons himself, of course.

Bash chuckled. "Gotta have all our bases covered, you know," he explained. "Just in case we screw something up."

"Screw something up?" Kane repeated.

"When we burn this place to the ground!" Bash said excitedly. Prescott chuckled again, skewering half of a plant-based McNugget on a piece of silverware and dunking it into Hot Mustard Sauce.

SAMANTHA SALIERI OPENED HER eyes in the dim light of a hospital room.

She ached all over. She didn't know what time it was. The last thing she remembered was—

No.

Where *was* everybody?

She tried to sit up, and cried out at a sharp pain in her neck as she did so. As she lay back down gingerly, a nurse walked into the room.

"Samantha?" she said soothingly. "How are you feeling?"

Samantha groaned.

"All right," the nurse said. "We can get you something for that. I'm Josie. You need anything for the rest of the night, you just hit that button there, okay. You're in pain?"

Samantha nodded carefully, one movement of her chin downward. Josie picked up a clipboard and made a note on it.

"How did I—" Samantha started.

"Now *that's* the big mystery we're all waiting to figure out," Josie broke in. "I was hoping you'd be able to tell *me* that!" She smiled.

Samantha thought for a moment as the nurse made another notation on the clipboard.

"Is there anyone else here?" Samantha asked. "I mean, did anyone else come in with me?"

"Just that little weirdo," Josie said. "Sorry. That kid with the spacesuit on. He's next door. Friend of yours? He didn't have any ID. A Star Trek pin, though! Trekkie here said it was a 'Science Officer's Badge'! But we haven't figured out yet who to contact about him."

Samantha's eyes grew large. *Kid with the spacesuit on? What the hell? Where's Martin? Where are Kane and Bash and EVERYBODY ELSE?*

Josie smiled at Samantha once before placing the clipboard back in its holder. "We contacted your mother down in Bradbury. She's coming up here as we speak. I'll be right back with something for the pain, Samantha," she said. "Right back."

"Wait," Samantha said. Josie paused at the door and turned around. "Did the kid—the weirdo—did he say anything? Is he awake?"

Josie burst into laughter. "Sorry, honey," she said. "Yeah, he said *something*, that's for sure! Kept talking about gettin' back to his 'spaceship,' and all that! Then he fell right back to sleep. Stressed *out* about that 'spaceship'!" Josie took a step back into the room and lowered her voice. "Pardon me, if he's a friend of yours, but *that* one's got a few screws loose, I'm thinking!"

Samantha had a sudden thought. "Yeah," she said, and tried a smile. It hurt. "Yeah, he's a little weird. Hey, did you say you guys got his Science Officer's Badge?"

Josie nodded.

"Could I hold onto it for him? He'll die if anything happens to that thing," Samantha said.

"Why, you are just a *sweetheart* aren't you?" Josie said, smiling broadly. "Takin' care of that kid. I think I got an idea what happened, honey, and if you don't want to talk about it, don't worry. But kids beating up other kids? That's a shame. We need a new world."

Josie stepped out of the room, leaving Samantha with her consternation and a major headache. A few moments later she reappeared with an incredibly effective pain medication and Geordi's Science Officer Badge, a thick plastic pin bearing two interlaced circles on the front.

It's a start, Samantha thought, turning the pin over and examining it. The pain meds started to kick in as she arbitrarily depressed the circles simultaneously with both thumbs.

She didn't even see the dull, orange light they emitted right after she did so, nor the transport beam shining down on Geordi Mifflin's unconscious body in the room next door, from which he disappeared corporeally without a trace mere moments later.

PAMELA STEPPED BACK INTO the meeting room at Ever, Nevers, & Co. to find her quarry grinning, laughing, and even engaging in the lightest degree of food fighting with a few French fries.

She literally stomped her foot in rage when they failed to notice her entry.

"*What* are you—" she began. Ward noticed her out of the corner of his eye, then waved a hand at her.

"Have a seat, Miss Stoyanova," he said. A chair slid out from under the table near her. She collapsed into it, whatever spell Ward had cast making it impossible for her to deny the request. Blind rage generated an acid plan of vengeance in her mind.

"Many apologies!" Grajug said, biting into a breakfast burrito. "We just needed time for everything to work out in the best possible way!"

"Indeed," Loah-Dath said. He sipped from a can of Dr. Pepper. "A word of thanks is in order to you, Miss Stoyanova, for the much-needed rest from our endeavors."

Pamela burned with a fury she never knew she had,

quaking in her seat.

Ward glanced at Loah-Dath, then at Grajug, who shrugged. Ward waved his hand toward Pamela again.

"*I will burn you all ALIVE for this!*" she screamed. Even the devilish horns sprouting from her skull appeared to strain toward them, eager for blood. "*You will not escape us! Franklin will—*"

The trio of late-lunchers burst into laughter again, drowning her out. Through the haze of anger, Pamela began to sense that there was, indeed, a chink in the armor of her plan. She glanced frantically at each of them.

Ward shook his head, ate a French fry, and stood up from his seat. "My dear Pamela," he said, pacing to the other end of the room and filling a glass from the water jug there. "Four hundred *years* of this, so far? Really? And you *still* don't get it?"

Pamela was literally huffing and puffing, no doubt intent on blowing Ward Chapman's house in. But a *very slight* cast of doubt appeared to beset her features.

"The world has *not* changed all *that* much, Pam," Ward continued. Loah-Dath and Grajug seemed intent on their food, almost deliberately ignoring the awkward exchange. As devilish a creature as Pamela Stoyanova in fact was, there was no reason to add embarrassment to the mix. "When we first met, you were understandably frustrated. Being basically sold to the nunnery at that time was, admittedly, a dastardly move on the part of your parents."

Loah-Dath inadvertently nodded his head. He met Grajug's eyes and they both shrugged.

"I don't blame your forward-thinking arrangements," Ward said to her, sitting in the seat directly opposite hers at the table. "But you must understand: the *anger* was never going to get you anywhere." He gazed at her furious eyes with absolute compassion. "Anger is merely a lack of faith in oneself, after all. You need to stop relying on others for your satisfaction."

Were those actual *tears* brimming over Pamela's pitch-black eyes, causing the flawless application of expensive mascara to run? Oh, but Ward Chapman's magic was *strong*, wasn't it!

Pamela, nonetheless, with typical demonic intracta-bility, refused to speak. She even seemed to be somehow, mysteriously, keeping the tears in her eyes from brim-ming over the lids. She would *refuse* to give in! Refuse, refuse, *refuse!*

"I'm sorry to have to tell you this," Ward Chapman said, lowering his voice, "but Franklin Fleurety is gone."

At this, several droplets of lachrymal fluid did, indeed, teeter over the brink of Pamela's lower eyelids. It was an embarrassing sight; Loah-Dath and Grajug committed themselves to "not noticing."

"Gone," Ward Chapman said again, "in the sense of being *fictionalized*." He stood up from his seat and waved a hand at Pamela, who suddenly felt her ethereal bonds released. "I'm letting you go, with the understanding that you are not to return here. Even now, the Story is being rewritten. Someone will be taking your place here at Ever, Nevers, & Co., shortly."

Pamela didn't move. Instead, she spoke. "Where is Frank?" she said.

"He has been *edited*," Ward answered. "Cut from this story. Though, in a very real sense, *consumed* and *metab-olized*."

Pamela whimpered, then seemed to notice that she had done so. "You haven't destroyed him—" she started, all sense of hellish energy having departed her.

"Indeed, I have not," Ward said. "Franklin made a conscious decision to attempt a return to Yuttelborough. *Old* Yuttelborough—which has been utterly consumed by the Children of Manifestation: *nothingness*."

Ward paused. When Pamela decided not to respond, nor to get up and leave, he continued. "Anger and sorrow, greed and fear—all these things are transient. Goodness need only *wait* for them to, inevitably, consume themselves."

Pamela glared at Ward. The horns sprouting from her head retracted into her skull, into the mass of blonde curls. The dark abysses of her eyes funneled into pupils resting in the midst of their usual bright blue irises. She stood, took one more glance around the room as if appraising its value, nodded, and left.

"Ought we set in place some sort of safeguard—" Loah-Dath began.

"No need," Ward said. "She will move on—another city, perhaps. Perhaps another world. There is no need to upset the balance of things further than has already been done. We must leave the choice of those who deal with her to those who might do so. We must give them a chance *not* to do so, voluntarily—without that, nothing changes."

"And Bash? Are you *certain* that he is..." Grajug sought for words.

"We will be hearing from Baeshazanam shortly," Ward said. "For now, let's at least clean up this mess." He snapped his fingers and the room was instantly immaculate.

Loah-Dath's eyes widened. "You'll have to teach me how to do that," he said simply.

Ward laughed. "After tonight, you've broken enough rules to be a member of the inner order, I think," he said.

Grajug laughed.

Prescott Mayhew extracted several key documents from a well-hidden safe located in the mansion. Following this, at Kane's insistence, Bash performed a simple enchantment that ensured all living creatures fled from the place and the grounds surrounding it.

All three stood outside the gates of the mansion. The first inklings of dawn had begun somewhere off to the east of Rookville as the buzzing and hopping and creeping of life made its way deeper into the forests surrounding them.

When the sound faded, Prescott removed a file of neatly collected papers from his briefcase.

"This negotiation is now ended; the contract is null and void," Prescott said, and tore a small stack of papers in two.

Instantly, the entirety of Thomas Graham's estate burst into sorcerous flame.

Kane and Bash gazed at the towering inferno that was once Thomas Graham's custom-built estate. It took mere seconds for the edifice to become a cone of smoke, like a reverse tornado, funneling into the sky.

A few seconds after that, there wasn't even a gate separating them from a new, vast expanse of ancient forest.

Prescott Mayhew pressed a button on his briefcase, resulting in the appearance ten minutes later of a long, black limousine.

"Gentlemen," he said as the chauffeur opened a door for them. "Please accept this complimentary accommodation. The driver will return you to your residence."

"Aren't you coming with us?" Kane asked.

Prescott shook his head. "A few more things to attend to here," he said secretively. "On your way, now! I'll be in touch."

Bash was already in the limo, pouring himself a drink from the selection displayed on one dimly lit wall of the cab.

"Want one?" Bash asked, holding up a fizzing glass.

Kane shook his head. "Not even a little bit," he said. He leaned back and closed his eyes as the car took off.

A WEEK LATER, THE world had changed for everyone.

Samantha's mother hadn't let her out of sight for almost seventy-two straight hours after they discharged her from the hospital. She basically moved in to Samantha's apartment and ensured that her every need was taken care of until it was demonstrated to her, quite clearly, that such a thing was *entirely* unnecessary—*many thanks, mom, love you, yes, yes, gonna be all right, I'll see you on Thanksgiving.*

Back at Ever, Nevers, & Co., Samantha thought she noticed a tremendous difference where there was, quite obviously, none. Vic Toronto, owner and editor-in-chief—as usual. Brie van Dorr, managing editor—as usual. Herself, Samantha Salieri, associate editor—nothing new there.

It was this weird—okay, the appropriate phrase would be "*exceedingly odd*"—new manuscript she found on her desk Friday morning that bugged her, with a post-it note on it that read: "*Proof by next Fri. K? —Brie.*"

It was called *How This Ends*. There was no author given—correction, "by Anonymous." She started reading it, all the while frowning and wondering.

Martin felt something very different when he suddenly realized that he stood in the middle of his apartment in Sagrada Circle, holding a bottle of Prosecca over three wine glasses. (He had never invested in champagne flutes.)

Samantha grinned widely. "So—are you going to pop the cork, or...?"

"Oh, right, yeah," Martin said. He had at least learned how to do *that*. He twisted the cork gently, easing it out of the top of the bottle. Pent-up carbonation released, and Martin poured. One for Samantha, one for Kane, one for himself.

Rowley rubbed up against his leg. He looked down at her, and she returned his gaze, licking her chops. *Tuna fish. Thank you.*

Kane lifted his glass. "To New Yuttelborough?" he suggested.

Samantha nodded. Martin lifted his glass thoughtfully, nodding as well. "Better," he said. "To Bash."

Kane's brow furrowed. "What happened to him?"

Martin sighed. "High-ranking dude, now," he said. "He and Grajug tend the Hesterian Fire. The new promise is that it actually *cannot* go out. I mean literally—they're the ones who make sure that the *Gah Quinkwe* can be freely consulted. That way, it can never be stolen again."

"But if it hadn't been stolen—" Samantha started.

"It would have been impossible to keep the promise that it would be recovered, one day," Martin finished for her.

Kane nodded. They clinked glasses and sipped their champagne.

"You met with Haz?" Martin asked Kane.

"Oh, yeah," he said. "Sure did. Gave him Quest Video."

"I didn't know you *owned* that place!" Samantha laughed.

"Neither did I," Kane said. "Looks like Prescott really *did* have his uses. Anyway, I've got enough to handle with managing the estate and dealing with the charities."

The three of them fell silent for a moment, all thinking the same thing. No one had seen Geordi since his disappearance from the hospital—apparently, most of the blame for the Rookville Mall Massacre had fallen on him, but the FBI was apparently at a loss for his whereabouts.

"What about the other two?" Samantha asked, looking to Martin. "What were their names again?"

"Off doing inner order stuff," Martin said, not naming them aloud. "Who knows? Maybe we'll run into them again?"

"The world's saved, though, right?" Samantha said. "The point-source is re-installed here, but on that island paradise, now?"

Martin recalled the scene. He had honestly thought he had more in common with Benjamin Crabbe, but the fact that the latter had insisted upon being stationed on a tropical paradise in the Pacific Ocean assured him he would be seeing little of his old teacher. Martin had to agree that it was, indeed, a damned sight better than being thrown in *jail*, after all! Talk about those Liquid Agent guys taking shit literally! The apologies for his temporary insanity, on the false assumption that Parisa had truly been destroyed, were profuse.

But Parisa was exactly where she was supposed to be.

Martin smiled and took another sip of his champagne. Everyone leaned back, relaxing for the first time in...had it really only been a week?

Timing—in the sense of a multi-dimensional egg large enough—might, in fact, be everything!

Martin recalled standing on the castle wall ledge and gazing out upon New Yuttelborough's expanse.

The City teemed with joy. Light ships darted in from numerous points in the sky, unerringly finding their way to homes re-built in perfect harmony, in perfect accord with their prototypes from the City that came before.

There stood Bash with Grajug to his left. Both creatures grinned and pointed, chuckling and speaking excitedly, literally hopping every now and then with joy at the rediscovery of their homeland.

It was a kept promise in itself, and this one, as all truly made promises do, would be kept forever—that was the new destiny of promises.

And yet, destiny is an odd thing, in that what seems good dances hand-in-hand with what seems evil, and the two often change places, and the worlds we love are sometimes the worlds we can never live in.

And yet sometimes, luckily, they are.

"SAMMY? I THOUGHT YOU were at lunch."

It was Vic, knocking lightly at her partially opened door.

Samantha looked up. "No, not yet," she said. "Just about to go. What's up?"

"That guy Martin Ready just called," Vic answered. "Professor at Rosewood. He said he could help you with *that* if you have any problems with it." Vic indicated the stack of pages Samantha had been reading.

"This?" Samantha said, glancing down at the pages.

"A *professor* wrote this? It's pretty weird—"

Fractional Spaces in Nonsymmetric Algebras. By Martin Ready, Ph.D.

"Wait—what?" she said.

"I know!" Vic said sympathetically. "I *know*! I'm sorry! But we don't have anyone else better than you at the moment to deal with this one! I promise I'll make it up to you."

"No, I mean—" Samantha stopped short. *Fractional Spaces in Nonsymmetric Algebras.* Chapter One. Dense Subsets of Compact Topological Spaces. *Following on Perelman's solution of the Poincaré conjecture, we will attempt to...*

W*hat the fuck?* Samantha thought to herself. She looked back up at Vic.

"Promise!" he said. "Hey, take a long lunch, or whatever. And just a once-over. I hear this guy's pretty good at sending stuff in near-mint condition, anyway."

Vic sauntered off.

Samantha looked back down at the manuscript. The post-it note was still there. "*Proof by next Fri. K? —Brie.*" But *where had the story gone...*

She shook her head. She'd go to Wednesday's and get a sandwich. Too much work, recently. Too much goddamned work.

IT RAINED FIERCELY OUTSIDE, which usually meant (for some reason Haz could never discern) a greater influx of customers than normal.

Tonight, however, Quest Video was peaceful, silent. He had decided to turn off the usual background movies, as well. As pleasant as it was to have the *Evil Dead* trilogy playing when patronage died down, he felt the quiet was more comforting tonight. Granted, the usual crowds of customers meant money, and money was always welcome and invited.

Sometimes, though, peace was more valuable than dollars, being, after all, what dollars were intended to buy for him in the first place.

Maybe he'd close the store early... To hell with it, he *would* close the store early. It was *his store*. He could do whatever he wanted with it.

Haz glanced down at the map on the back counter. He had taken it out to assist a customer, earlier, to show them how to get to the Hampton downtown without having to get back on the highway, when he noticed something strange.

Or didn't notice something.

Really, he didn't understand *what* it was that he either

noticed or did not notice, but he knew one thing: *the map didn't look the same.*

The same as *what*, precisely?

Well, that was problematic as well, since Haz couldn't tell you what seemed to be missing—or added—or whatever. But it almost certainly had *something* to do with this spot over on one end of town—hadn't there been a big house there before? A mansion, even?

That was crazy, of course. The area was utterly uncultivated forestland off I-64. If there ever *had* been a building in that spot, it would have had to have been built and leveled well over a hundred years ago...

Haz shook his head. Looking at the map was giving him a headache. Not to mention the fact that he remembered something else which was *right there*, but simply *would not* give way to mundane conscious awareness... something about *smoke*, wasn't it?

When the smoke clears.

Why did that bother him? Why did that seem significant?

He turned off the buzzing neon OPEN sign and locked the front doors. One by one, he turned off the five television sets and double-checked to make sure the store seemed in readiness for his morning manager to take over tomorrow.

Cash register till—check. Alarm on—check.

Haz headed out the front door, locking it behind him, and made a beeline for the little Subaru with the abundance of bumper stickers parked at the back of the lot. It took him a rain-soaked second or two to get the door open and get inside.

Rain pattering on the roof. Quiet. He loved that sound.

He turned the ignition, adjusted the rear-view mirror—

and froze.

Gazing back at him from the back seat of the car were a pair of glowing green eyes.

Haz jumped and turned in his seat.

Nothing. No one there.

He turned forward again, breathing heavily, heart racing.

There, taped neatly to his steering wheel, was an envelope with his name on it, printed in neat calligraphy. *HAZ*.

His heart wouldn't stop racing. He glanced around the parking lot; through the rain and the shadows cast by the several parking-lot lights, he saw no one. Quest Video was always the last of the shops to close in this area.

He looked back down at the steering wheel. *HAZ*.

Trembling, he removed the tape and turned the enveloped over several times.

He opened it.

Hazzard Groschen, it read. *I know what they did to you, and I can help, but I will need you to agree to do a few things for me in exchange. I promise that the experience will be rewarding in every possible manner—despite, perhaps, the presence of some "old friends." If you would like to know the terms, meet me in the forest that has confused you as soon as possible.*

Don't worry—I will know when you arrive and I will be there.

Following this was a single word that, when he brushed over it with his eyes, caused him almost to cry out in longing.

PAM.

The car tires screeched as he swung out of the parking lot, heading for the highway and the wildness of the forest beyond.

THE END

FORMER HEAD OF THE now-defunct "Werewolf Coven" (1987-1995) and occasional college mathematics instructor **DAMIAN STEPHENS** lives at the edge of a dark forest in Virginia, within which he can often be found chanting baleful incantations to Yog Sothoth or evoking demons from the Pit to physical appearance. Currently, his research includes: applications of Bruno's *De umbris idearum* to quantum entanglement (via microtubule configuration); fractal multiplication of the *elixir rubeus* (macroscopic treatment); Vaihinger's *Die Philosophie des Als Ob* as Husserlian device in many-worlds travel; "PDEs and Parzival: The Differential Geometry of Mithridatist [sic] Architecture" (a presentation for the Noisy Bridge Rod & Gun Club) ; and an encyclopedic analysis of agonistic tropes in *Finnegans Wake*. All of these themes and more are pursued, heavily camouflaged, in his fiction.

Made in the USA
Middletown, DE
17 May 2019